VALOROUS

A QUANTUM NOVEL

BY: M.S. FORCE

Valorous
A Quantum Novel
By: M.S. Force

Published by HTJB, Inc.
Copyright 2015. HTJB, Inc.
Cover Design by the Designing Women: Courtney Lopes and Ashley Lopez
Cover Models Zeb Ringle, Danielle Tedesco, Scott Hoover Photography
Interior Layout by Isabel Sullivan, E-book Formatting Fairies
ISBN: 978-1942295129

All characters in this book are fiction and figments of the author's imagination.

www.marieforce.com

The Quantum Trilogy
Book 1: Virtuous
Book 2: Valorous
Book 3: Victorious

CHAPTER 1

Flynn

She's in shock. That's the only possible explanation for the glazed look in her gorgeous brown eyes as well as the unusual and pervasive silence between us. She's trembling so violently that I want to call a doctor to give her something to calm her down. I'm at a total loss as to how to comfort her.

I've brought her to my home, hoping to protect her from the feeding frenzy going on outside hers. All my worst nightmares have come to life, but my worst nightmares have nothing on hers. With her painful past made public for the world to dissect, she's lost her job as well as her anonymity, and it's entirely my fault.

I want to get on the phone with my people—lawyers, publicists, anyone who can get me the blood of the man who hurt her. I want to get Leah over here, because Natalie needs a friend. But I'm afraid to leave her alone for even the short time it would take to make calls that might help. Her silence is freaking me out. I liked it better when she was sobbing. That I understood. The eerie silence… That scares me.

Then I remember how she admired the big tub in my bathroom—the one I've never used in the ten years I've owned this place. Leaving her curled up on my bed, I go into the bathroom and start the bath. Under the counter, I find a bottle of body wash that can be used to make bubbles. Keeping one eye on her and another on the tub, I wait until it's three-quarters full before I turn it off and return to her.

Sitting on the edge of the mattress, I kiss her cheek, which is cold under my lips. "Hey, Nat, I ran you a bath. It might feel good to warm up."

She doesn't protest, so I help her up and out of her clothes and then pick her up to carry her into the bathroom, where the tub full of steaming water and bubbles awaits. Two nights ago, we made love for the first time, yet nothing about this is sexual. When I deposit her into the water, I end up with wet sleeves, so I remove my shirt and take a seat next to the tub.

"Sweetheart, will you talk to me?"

"Nothing to say." Her voice is dull and flat, as are her eyes. The tears that roll silently down her cheeks break my heart and threaten my own composure. I have to do something—anything—to help her.

"I'll be right back." I get up to go into the other room to find my phone and a dry shirt. I've missed thirty-two calls and forty-six text messages. I ignore all of them and call Gabe at Quantum. He runs our BDSM club and acts as Quantum's head of security in New York.

"Flynn," he says, "are you all right?"

"I've had better days. I need a doctor for Natalie. Do you know someone who can come here and be discreet?"

"My cousin. I'll call and set it up."

"Thanks, Gabe."

"Let me know if there's anything else I can do. We all want to help."

"I will, thanks again."

I return to the bathroom, where Natalie hasn't moved from where I put her. Tears continue to leak from her eyes, every one of them a knife to my heart.

"Flynn," she whispers.

"What, honey?" I kneel beside the tub. "I'm right here. What do you need?"

"I'm going to be sick."

I grab the trashcan from the floor and get it to her just in time to hold back her long dark hair as she heaves violently. "I need to get Fluff," she says, still gasping from being sick.

"I'll ask Leah to bring Fluff here. Don't worry about anything." I settle her back against the towel I've rolled into a pillow for her in the tub. I wet a washcloth under cool water and kneel next to the tub to wipe her face and mouth. "I'll get your phone so we can text Leah."

Tears continue to roll unchecked down her pale cheeks.

In all my thirty-three years, I've never felt as helpless as I do right now. I don't want to leave her for even the short minute it takes to retrieve her phone from where we left it with her purse in the living room. "I'll be right back, okay?"

She nods, and the weary resignation I sense in that small gesture crushes me. This is my fault, and I'm going to fix it for her or die trying. I bring the phone back to the bathroom. "Do you want to punch in your code?"

"You can do it," she says. "It's zero one one eight."

I'm strangely moved to be trusted with her code. What can I say? I'm a disaster where she's concerned. After punching in the code, I see that her phone is alight with messages and voice mails. Ignoring all that, I open a text to Leah.

Hey, it's Flynn. Natalie is asking for Fluff. How do you feel about bringing her to us at my place?

She responds immediately. *So glad to hear from you. How is she? Of course I'll bring Fluff. Whatever I can do.*

Thanks. Not so good… Fluff will help.

I send another text with info about how to get into the garage at my place, which is not something I give to just anyone. But right now, I can't be bothered with things I'm normally obsessive about, such as protecting my privacy. All I care about is Natalie and whatever I can do for her.

The buzzer on the elevator sounds, and I'm once again torn over leaving Natalie alone, even for a minute. "Fluff is on her way with Leah. I'm going to get the door. Be right back."

She doesn't reply. Tears continue to roll down her cheeks, but she's completely unaware. The vacant look in her eyes terrifies me.

I run for the elevator. "Yeah?"

"It's me." Addie.

Without hesitation, I hit the buzzer to let in my faithful assistant. A minute later, she steps off the elevator, drops her bag in my foyer and hugs me. "What can I do?" She's become like a little sister to me in the five years she's worked for me. There's nothing either of us wouldn't do for the other, which she's just proven once again.

"I don't even know what I need right now."

"Whatever it is, I'm here for both of you."

"How did you get here so fast?"

"I jumped on a plane an hour after the news hit the Web. Liza is coming, too," she said of my publicist, "but I told her not to come here tonight. Tomorrow will be soon enough."

"Good call, thanks. I need to get back to Natalie. She's in the tub. Gabe is sending his doctor cousin over."

"I'll make tea."

"She likes hot chocolate."

"I'll make that, then." She grasps my arm. "You're not in this alone. The entire Quantum army is circling and out for blood."

"Thanks for coming, Addie."

"Just doing my job."

"You're doing much more than that, as you well know."

"Go to her. It's all going to be okay."

Though I'm soothed by Addie's assurances, one look at Natalie's ghostly white, tearstained face tells me it's going to be a very long time—if ever—before things are all right again. "Let's get you out of there, sweetheart." As if she's a child, I help her up and out. I dry her and wrap her up in a warm robe of mine. Then I towel-dry and brush her hair.

All the while, she stares blankly at the wall, barely blinking even as tears keep on coming. Where the hell is that doctor? "Let's get you to bed." She doesn't so much as blink when I pick her up and carry her to my bed. After she's tucked in under the thick down comforter, I sit beside her, holding her hand and wishing I knew what to do for her.

Addie comes in with a mug of hot chocolate and silently puts it on the bedside table before leaving us alone.

"Addie made you some hot chocolate."

"What's she doing here?"

The question is a huge relief to me. "She came to help us."

"There's nothing she can do."

The absolute desolation in her voice is another arrow to my broken heart. "There's a lot we can do, and we're going to do all of it after we take care of you. You're the only thing that matters."

"Your career, what they must be saying…"

"Fuck that. I couldn't care less about my career right now. I care about you. I love you, and I hate that this is happening to you because of me."

"I just… I don't understand… Why? Why would he do this?"

I wipe the tears from her face while holding back my own. I can't remember the last time I cried about anything, but I fear if I start now, I might never stop. "Who did it, Nat?"

"It had to be the lawyer in Lincoln. I paid him a lot of money to help me change my name after everything that happened. Why would he do this?"

"Money." I'm gutted as the pieces fall together. "After you were seen with me, he recognized the chance to cash in."

"I was his client," she says on a sob. "He's not allowed to talk about me."

"You're damned right he's not. I'll see to it that he's disbarred and charged criminally for what he's done to you. Not to mention we'll sue his ass off."

"It's like it's happening all over again… Feels just like it did then."

She's referring to being raped at fifteen, which the whole world is now hearing about thanks to a fucking lawyer in Lincoln, Nebraska, who sold her out to make a buck—probably a lot of them.

I can barely breathe through the rage. I want to cry along with her at knowing I caused her to be victimized all over again. I dragged her back into a nightmare that she'd long ago put behind her. If I'd had any idea something like this was even possible, I never would've been seen in public with her.

"It's not your fault," she says softly.

Though I'm relieved to see a spark of life in her normally luminescent eyes, I refuse to be let off the hook. "It's absolutely my fault. Because you were seen with me, they wanted to know more about you, so they dug until they found someone willing to talk for a price."

"I don't blame you. I blame him."

I adore her for being concerned about me at a time like this. "What's his name, sweetheart?"

"David Rogers. He's the only person, until today, who knew me by both names. It had to be him."

"You've never told anyone, even your family?"

She shakes her head. "I haven't seen or talked to my family in eight years."

I'm saddened to be reminded of how alone she's been for all these years. Well, she's not alone anymore. I want every detail of what happened to her, but asking for that now isn't what she needs. So I sit with her, holding her hand and offering her sips of hot chocolate until a knock on the door announces the doctor's arrival.

I'm relieved that Gabe's cousin is a woman. I'm further relieved when she doesn't make a thing of who I am. Rather, she focuses all her attention on Natalie.

"Hi there, I'm Doctor Janelle Richmond." She shares dark hair, eyes, complexion and a general family resemblance with Gabe.

I get up to shake her hand. "Thanks so much for coming."

Natalie glances at me, her trepidation palpable. "You called a doctor?"

"I thought it might help to get something so you can sleep."

"Maybe I could have a moment alone with Natalie?" Janelle asks.

I don't want to leave, but I defer to her. "Is it okay with you?" I ask Natalie.

She grasps handfuls of the down comforter on my bed. "I guess."

"I'll be right outside the door. Call if you need me." I lean in to kiss her forehead before I leave the room, closing the door behind me.

Addie finds me in the hallway. "How is she?"

"A little better than she was." I run my fingers through my hair repeatedly. "Can you call Emmett for me?"

"Sure." She goes to the living room to get her phone and returns to my post outside the bedroom door. "Here you go."

I take the phone from her. "Emmett."

"What can I do, Flynn?" As the chief counsel for Quantum, Emmett Burke is a friend as well as a colleague. He's also a member of Club Quantum, our secret BDSM club. "I can't even imagine how upset you must be."

"I've moved past upset straight to enraged. A lawyer named David Rogers in Lincoln, Nebraska, handled Natalie's legal name change. She says he's the only person on earth who knows her by both names. I want him buried."

"I'm all over it." After a pause, he says, "Flynn… I know you've been tending to Natalie, but what they're reporting about what happened to her… You… um… You need to prepare yourself before you read it. It's h-hard-core, man."

In ten years in business together as well as a close personal friendship, I've never heard the supremely confident Emmett Burke stutter or stammer. That he is doing both now only adds to my anxiety. "Give me the highlights—or lowlights." I brace myself for what I'm about to hear.

His deep sigh comes through the phone loud and clear, letting me know how difficult it is for him to tell me these things. "Her father was a top aide to former Nebraska governor Oren Stone. They were lifelong best friends. The families were close, and Natalie—or April, as she was known then—babysat Stone's kids. She traveled with them on family vacations and spent many a night at the governor's mansion."

My stomach knots with tension as the story unfolds. Her name was April…

"Apparently, Stone arranged for Natalie to babysit for a weekend that his wife and kids were going to be out of town. He held her there all weekend, raped her repeatedly and threatened her family if she told anyone."

I feel like I've been gut-punched. "Son of a fucking bitch."

"She went straight to the cops."

I close my eyes in awe of her strength and courage as a brutalized fifteen-year-old who had the guts to take that bastard down.

Then Emmett drops the next bomb. "Her parents sided with Stone."

"Are you fucking *kidding* me?"

"I wish I was. The case made national news. Stone made a lot of enemies on his way up the ranks. A bunch of people stepped up to support her through the trial. She filed for and was granted emancipation from her parents. She testified against Stone, and her graphic, detailed testimony sealed his fate. He was sentenced to twenty-five years to life in prison. About four weeks after he went to jail, he was raped and murdered in the shower by another inmate."

I experience a perverse feeling of pleasure at knowing he suffered even a fraction of what he'd inflicted on her.

"She disappeared after the trial. There's no mention of her anywhere online after the day Stone was sentenced."

"That must be when she changed her name."

"Natalie Bryant made her debut a couple of years later as a freshman at the University of Nebraska. There's no mention anywhere of how or where she spent the years between the trial and college. She graduated in four years and then moved to New York to take a position as a teacher at a charter school."

"Tell me there's something we can do about this Rogers guy."

"Oh, there's a lot we can do. I'll be making a call to the Nebraska bar to start with and preparing a civil suit as well as demanding criminal charges be brought against him. He's going to be very sorry he ever fucked with her—and you."

"Whatever we do, we can't make this any worse for her than it already is."

"I hate to say it's likely to get worse before it gets better."

The thought of it getting any worse makes me sick. I lean against the wall, closing my eyes when they fill with tears. Hearing the details of what happened to Natalie shreds me. My emotions are all over the place. "I want to protect her, but I don't know how."

"The most important thing you can do is keep her off the Internet and away from TV. She knows what happened. She doesn't need to see it playing out for all the world to see—again. I've spoken with Liza, and we're on it. Just take care of her and try not to worry. It'll blow over in a couple of days."

That may be true, but would Natalie ever be the same joyful, sweet person she was before her life and painful past were exposed to the world?

When the bedroom door opens, I tell Emmett I have to go. "I'll call you tomorrow."

"Talk to you then."

I stash Addie's phone in my pocket. "How is she?"

"She gave me permission to tell you she's definitely in shock and having a physical reaction to it, thus the trembling and crying. I gave her a very light sedative to help her get some rest." She hands me her business card. "If she's still feeling anxious or has trouble sleeping, call me tomorrow and I'll call in a script."

"Is she… Will she be okay?"

"Eventually, but it's going to take some time for her to process what's happened. You'll need to be patient and let her work through it in her own way."

Patience isn't exactly my best quality, but I'll become the most patient man on earth if that's what Natalie needs from me.

"Please call me if I can be of any further assistance to either of you."

"Thank you so much for coming."

"Of course. Gabe speaks so fondly of you and the others at Quantum. I know how much you mean to him."

"He's one of the good ones for sure."

"I'll let myself out so you can get back to Natalie."

"Thanks again." I step into the bedroom, where the only light is coming from the bathroom. Natalie's eyes are closed, but her cheeks are still wet with tears. As I get closer to the bed, her eyes open. Even in the midst of despair, I feel the connection that has drawn us together since the day we met. And now that connection has ruined her life.

"Can I get you anything?"

She shakes her head. "Will you… Can you…"

"What, honey? Anything."

"Will you hold me?" Her voice breaks on a sob. "Please?"

"There's nothing else in this world I'd rather do." I'm thankful—and humbled—that she still wants me close to her after the mess I've made of things. I strip off my shirt and drop my jeans into a pile on the floor and crawl into bed with her.

Releasing an anguished moan, she turns into my embrace, pressing her face into my chest.

Tears fill my eyes and spill down my face. I can't bear her pain. It's as if someone is sticking a knife straight through my heart. "It's okay, baby. I'm right here, and everything is going to be okay. I promise."

I run my hand over her back, which is covered by my bulky robe. Her shoulders shake with the power of her sobs. "Everyone will know," she says so softly I almost don't hear her. "The whole world will know what happened to me."

"And they'll know you survived and thrived in spite of it. They'll know that part, too."

"I didn't want anyone to know. I didn't want you to know."

"Baby, nothing could ever change the way I feel about you. If anything, I love you even more than I did this morning, and I wouldn't have thought that was possible."

"It's humiliating."

"Remember what you said to me once? That it took years of therapy to be able to realize this was done *to* you? It wasn't your fault? Same thing now. You didn't do this. Someone else did, and we're going to make him pay. I promise you that."

"What will it matter if he pays? Everyone will still know. You'll know."

"Natalie, sweetheart, it doesn't change anything for me. I'd still choose you a thousand times. A million times."

She burrows her face into the nook between my neck and shoulder, and I hold her as close as I possibly can. We stay that way, her sobs gentling, until we hear a telltale yip from the hallway.

"Fluff!"

The excitement I hear in her voice fills me with hope. "Stay right here. I'll get her for you." I kiss her forehead and get up from the bed, taking a minute to pull on my jeans before I open the door to Leah and Addie, who are about to knock.

Fluff sees me and shows me the ten teeth she has left in her fourteen-year-old mouth.

"Fluff," Natalie says. "Come to Mama."

The little white ball of fur bolts into my room and onto my bed, where she's reunited with Natalie.

"Thanks, Leah." Natalie's roommate is trying not to stare at my bare chest.

"Um, sure. Could I see Nat? Just for a minute?"

"Of course. Go on in." I step aside to let her enter the room.

"You have a dog in your bed," Addie says, going for a bit of levity.

"So it seems." A herd of elephants can invade my bedroom if that will make Natalie happy. "And isn't it just my luck that Fluff is immune to my many charms?"

Addie suppresses a laugh. "So you've finally encountered the one female on earth who isn't bowled over by Flynn Godfrey?"

"So it seems. She actually bit me and drew blood the day I met Natalie."

"I might've heard about that."

"Hayden's been telling tales out of school again, huh?"

"I'll never reveal my sources."

My best friend and business partner is crazy about Addie, not that he'll ever admit it to himself or to her. I suspect the attraction runs both ways, but Addie doesn't talk about him to me, and I don't ask.

I run my fingers through my hair repeatedly until I'm certain it has to be standing straight up. "Tell me what to do here, Addie. I'm at a total loss."

"Just be there for her. She needs to know nothing has changed for you because of what happened today."

"I've told her that already. I don't know if she believes me."

"Keep telling her until there can be no doubt."

"I never expected to feel this way about anyone."

Addie smiles at my confession. "It happens to the best of us."

"I can't lose her over this. I just can't."

"You won't. When the dust settles, and it will, she'll remember that you were with her through it all. That'll matter."

While I appreciate Addie's vote of confidence, I wish I could be more certain that Natalie and I will get through this intact. How long will it take for her to blame me for ruining everything for her?

Chapter 2

Natalie

I've wondered at times what it might be like if my secrets were revealed, but nothing could've prepared me to have the scab ripped off my wounds so suddenly and violently.

I feel violated all over again.

Fluff goes right into caretaker mode, licking away my tears the way she has since the beginning of my long nightmare. I'm happy to see Leah, my friend and roommate, but I can tell she has no idea what to say to me.

"I... um, for what it's worth, everyone is pissed at Mrs. Heffernan for firing you," Leah says. "My phone has been buzzing nonstop with texts from school. Sue even threatened to quit unless she hires you back." Sue is the administrative assistant who runs the office at the Emerson School where Leah and I are first-year teachers.

Or I was until earlier today when I was fired for lying on my background check and for causing a disturbance at school. As if I invited the throngs of reporters to stake out my school hoping for a glimpse of me in my humiliated state.

"I know you don't want to talk about it, and I totally respect that," Leah says haltingly, "but I need you to know how sorry I am for everything you've been through, and how sorry I am for mocking you for being so virtuous all those times. I didn't know, Nat."

Her voice breaks, and I see she's on the verge of tears.

I take hold of her hand. "Please don't apologize. You didn't know because I didn't tell you or anyone. I wanted to forget it ever happened, but I found out today how easily the past can catch up to us."

"Flynn must be dying over this."

"He blames himself. It's not his fault."

"You can see how he'd think so. I mean, before you met him, no one would've cared about your past."

"It's still not his fault. He's almost as upset as I am."

"You might have to keep telling him you don't blame him."

I'm so tired. Whatever the doctor gave me to help me sleep is kicking in, and I'm having trouble keeping my eyes open.

"I'm going to leave and let you sleep. Can I call you tomorrow?"

"I wish you would." I squeeze her hand. "Thanks for bringing Fluff over."

"I was just glad to be able to do something for you."

"Leah…" I force my eyes open to look up at her. "You've been the best friend I've had since my life fell apart. I just want to thank you for that."

"Oh God, Nat, I've been an *awful* friend to you, always pushing you to step outside your comfort zone—"

"No, you've been wonderful, and most of what you said is true. It's real between us, despite our differences. You have no idea how much I loved our normal, humdrum lives in that apartment."

Leah wipes tears from her face. "You won't be able to come back now, will you?"

"I have no idea what I'm going to do. Everything is a huge mess. I don't know how I'll be able to make the rent without a job."

"The rent has been paid for both of you for the rest of the year," Flynn says from the doorway. "I've also arranged for security for Leah until things die down."

I can't believe what I'm hearing. "You… you paid our rent for a *year*?"

"Yes, I did, and don't try to tell me I shouldn't have. None of this would be happening if you hadn't met me. Paying your rent and making things easier for both of you is the least I can do in light of the trouble I've caused you."

I hold out my hand to Flynn. "Come here."

Leah gets up to make room for Flynn to sit next to me on the bed.

"It's not your fault. You didn't do this to me."

Leah clears her throat. "I'm, ah, gonna go and give you guys some time alone. I'll call you tomorrow?"

"Sounds good. If you see my kids… Tell them I love them." The thought of never seeing them again is the worst part of a heartbreaking day.

"I will. I'll get your stuff from your classroom, too." She starts to leave, but turns back. "I hope you know—you getting fired over this—it's a lawsuit in the making. She had no right."

"Trust me," Flynn says, "I've got lawyers all over it. If there's any way to make it happen, we'll get Natalie her job back."

"Good. Try to get some sleep. I'll talk to you tomorrow."

"Thanks again for bringing Fluff." At the sound of her name, my beloved dog raises her head to see what's going on before she goes back to snoring contentedly in my arms.

After Leah is gone, I return my attention to Flynn. "Thank you for letting me have Fluff here."

"You can have whatever you want. Don't you know that by now?"

"Still… She's not very nice to you, and now she's in your bed."

"So are you. If I have to take the bad with the good…"

Despite the attempt at humor, he looks so sad and undone. I hate being the cause of that. I take hold of his hand and link our fingers. "It's not as bad as it was before."

"What isn't?"

"All of it. The last time my life blew up in my face, I was very much alone. This time, I have you and Leah and Addie and everyone you have helping us."

"You're far from alone," he says fiercely, his brown eyes shimmering with love and intensity. "I'd kill for you, Natalie."

"Please don't do that. I need you right here with me, not doing hard time."

He raises our joined hands to his lips and runs them over my knuckles. I love the feel of his stubble against my skin. He's so fierce and beautiful, and he's shown how much he loves me with the way he's cared for me tonight.

"Come to bed with me."

Fluff's low growl is full of warning, and I can't help but laugh at how ridiculous she's being.

"It's nice to hear you laugh."

I pick up Fluff and move her to the side he's currently occupying. "I think it's safe."

He gets up and goes around to the other side, takes off his jeans and gets back into bed.

Fluff starts barking frantically when he snuggles up to me.

I find the whole thing ridiculously funny and can't stop laughing. And then I'm crying again as I recall that I have nowhere to be tomorrow, that my kids won't understand why I'm not there, that the entire world is hearing about my sordid past and dragging Flynn's name through the mud, too.

"Nat," he says with a sigh. "Come here."

I leave Fluff to her rage and turn toward Flynn. As much as I love Fluff, I need Flynn's comfort the most right now. He wraps his arms around me, and I make myself comfortable in his embrace.

Then he jolts and lets out a cry of pain. "*Shit!*"

"What happened?"

"She bit me. Again." He holds up his hand to show me the red marks, but fortunately there's no blood this time.

"Fluff! No! No biting!" I sit up and turn to my obstinate little dog. "No, *no*!" She gives me a look that tells me she isn't sorry and she'll do it again if the opportunity presents itself. "I'm so sorry." Turning back to Flynn, I find him laughing.

"What is so funny?"

"She totally gave you a 'fuck you' look."

His accurate assessment makes me laugh, too. "She's awful! You shouldn't have to be worried about getting bit in your own bed."

"So much I could say to that..."

"Flynn! I'm being serious. She's out of control."

"She's protective of you. I respect that." He holds out his arms to me. "Come back."

Pointing a finger at Fluff, I use my sternest voice when I tell her, "*No biting. Or else.*"

"I'm incredibly turned on right now. Will you chastise me sometime?"

His irreverence makes me laugh, and I forget, for a moment, about the nightmare my life has become.

Back in his arms, I try to settle the turmoil inside me so I can rest. At some point in the last few days, his scent has become the scent of home to me. His chest has become my favorite place to lay my head, and wrapped up in his embrace, I find my happy place. Even in the midst of my worst nightmare, I feel safe and loved because of him.

The medication the doctor gave me is dragging me under, but I can't sleep until he knows how I feel. "Flynn?"

"What, honey?"

"I just want you to know… I've been afraid of this happening for so long, I don't remember not being afraid of it. But being here with you… I'd be losing my mind if it weren't for you telling me it's going to be okay."

"It *is* going to be okay. I promise you that. I don't want you to worry about anything. Close your eyes and go to sleep. I'll be right here with you."

I want to talk to him. I want to be with him. But I can't fight the effects of the medicine any longer. "Love you," I whisper.

"I love you, too. More than anything in this world."

Flynn

I want to find the bastard who did this to her and fucking kill him with my own hands, but not until I make him suffer. I'm so full of rage, I don't know what to do with it. And with Natalie sleeping in my arms and her wildebeest of a dog snoring on the other side of her, there's nothing I can do but fume.

I'm awake most of the night thinking about what needs to be done. When my tired brain can't take another second of thinking about the hell I've brought down on the woman I love, I let my mind wander and revisit the time I've spent with her. From that first fateful meeting in the park in Greenwich Village to this past weekend in Los Angeles, it's been a whirlwind of romance and passion and desire.

I never expected to fall in love like this. After my marriage ended, I was happy to be a jaded, cynical playboy who went through women the way other men go through beer. I worked hard, and I fucked harder—as much and as often as I could. Weekends at Club Quantum were my reward for hard work. The BDSM club I started with four of my closest friends and colleagues was at the center of my life until I met Natalie and decided I need her more than I need the lifestyle.

Last weekend, she told me she'd been raped. Hearing that, I knew there was no chance of ever introducing my dominant side to her. So it had come down to a choice—her or the lifestyle. I'd chosen her. I'd choose her every time. I need her more. It's that simple.

She's everything I didn't know I needed until she literally slammed into me and turned my life upside down. And now I've returned the favor by ruining the life she's worked so hard to build for herself.

By the time the sun comes up, I'm no closer to knowing what to do to fix this than I was before. Natalie is still sound asleep, but I need to do something—anything—so I get up, take a shower and pull on sweats and a long-sleeve T-shirt.

Addie, who spent the night on the sofa in my office, is already up and has coffee ready. She hands me a mug with cream and a touch of sugar, just the way I like it. "You need to see this." She hands me her phone.

I'm scared to look. "Tell me it didn't get worse overnight."

"Just read it."

It's a tweet from my best friend and business partner, Hayden Roth. *Some things are none of our goddamned business. #TeamNatalie #NoneOfOurBusiness*

I'm incredibly moved by my friend's gesture. He hasn't been Natalie's biggest fan because he's afraid for me getting involved with a woman whose lifestyle is so different from mine. He lived through the demise of my marriage after my wife discovered my sexual preferences and then got even with her "depraved" husband by having an affair with our director at the time. The fallout was hideous, and I've avoided commitment ever since.

Until now. Until Natalie.

"Click on the hashtag," Addie says. "There's more."

From my close friend Marlowe Sloane: *Sending love and hugs to my dear friends @FlynnGodfrey and Natalie. #TeamNatalie #NoneOfOurBusiness*

From my sister Ellie: *Much love to @FlynnGodfrey and his love, Natalie. #TeamNatalie #NoneOfOurBusiness*

From one of my partners in Quantum, Jasper Autry: *Fucking paparazzi has crossed a line. Butt the fuck OUT! #TeamNatalie #NoneOfOurBusiness*

Another Quantum partner, Kristian Bowen, tweeted: *Total bullshit to do this to someone who's already been victimized once. Enough! #TeamNatalie #NoneOfOurBusiness*

I'm overwhelmed by the show of support from my family and friends. A lot of other people I don't know have weighed in as well, accusing the media of going too far by publishing Natalie's story.

"People are pissed," Addie says bluntly. "TeamNatalie is trending."

"Good. People should be pissed. This whole thing is outrageous."

"Emmett called late last night. He's been in touch with the attorney for Natalie's school. I'm afraid the news there isn't good. Her contract stipulates that she can be released 'for cause' at any time, and there's no appeal process."

"You've got to be kidding me."

"I wish I was. I didn't think either of you needed to hear that last night."

"So what are they citing as the so-called cause?"

"Technically, she did lie on her background check when she said she'd never been known by any other name."

"She did that for a good reason!"

"You and I know that, and Emmett said the lawyer acknowledged she had a good reason, but the principal isn't willing to budge."

"I can't fucking believe this. Natalie will never forgive me."

"Flynn… Come on. She knows this isn't your doing."

"*How* is it not my doing? If I hadn't taken her to the Globes, none of this would be happening."

"Did you know about what happened to her? Before last weekend?"

I shake my head. "I knew she'd been assaulted when she was a teenager, but not the rest."

"Then how could you have protected her from something you didn't even know about?" Before I can form an answer, she says, "You couldn't have. It's not your fault. It's the fault of the man who attacked her. It's the fault of the person who sold her out to make a quick buck for himself. It is not *your* fault."

"You should listen to her, Flynn," Natalie says from behind me.

I spin around, and there she is, wearing my robe and holding Fluff to her chest. Her face is unusually pale, and dark circles under her eyes mar her otherwise flawless complexion. "Hey, sweetheart." I hold out my hand to her.

She comes to me. "Addie's right. None of this is your fault. I went with you last weekend knowing what was at stake. I trusted someone who didn't deserve that trust. If he'd done his job and kept his mouth shut, none of this would be happening."

"How about I take Fluff out for a walk?" Addie says.

"Thanks, Addie." Natalie spots the leash on the counter with some of Fluff's toys and clips it on the dog.

Thankfully, Fluff doesn't seem to care that she's leaving with someone other than her beloved Natalie. I send Addie a grateful smile. Walking my girlfriend's dog is definitely not in her job description.

"If you hadn't been seen with me," I tell Natalie when we're alone, "his story wouldn't have been worth anything."

"Again, not your fault. Last week, I did a search online for my name, and there was nothing to be found other than where I went to college and my job here. Because of that, I felt confident about going public with you." She comes to me and lays her hands on my chest. "It's not your fault. I want you to say that."

I force a smile for her benefit. "It's not your fault."

"Flynn…"

Sighing, I give her what she needs. "It's not my fault."

"Keep saying it to yourself until you believe it." Natalie goes up on tiptoes to kiss me. "I wouldn't trade one minute of our magical weekend. It was the best time of my life."

I put my arms around her to keep her close. "Mine, too, sweetheart, and winning the Globe was the least of it." The night I won the biggest award of my career and made love to Natalie for the first time seems like months ago rather than only a few days. After enjoying the pleasure of holding her for a moment, I draw back so I can see her gorgeous face. "You seem a little better."

She shrugs. "I guess."

"Hayden started a TeamNatalie hashtag on Twitter that's trending."

"He did? Really?"

"Uh-huh. The outpouring of support has been amazing. Everyone is furious about what was done to you."

"It's nice of him, especially since he doesn't even like me."

"That's not true. He doesn't know you. You guys got off to a rough start the day we met. It'll be fine when you get to know each other." Because she seems so much better than she was last night, I hate that I have to tell her what Emmett found out about her job.

As always she's tuned in to me in a way that no one else has ever been. "Whatever it is, just say it."

"My lawyer looked into your situation at school."

"And…"

"The contract is pretty solid. They can fire you 'for cause.' It doesn't define what constitutes cause. Apparently, it's at the principal's discretion."

"So Stone-face Mrs. Heffernan can get rid of me, and there's nothing I can do."

"Essentially." I'm careful here, because I don't want to upset her again. "Did you know that when you signed the contract?"

She bites her bottom lip and nods. "I never imagined I'd give her cause to fire me." Her eyes fill with tears. "I'm going to miss those kids."

As I brush away her tears, an idea occurs to me. I'll need her phone to make it happen, though. "How about some coffee?"

"Yes, please." I fix her coffee exactly the way I like mine. It's one of many things we have in common when it comes to food and drinks. "So what do I do now? Everyone knows about me, my job is gone, and I can't go to my apartment because it's overrun with media."

"I have an idea of what we can do."

"I'm listening."

"Let's go back to LA and hang at the beach until this shit dies down."

"You're serious."

"Dead serious. Hayden has a place down the road from Marlowe's in Malibu. I know he'd let us have it for as long as we need it. No one would think to look for us there."

"So we just get on a plane and go to California?"

"Why not? If we stay here, we're going to be stuck inside. If we go there, at least we can enjoy the warm sunshine and the beach."

"It's weird not to have anywhere to be."

"I know, sweetheart. I'll do whatever you want. It's totally up to you."

She glances up at me, those brown eyes slaying me the way they always do. "Could I bring Fluff?"

"Of course you can."

"That's very nice of you, especially after she bit you in your own bed."

"She doesn't scare me." With my hands on her shoulders, I look into her eyes. "The only thing that truly scares me is losing you now that I've found you."

"You're not going to lose me, Flynn. Remember, you're blaming yourself for all this. I'm not."

Filled with gratitude for her, I rest my forehead against hers. "So LA. Yes?"

"Yes, let's do it."

CHAPTER 3

Natalie

I'm deeply saddened to be leaving the city I've come to love, but Flynn has convinced me it's for the best. He asks if he can borrow my phone so he can consult with Leah about the apartment. I hand it over to him.

"Do you want me to check the voice mails and texts for you?"

"You don't have to. I'll do it when I feel up to it."

"Nat… It's probably best if you don't go online."

"Trust me, I have no desire to read about my private hell online. Been there, done that eight years ago. Once was more than enough."

"I hate that this is happening to you again. I hate it so much."

"I know you do, but in some ways… It's a relief. Everyone knows now. No more secrets to be guarded."

"They were your secrets to release or not on your own timetable. It shouldn't have happened this way."

"Maybe not, but I refuse to give that monster any more of my life than he already stole from me. If I curl up into a ball in defeat, then he wins. That can't happen."

"I'm so fucking in awe of you." He cradles my face in his hands. "You're the strongest person I've ever known."

"No, I'm not."

"Yes, you *are*. This awful thing happened to you when you were too young to understand, and then to have to cope with it entirely on your own…"

"I wasn't completely alone. I was lucky that by the time he attacked me, Stone had made a lot of enemies. They were happy to support me if it helped to bring him down."

"Your parents really turned their backs on you?"

Shrugging, I look up at him as it becomes obvious that he knows the details of what happened to me. "Stone was their bread and butter. My father worked for him. They told me I needed to be more concerned about my family than I was about myself."

"Fucking unreal."

"What they never understood is that I did it for my sisters. Candace is four years younger than me. If I kept my mouth shut, he might've gone after her next."

"So brave."

"I was so scared. He told me he'd kill me if I told anyone."

When Flynn wraps me up in his strong arms, I can feel him trembling.

"Since everything happened, I haven't felt safe, truly safe, until I found you."

"Natalie…" He buries his face in my hair. "No one will ever hurt you again. I swear to God."

I hold on to him and his assurances even as my heart breaks over the loss of my happy new life in New York.

On the way to the airport in Teterboro, New Jersey, later that day, Flynn tells me we have a stop to make before we leave the city. We're in one of two SUVs full of the security personnel he hired to keep me safe. I'm surprised to hear we're stopping anywhere when he's so anxious to get me out of New York, where rabid reporters have staked out his place and mine.

Addie is riding with us and will be flying back to LA on the plane Flynn chartered to make the trip. She's been quietly supportive all day, working the phones and taking care of details like arranging to have the bags Leah packed for me picked up at our apartment.

It's a relief not to have to consider logistics at a time like this. "Thanks for everything you did today, Addie." Fluff squirms in my arms, but I keep a tight grip on her so she can't cause any trouble.

"I was happy to help."

Flynn's publicist, Liza, wanted to come by to talk to us, but he put her off for now. He spent an hour on the phone with her earlier, during which he did a lot of yelling. I hate how upset he is and that he's still blaming himself.

We pull up to a curb on a street I don't recognize. Flynn takes me by the hand and leads me from the car. The security guys are all over us as we enter what looks like a family-style restaurant that's largely deserted before the dinner rush. We follow Addie through the restaurant's dining area to a room in the back.

I'm about to ask Flynn what's going on when I'm rushed by third-graders. The kids all talk at once as they hug me. Leah is there, as are several of the other teachers from our school. I also see Sue from the office and the children's parents, including my good friend Aileen. Her son, Logan, is one of my favorite students.

Aileen hugs me the minute she can get close enough. We're both in tears as we cling to each other. "This is such *bullshit*," she whispers. Her body is thin and bony from the battle she's waging with breast cancer, but her voice is fierce.

"I can't believe you're all here," I somehow manage to say. I'm so completely overwhelmed that I can barely breathe.

"It was Flynn's idea. His assistant, Addie, and Leah put this together so you could see the kids before you leave."

I glance at Flynn, so filled with love and gratitude I don't know how I'll ever express it to him properly.

He smiles at me, but I can see the disquiet that remains within him because this gathering is necessary in the first place. Then my kids want my full attention, and I give it to them, not knowing how long it will be before I see them again. They have a lot of questions, for which there are no easy answers.

"Why can't you be our teacher anymore?" Clarissa asks.

Tears fill my eyes, but I'm determined to leave them with happy memories of me, not tearful ones. "It's really complicated, honey, but it's not because I don't want to be your teacher. I want that more than anything, but sometimes you can't have what you want."

"Like at Christmas," Micha says, "when Santa brings you some of the toys on your list but not all of them."

"That's exactly right. But I want you all to do me a favor and work really hard for your new teacher and show her how much we've already learned this year. I know you'll be super well behaved because you always are."

"I'm sad that I won't see you every day," Logan says.

My heart breaks over the thought of not seeing him either. The poor kid already has more than enough to contend with worrying about his mom. I hug him tightly, knowing I'm likely to see him again because I intend to remain in touch with his mother.

Flynn has provided a spaghetti dinner for the kids and their parents, and as we all sit down to eat, it feels like a big family gathering. If only I wasn't trying not to cry the whole time, I might be able to believe that this is just another night and tomorrow I'll be right back in the classroom where I belong. Instead, I'll be holed up in a Malibu beach house waiting for the media to lose interest in me.

Flynn's hand on my back calms and steadies me. He is right by my side through it all, reminding me I'm not alone and I'm loved. I feel his love in every look, every touch, every word he says to and about me. I've known him for twelve days, and my life has changed in every possible way since then—mostly for the better.

I could live without the feeding frenzy currently unfolding online and in the tabloids, but Liza has assured him—and me through him—that the story doesn't have "legs." Most people, she said, are horrified by the violation of my privacy.

Hayden's hashtag has apparently gone viral, with everyone who's anyone in Hollywood jumping on board to denounce the media. I look forward to the opportunity to thank Flynn's best friend and business partner for his support while we're in LA.

"So what're you going to do now?" Aileen asks me quietly.

"We're going to LA tonight. Flynn's friend has a house at the beach. The plan is to hide out for a while. And then I guess we'll see what happens."

"I know this is a nightmare for you, but I hope you'll try to enjoy the time off and the getaway with that amazing man of yours."

I force a smile for her benefit. "He does make the glass seem a little less empty, doesn't he?"

"Um, yeah, he certainly does," Aileen says with a dirty laugh that makes me laugh with her. She takes hold of my hand. "Let me give you some unsolicited advice. You have your health, Natalie. You have a man who's crazy about you and friends who care deeply. Please don't let this setback derail your life. Promise me."

"I won't. I promise."

"Remember what's most important."

Appreciative of the timely words of wisdom, I hug her tightly. "Do you promise you'll keep in touch?"

"Always. Just so you know—a bunch of us parents are getting together with the Emerson board tomorrow night. We're not letting this go without a fight."

I'm stunned speechless. "You... you're..."

"We're fighting for you, Nat. Teachers like you, who care about the kids the way you do, should be given the benefit of the doubt, especially in light of what you've already been through. You should be treated like the hero you are and not vilified for making a new life for yourself. And by the way, as your friend, I'm truly proud of you for standing up to that monster the way you did."

I wipe away tears that blind me. I haven't cried this much in eight years. "I don't even know what to say."

"You don't have to say anything. We're on your side, and we're not going to be happy until they bring you back where you belong."

I hug her again. "It's been a long time since I've had real friends."

"You've got a lot of people pulling for you. Don't get too comfortable out there in California."

Laughing through my tears, I marvel at the show of support from the parents of my students.

After chocolate cupcakes and ice cream for dessert, the kids start to say their good-byes. I spend a few minutes with each of them, and I'm a weepy disaster by the time I say good-bye to Logan, Aileen and her daughter, Maddie.

"Thank you so much for everything you did for us this year, Natalie," Aileen says as she hugs me. "Despite what's happened, I want you to know that you— and Flynn—have made such a difference for our family."

"That means the world. Thank you."

Aileen also hugs Flynn and thanks him profusely for the huge donation he made to the fund we set up at school for their family.

"I don't know what you're talking about," he says with a smile and a wink. He's denied making the half-million-dollar donation we all know came from him.

"Sure you don't. You'll never know how much it means to me." She glances at me. "Take good care of our girl. She means a lot to us."

He puts his arm around me. "It'll be my pleasure to take good care of her."

Aileen fans her face dramatically and leaves us laughing as she escorts her kids from the room.

Sue, the admin from the office, hugs me. "Hang in there, kiddo. If it makes you feel any better, the entire faculty and most of the staff are pissed with Mrs. Heffernan over this. We all think it's ridiculous."

"Thank you for that and for being here. I appreciate it so much."

Sue whispers in my ear, "I thought you'd want to know that your sexy friend has paid for breakfast and lunch for every kid in the school for the remainder of the year."

I'm staggered by this information as Sue squeezes my arm and leaves me reeling.

Leah is the last one to depart. "I fucking hate this," she says with her usual bluntness.

"Me, too."

"I'm going to miss you and Fluff so much."

"We'll miss you, too. Maybe you can come see us in LA?"

"I'd love to." She pauses and clears her throat. "I want you to know… The way you're handling this is so admirable. I'd be rolled up in the fetal position if any of this shit happened to me, but you… You're amazing, Nat. We all think so, and I just wanted you to know that."

I hug her tightly. "You've been the best friend I've had in years. Thank you for my little slice of normal in our cozy apartment. I'll never forget it."

"Me either. But you won't get rid of me that easily. I'll drive you crazy texting you every day."

"Please do."

I release her, and she hugs Flynn.

"You're the nicest movie star I've ever met, and if I didn't love Nat so much, I'd be green with envy."

Laughing at her typical cheekiness, he says, "Thanks for everything today and for being such a good friend to Natalie. We'll see you soon."

"I'll look forward to it." She steals one more hug from me before she leaves.

Addie has taken Fluff out to pee, so Flynn and I are left alone in the room. I place my hands on his chest and look up at him. "Thank you so much for this. It's the sweetest thing anyone has ever done for me."

"Least I could do."

"You're not still blaming yourself, are you?" I ask with a teasing smile.

The deep sigh that escapes from him as he hugs me says it all. "I wanted you to have closure with the kids if things don't work out with the school."

"I'm so glad I got to see them and try to explain what's happening. I'd hate for them to think I left because of them for some reason."

"You were great with them. They'll never forget you."

"I hope not. And you… paying for breakfast and lunch for every kid in the school… Flynn, my God!"

He shrugs. "You know how I feel about hungry kids," he says gruffly.

I hug him. "You're amazing. Truly. I love you so much for doing that."

Wrapped up in his arms with his forehead resting on my shoulder, I feel the tension beating through him. He's like a live wire that's been set loose in a tight space. I worry what will happen when his rage boils over. But not for one second am I afraid for myself. Mostly I'm afraid for him.

Addie returns with Fluff. "Are you guys ready to go?"

Flynn glances at me.

I take a look around the room that was recently filled with people who mean the world to me. And then I take the hand of the man who has come to mean everything to me. "Yeah, let's go." Other than a few close friends with whom I'll stay in touch, there's nothing here for me anymore.

Flynn

Seeing Natalie with her kids has toughened my resolve to fix this for her somehow, some way. I'm not used to being told there's nothing I can do. There's always *something* that can be done, and I'm going to fight the injustice that's been perpetrated upon Natalie with everything I've got. I'm sure I've driven my friend and attorney Emmett to drink today with at least twenty phone calls looking for updates that have been slow in coming.

He's been in touch with the Nebraska Bar Association about the scumbag lawyer, David Rogers. Emmett also has a private investigator looking into Rogers, and so far they've discovered that the lawyer was up to his eyeballs in debt until a large deposit recently landed in his account.

He probably saw Natalie with me at the Golden Globes and thought he'd found a way out of his financial crisis. Well, he fucked with the wrong movie star if he thinks he's going to get away with ruining her life to enrich his own. I'm going to destroy him.

Natalie's yelp of pain makes me realize I'm squeezing her hand a little too tightly.

Cuddled into a ball in Natalie's lap, Fluff raises her head and shows me her ten teeth.

"Sorry, sweetheart."

Natalie leans her head against my shoulder as we're driven to the airport by one of the security guys. Addie is riding in another car to give us some privacy. "You're rigid with tension."

Because driving is one of the few freedoms my fame affords me, I can't stand being driven anywhere, but until we're out of New York, I'm doing what's necessary to ensure her safety. In light of her observation, I make an effort to relax even as my body hums with the kind of stress I've rarely experienced in my charmed life.

"Flynn…"

"What, honey?"

"I can feel you about to boil over."

"I can't help it. I feel like my skin is too tight for the rest of me or something."
I lack the words to properly convey what's going on inside me. It seems, however,

that the more wound up I get, the calmer she is. That said, I much prefer her serenity to the blank shock of the night before. I don't ever want to see her like that again.

"I hate that you're blaming yourself."

"Can't help it."

"Are you doing everything within your power to deal with it?"

"You know it."

"Then let it go and let the people who work for you do their jobs. You've done everything you possibly can for me and then some." She wraps her arms around my right arm. "Aileen gave me some really good advice tonight."

I squeeze her thigh. "What was that?"

"To remember I have my health and a man who's crazy about me. At least I think he is…"

"You know he is."

"She said we should enjoy this little escape from reality while we can and try to focus on all the positives."

"She does make a good point."

"It's hard for me to see you so upset."

"It's hard for me to see your life upended because you got involved with me."

"That's not why my life was upended. It happened because someone I trusted got greedy."

"Which wouldn't have happened if I hadn't dragged you into my life."

She surprises the shit out of me by moving Fluff to the seat next to her and removing her seat belt so she can crawl into my lap. Fluff is extremely put out by the disruption and growls to show her displeasure.

I want to growl with pleasure as Natalie straddles my lap and forces me to look at her. "May I say something and will you listen to me? Really listen and believe me when I tell you that if someone had told me I was going to lose my job, my home and my anonymity but that the trade-off was going to be the love of the most extraordinary man, I would choose love over everything else. Do you know how long it's been since anyone has loved me?"

I wrap my arms around her and hug her as tightly as I can. "Christ, Nat." I want to give her the stars, the moon, the entire universe—anything and everything I possibly can to make up for all the years she was so painfully alone.

"What you did for me tonight, bringing my kids to me, knowing how badly I needed to see them… No one has ever done anything like that for me before. I know you want to fix everything for me, but even you can't put the genie back in the bottle. My cover's been blown, and I'm going to have to figure out how to live with that. But knowing you're here with me, that I don't have to go through this alone… That's huge. This could've happened at any time. Someone could've put two and two together with the girl who brought down the governor of Nebraska. I can't imagine what it would've been like to go through this alone, without you and Addie and your army of people out for vengeance on my behalf. You're already making everything better by calling in your army and just by being here and holding me and loving me."

She brings me to my knees. She makes me want to be a better man so I'll deserve every sweet inch of her and the trust she has placed in my hands. I hold her close to me, breathing in the addicting scent of her hair as it brushes against my face. For the first time since Addie sent the 911 message yesterday and I heard what was happening to Natalie, I take a deep breath and feel myself begin to relax ever so slightly.

That Natalie doesn't blame me for what's happened to her makes me the luckiest bastard on earth. Rather than pushing me away as I feared she would, she's turned to me and pulled me closer. "I love you so much, Nat. More than I ever thought I could love anyone."

"I love you, too. Every time I think I've seen the full extent of who you are, you go and top yourself by arranging a spaghetti dinner for my class and then paying for the whole school to eat for the rest of the year!"

"Technically, Addie did the arranging and stuff."

"Whose idea was it?"

"Mine. I guess."

"See? There you have it. My guy is the most thoughtful, wonderful man in the world." She takes my face in her small hands and forces me to look at her as she kisses me. Hearing her call me *her guy* winds me up in knots that have nothing to do with stress and everything to do with desire. After the momentous step we took together the other night, I hadn't expected to spend these last few days dealing with her worst nightmare come to life. I'd hoped to spend them wrapped up in her, making love to her over and over again.

Nothing has gone according to plan since we got home from LA on Monday night.

We arrive at Teterboro and are driven onto the tarmac where a Lear awaits us. I've requested a plane with a bed for this trip and not for obvious reasons. I want Natalie to get a good night's sleep while we fly. If other stuff happens, too, well, so be it. Our security detail wishes us well and ushers us onto the plane where a flight attendant named Miranda greets us.

I can tell she's trying to be professional, but she wants to do that screaming thing women do when they meet me. Thankfully, she manages to contain the urge. Natalie, Addie and I buckle in for takeoff, and as soon as we're airborne, I get up and hold out a hand to Nat.

"We're going to get some sleep," I tell Addie. "Will you be okay out here?"

"I'm great. I've got a ton of work to do, and then I'll sack out on the sofa. See you in LA."

"Don't work too hard."

She gives me a small smile that's full of sympathy for what we're going through. She's been almost as upset as we are, and she's out for blood on our behalf.

I lead Natalie to the back of the cabin and into the bedroom.

"Holy cow," she says when she spies the full-size bed. "This is the life."

"I'm glad you think so, because it's your life from now on."

"I'm still trying to wrap my head around that."

I drop a quick kiss on her lips. "Take all the time you need to get used to it. You want to use the bathroom first?"

"Sure, thanks." She takes her purse with her into the tiny bathroom that adjoins the bedroom.

While she's in there, I unbutton my shirt and remove it and the T-shirt under it. I remove my jeans and then pick them up off the floor so Natalie won't trip over them. A few minutes later, she emerges from the bathroom wearing only a T-shirt. Her hair has been brushed and the minty scent of toothpaste follows her.

I take my turn in the bathroom and make use of the toothbrush and toothpaste the airline provides. And then I take a minute to remind myself that I need to be gentle with her tonight and keep the rage that's overtaken me out of our bed. It has no place there, especially in light of what's happened to her in the past.

When I feel calm enough to be what she needs, I leave the bathroom and crawl into bed beside her. "This is becoming my favorite place to be."

"In bed on an airplane?"

"No, in bed with you." I reach for her, and I'm greeted by a snarl and a bark that remind me we're not completely alone. "Fluff, you and I need to come to an understanding."

The little brat shows me her pathetic fangs.

"Maybe we'll do that tomorrow."

Natalie giggles like a little girl, which goes a long way toward helping me relax. If she can laugh like that, maybe I can chill the fuck out until tomorrow, when I'll rejoin the war already in progress. Natalie sits up to settle Fluff at the foot of the bed.

The dog reacts by whimpering in protest. I can't say I blame her for wanting to sleep cuddled up to Natalie.

"Stay." Natalie's stern tone turns me on. Hell, everything about her turns me on.

Satisfied that Fluff will stay put, she turns on her side so she's facing me. "How you doing?"

I caress her cheek and let her silky hair slide through my fingers. "I should be asking you that."

"I'm not the one who's about to spontaneously combust from stress and rage and a host of other unpleasant emotions."

"How are you able to be so calm?"

"I don't know exactly." She worries her bottom lip with her teeth, which is so freaking adorable. "I guess when you worry about the worst possible thing happening and then it does, you don't have to worry about it anymore. Does that make any sense?"

"It makes a ton of sense. It's almost a relief that the worrying is gone."

"Yeah, exactly."

"I'm so sorry you lost your job and your kids. I don't know if I'll ever get over that happening because of me."

She gives me that stern look she normally reserves for Fluff. "It's not your fault. I'm going to keep saying it until you believe it, too."

"That might take a while, sweetheart."

"Well, apparently we have nothing but time to spend together."

I have a million things I need to be doing with a new film heading into postproduction, decisions to be made on upcoming projects and meetings galore about the hunger foundation I'm starting. But nothing is more important than her and whatever she needs.

I'll put everything else on hold until this crisis has passed and I'm certain she's really okay, not just acting the part for my sake.

Her hand on my chest demands my full attention when she slides it down the front of me, coming to rest on my stomach.

"What're you up to?"

"Just touching you. Is that okay?"

"Fuck, yes, that's okay."

Smiling, she goes up on her knees and bends over me, peppering my chest with kisses and little bites that make me hard as a fucking rock in about two seconds flat.

"Nat... What're you doing?"

"Touching you."

"*Fuck...*"

Then she laughs, and my heart literally contracts in my chest because the punch of love is that strong. I'm willing to put up with any torture she has in mind if it means she'll laugh and smile. Then she closes her teeth around my nipple, and my mind goes blank. I grasp handfuls of her hair, trying to retain some control, but she won't be controlled.

Holy motherfucker...

She kisses her way down the front of me and uses her tongue to outline the hills and valleys of my abs. I thank Christ for every second I've spent in the gym. It becomes worth it right here and now. Her chin brushes against my cock through my boxer briefs, and I nearly lose my shit. That's all it takes to put me right on the edge.

"Could I... Can I..."

I groan loudly. "*Nat.*"

She rests her face on my quivering stomach, her hair soft against my fevered skin. "I suck at this."

"Oh my God, you do not! You're about to make me come just by *thinking* about what you want to do."

She turns so her chin is propped on her hand and she's looking up at me. "I am? Really?"

"*Yes,*" I say through gritted teeth.

Her smile stretches across her face, making her eyes dance with joy. I'm swamped with love for her.

"You're quite pleased with yourself, aren't you, sweetheart?" I ask with a grunt of laughter. She's so fucking adorable.

"You have to admit that making a guy like you tremble does come with a certain amount of thrill."

"A guy like me... What's that supposed to mean?"

"Strong," she says, kissing between my pecs. "Sexy." More kisses, some tongue action and fucking hell... teeth. "Commanding." She nuzzles my happy trail, and my dick surges, wanting in on this right now. I don't know what I need more—for her to touch me where I'm dying for her or to hear more words that describe me from her point of view.

Touch. I definitely want her to touch me right fucking now. "Natalie... Have some mercy, will you?"

She hooks her fingers into the waistband of my briefs and draws them down slowly, so fucking slowly she nearly finishes me with only the drag of elastic over my rigid erection. I've never been so fucking hard in my life.

I grab the hem of her T-shirt and pull it up. "Can we take this off?"

She hesitates, but only for a second before the shirt clears her head and hits the floor. Her full, gorgeous breasts fall into my waiting hands.

She twists out of my reach. "No! You're not taking over my show."

"What?" For a fraction of an instant, I forget who I am with her, and I nearly remind her who's in charge here. Thankfully, I catch myself before I can make that critical error, but the near miss humbles me.

"Relax and let me love you."

I blow out a deep breath and summon the will to control myself without controlling her, too. I don't surrender to anyone. But Natalie isn't just anyone. She's become my whole life, and if she wants to control me, albeit briefly, I'll allow it. Somehow.

She rolls her bottom lip between her teeth as she wraps her hand around the base of my cock and begins to stroke me. She watches with fascination as a bead of moisture appears at the tip. Then, in the single most erotic sight I've ever witnessed, she bends her head and licks me clean.

"Nat," I say on a gasp. "Wait a sec."

She looks up at me.

"The last time we did this… Don't do it if you don't want to." I can't forget the flashback that hit her without warning the first time she tried to take me into her mouth.

"I'm okay." Her lips encircle the tip, and her tongue slashes me.

It's all I can do to refrain from pulling her head down onto my dick. That's what I'd do with any other woman, but Natalie isn't any other woman. She's *the* woman. So instead of grabbing her, I fist handfuls of the comforter and hold on for dear life as she sets out to drive me mad with her experimentation.

"Does it feel good?" she asks.

"Yeah. It feels fucking amazing."

Hearing that pleases her, and she goes back for more, taking me in farther this time. I want to tell her what to do. I want to tell her to suck me, squeeze my balls and stroke me hard. I have to bite my tongue to keep from barking out orders when it's far more important that she become used to me in her mouth than it is that she do this exactly the way I want it done.

Besides, it apparently doesn't matter what she does, because she's got me on the verge of losing it in no time at all.

"Babe." The sight of her lush lips stretched to accommodate my dick takes me right to the brink. "*Natalie.*"

Not seeming to understand my urgency, she withdraws slowly, torturously.

I take hold of my cock and jerk my hips to avoid coming in her face. "*Fuck.*" The orgasm blasts through me with powerful intensity. I'm left panting and trembling while Natalie looks on with a look of satisfaction that might even surpass mine. "Jesus."

"It was good?" she asks.

"Yeah." I grunt out a laugh between deep breaths. "But good might not be a significant enough word to describe what that was."

"Really?"

I want to hold her and touch her and kiss her everywhere. "Hand me my shirt, will you?" I use the shirt to mop up the mess I made on my stomach and chest and then toss it aside. "Come here." Holding my arms out to her, I gather her close to me. The press of her breasts against my chest is all it takes to start my motor running all over again.

Fluff lets out a snore that makes us laugh.

"I can't believe she didn't try to bite my dick off when you were giving it attention."

"I'd never let her bite you there."

"Thank God for small favors."

"There's nothing small about it."

"If I wasn't already madly in love with you, I would be now."

"Flynn?"

"Hmm?"

"Will you make love to me? The way you did the other night?"

"You're not sore anymore?"

"I'm not sore," she says as she drags a fingertip across my abdomen, "but I am achy."

I feel like I've been electrocuted. The way she looks at me, the way she touches me… This can't possibly be real. I reach over to caress her face before I draw her into a kiss. "What's happened to my shy, reserved Natalie?"

"She got a taste of heaven in your arms, and now she wants more."

"Are you sure? With everything—"

"I'm sure."

"I'm so afraid I'm going to do something to scare you."

"You won't. You've got nothing at all in common with the man who hurt me."

I want to remind her I have one thing in common with him, and that particular part of me wants to be inside her more than I've ever wanted anything. "You have to promise you'll stop me if you're scared or worried or—"

She brings me into a kiss that starts off sweet and becomes something else entirely in a matter of seconds. Her arms encircle my neck, keeping me right where she wants me. This aggressive, passionate Natalie enthralls me. Maybe I could, we could… Visions of her tied to the headboard, her ass raised in the air, dance through my mind like the best movie I've ever seen. No. That's not happening. I have to remember to control my baser urges with her.

I roll her under me and look down at her. She's flushed and wide-eyed and flat-out gorgeous. Her lips are swollen from the blowjob. So fucking beautiful.

"What?" she asks. "Is something wrong?"

"No, love, everything is just right." I kiss her before I get up from the bed to find a condom. "Crap, the condoms are in my other bag, which I left out there." I pull on my jeans and somehow manage to get them zipped over my rampant erection. "Be right back."

"Hurry up."

Her excitement and urgency only make me harder. In the main salon, Addie is hard at work on her laptop. The glass of red wine sitting next to her computer tells me she's attempting to relax. She glances at me as I grab the backpack I left in one of the chairs.

"You're supposed to be sleeping," I tell her.

"So are you."

"Don't stay up too late."

"Hey, Flynn…"

"Yeah?" As I turn to face her, I hold the backpack in front of me.

"I've been emailing with Liza. She wants to schedule an interview so Natalie can tell her story—"

"That's not happening." The very thought of it enrages me.

"Liza's theory is that if Natalie tells her story, then the feeding frenzy will stop that much sooner."

"Not. Happening. Feel free to quote me on that to Liza."

Addie gives me a challenging look that I recognize all too well.

I release a deep sigh as my hard-on all but disappears at the reminder of our situation. "What is it you wish to say?" Addie always speaks her mind with me, and I always encourage her to do so because she's extremely savvy and always has my best interests at heart.

"For what it's worth, I think you ought to consider Liza's advice. You pay her a lot of money to tell you what to do in these situations. I happen to agree with her. If Natalie tells her story in her own words, that makes it impossible for anyone else to tell it. It would put an end to the salacious innuendo that has overtaken the Internet."

"You know what I hate most about this?"

"What?"

"Every time her name is mentioned for the rest of her life, this story will be tied to it. That's why she changed her name in the first place."

"I hate that, too. We all do. But the cat's out of the bag. You can't pretend it's not happening, as much as you'd like to."

She's right, and so is Liza, but all I can think about is Natalie and asking her to go on national TV to talk about the most painful thing in her life. The very idea of it makes me nauseated.

"Get some sleep, Addie."

"Night, Flynn. And good luck in the morning, not that you'll need it."

"Thanks." Her comment reminds me that Oscar nominations are coming in the morning, something that would normally be foremost on my mind. But I don't have the capacity to care about anything other than what's happening with Natalie right now.

I return to the bedroom, where Natalie is propped on her upturned hand waiting for me. The sight of her bare shoulder reminds me of what was about to happen before I left the room. Retrieving the box of condoms, I drop my pants onto the floor and crawl back into bed with her.

"What's wrong?"

I force a smile and hold up the box of condoms for her to see. "Nothing now."

"Don't lie to me, Flynn. Something happened while you were out there. I can tell just by looking at you."

"How'd you get to know me so well so fast?"

"The same way you got to know me." She caresses my face, and her tender touch makes me melt on the inside.

I love her so fucking much, and I want to protect her from anything and everything that could ever hurt her. "Addie has been talking to Liza. They think we ought to do an interview to give you the chance to tell your story in your own words to put an end to all the speculation." I watch the light in her eyes go dim.

"Oh."

"I told them it's not happening. I'd never ask you to talk about something so painful on TV. The thought of it makes me sick. I can only imagine how you must feel."

"If we did this, the interview, I mean… Do they think it would put an end to people talking about me? About us?"

"It might put an end to people talking about what happened to you years ago. It's probably safe to say they'll continue to talk about us."

"I'll do it."

"What? No. You're not doing it, and that's the end of it. I told them the same thing."

"Flynn." She uses the hand she has on my face to turn me toward her.

"You're not doing it."

"Yes, I am."

"No! No fucking way. And that's the end of it."

She smiles at me! The angelic, beautiful smile that slays me every time.

"Why are you grinning like a loon?"

Her smile gets bigger. "You're awfully cute when you're being bossy."

She hasn't begun to see the full extent of how bossy I can be. The thought of showing her my dominant side reawakens my cock.

"I'm doing the interview."

"No, you're not."

"Yes, I am."

I kiss her to make her stop talking, taking possession of her lips and mouth in the fiercest kiss we've ever shared. It's all lips and tongue and teeth. I keep expecting her to push me away in shock that I would dare to kiss her this way, but instead she meets every stroke of my tongue with one of her own. She makes me crazy with desire and the most intense need I've ever experienced.

I break the kiss and move down, cupping her breasts and sucking on her nipples. While I keep expecting her to stop me, she encourages me by arching her back and wrapping her legs around my hips.

I'm lost, completely fucking *lost* to her.

CHAPTER 4

Natalie

Something is different. He's wilder, untamed, ravenous. Is it because I defied him about the interview? Whatever the reason, I'm not complaining. I like him this way, a little unhinged and overtaken by desire. As his teeth clamp down on my left nipple, I want to beg him to hurry, to take me, to relieve the aching pressure between my legs, but I can't seem to find the words. He's stolen them, along with the breath from my lungs.

I'm on fire for him. He leaves my nipples stiff and aching to kiss his way down my body. His hands are everywhere, touching and caressing and coaxing. I can't get close enough.

He settles between my legs, his broad shoulders pushing them as far apart as they can go.

Every cell in my body is on high alert in anticipation of what's about to happen. The first time he did this, I nearly lost my mind. Even knowing what to expect can't properly prepare me for the first stroke of his tongue or the slide of his fingers into me.

"God, I love the taste of your sweet pussy," he says in a low growl that sends a flashpoint of heat blasting through me. "I could live right here and never want for anything." His fingers surge in deeper. "So hot and so tight."

I'm not sure whether his words or his actions are having the greater effect, but the combination is positively incendiary. I'm on the verge of a powerful release, and he's barely begun.

"Flynn…"

"What, honey? Talk to me. Tell me what you want."

"I…" I don't have the words.

He sucks on the very heart of me, and an orgasm rips through my body, making me burn from the inside. He stays with me through it all, coaxing me up and then bringing me back down.

And then he's pressing into me, stretching me to accommodate his thick erection. It's the most indescribable feeling I've ever had, his body joining with mine so intimately as he hovers above me, watching over me for any sign of distress.

My hands coast from his back to his ribs and down to his firm ass.

With a low growl, he drives into me, making me gasp from the impact.

He freezes. "Oh my God, Nat. I'm so sorry. I'm being rough with you."

I pull him closer to me and wrap my legs around his hips to keep him from withdrawing. "Don't stop. Please don't stop. It feels so good."

He reaches under me, grasps my bottom and then turns us so I'm on top of him, looking down at his exceptionally handsome face as he stares up at me with those soft brown eyes. "So fucking sexy."

"I… I don't know what to do. Tell me what to do."

"Ride me, baby. Move your hips. *Yes*," he hisses through clenched teeth. "Just like that. *Fuck*."

It's the most incredible thing I've ever felt. He's so deep inside me, and I'm stretched to my absolute limit by the size of him. Then he touches a spot deep inside that triggers something… Oh my God… His fingers press between my legs, and the combination sets off another orgasm. This time he goes with me, pushing deeper as he comes, too.

I bite my lip to keep from screaming.

He tugs me down to him, our mouths capturing my scream and his groan.

"Fucking Christ," he whispers against my lips. His arms come around me, anchoring me to him.

With my head on his chest, I can hear the hammering beat of his heart. His fingers burrow into my hair, making my scalp tingle. It never occurred to me before that my scalp could be an erogenous zone. As he continues to pulse and throb inside me, I shiver with aftershocks from my explosive release.

Without losing the connection between us, Flynn pulls the covers up and over me.

Memories of the man who hurt me are never far from my consciousness, but Flynn leaves no room for them. When we are together this way, there's no time or space for thoughts of anything other than what's happening right here and now.

"Is it always like this?" I ask him after a long period of silence. "The way it is with us."

"It's never like this. Ever."

His fiercely spoken response makes me smile as his chest hair tickles my nose.

"I'm doing the interview."

"No, you're not."

"Yes, I am."

He gives my hair a gentle tug. "You're being a brat."

"And you're being obstinate. I've run my own life for a long time. That's not going to stop just because you're part of it now."

"This is different. I have a lot more experience with these kinds of things than you do, and I know all the ways it can go very, very wrong."

"How can it go any more wrong than it already has?"

He starts to say something but seems to think better of it. "You'd be surprised how that can happen."

"I don't want to spend my life hiding out and worrying about what's around the next corner. I want to face it head-on and put it behind me."

"I know I've said this before, but your strength truly astounds me, Nat." He spins a lock of my hair around his finger.

"Your love and support make me stronger than I've ever been."

"Somehow I doubt that."

"So I'm doing the interview."

He sighs deeply. "We'll talk about it tomorrow. Go to sleep."

"I'm doing it."

I hear a chuckle rattle through his chest and fall asleep with a smile on my face.

I wake much later to intense pressure between my legs and Flynn's hand on my belly, holding me still as he enters me from behind. Holy moly, that's hot!

"Does it hurt?" he asks.

"No, God, no. It feels amazing."

"We've got to get you on something so we can forgo these fucking condoms. I want to feel your hot, tight pussy with nothing between us."

"Flynn…" I cover the other hand that's rolling my nipple between two fingers.

"Do you hate when I say things like that?"

"No… That's never been my favorite word, but when you say it…"

"You get really, really wet when I talk dirty to you."

Embarrassment sends a flush of heat to my face and breasts.

"Yeah, like that." He pushes harder, and I feel the course hair that surrounds his penis rub up against my bottom—another part of me that seems to be an erogenous zone. Hell, my whole body is erogenous when he's touching me.

As if he can read my mind, he moves the hand that was on my belly to my bottom to squeeze and caress me there. His fingers slip between my cheeks to press against my back entrance, making me startle with shock and pleasure.

"Too much?" he asks.

"No." My voice sounds high and squeaky.

He moves his fingers to where we're joined and then returns them, slick with wetness, to my anus. Good God… The combination of his thick cock stretching me and his fingers teasing me is almost more than I can take. Then he moves his other hand down between my legs and makes me come so hard I have to bite the pillow to keep from screaming from the pleasure.

I come down from the incredible high to discover his finger is now inside me, not far enough to cause pain, but far enough to force me to confront the dark pleasure of yet another part of my body that's been awakened to passion.

"I want to fuck you here," he growls in my ear as he pushes his finger deeper inside me.

I can't begin to fathom how he'd ever fit there, but I trust him to show me how amazing it could be. I want to give him everything, every part of me.

Fully seated inside me, stretching me to my physical and emotional limits, he doesn't move anything but his finger, in and out of my bottom. "So hot, so tight… I can't wait to feel your ass gripping my cock."

I'm losing my mind one small piece at a time. He plays me like a maestro, tuned only to me. And then I'm coming again, harder and stronger than before. He's right there with me, gasping into my ear as he drives his finger and cock into me at the same time.

I'm a shuddering, trembling mess afterward. My heart beats so fast, I wonder if it will burst free from my chest.

An announcement from the pilot brings me back to reality and reminds me we're on an airplane. "Good morning, Mr. Godfrey and Ms. Bryant. We hope you slept well."

Flynn snickers and squeezes my breast gently. "We slept great," he whispers in my ear.

"We're about forty-five minutes from arrival at LAX, and we expect a smooth landing. It's just after eleven p.m. in LA. We'll have you on the ground shortly."

"I need a shower," Flynn says. "Join me?"

"It's too small for both of us. You go first."

"Are you sure?"

"Yeah, go ahead."

He kisses my shoulder and withdraws from me slowly and carefully.

The muscles between my legs contract and spasm, making me squirm. I don't know how I'll ever look at him again after what we just did. A week ago, the idea of having sex with any man was unthinkable, and now I'm having dirty sex with Flynn and loving it.

He's certainly given me plenty to think about—and to anticipate. I can't wait for more.

Flynn

I'm a fucking animal. That's the only possible explanation for what just happened. What was I thinking? This is a woman who was sexually assaulted as a teenager. I'm her first lover—ever. And I'm already pushing her for things far outside the comfort zones of most women, let alone one who has been assaulted. I'll be lucky if she doesn't leave me the second we get off this plane.

My hands are shaking as I wash my hair and body. I thought I could control this thing, but I've just proven to myself—and her—that I can't control anything unless I control everything. If I show her that side of me, she'll leave me for certain, like my ex-wife did, calling me a depraved monster on her way out the door.

If Natalie ever looks at me the way Valerie did, I'll never survive it. The parallels are not lost on me. The situation now is similar to what it was then, except I love Natalie more than I ever loved the woman I married. It took years to get over the demise of my marriage. If Natalie leaves me, I already know I'll never get over her.

What just happened can never happen again. I need to watch my fucking mouth with her and keep my hands where they belong. There's far too much at stake to risk driving her away by showing her the depths of my desire for her.

I want to fuck you here. God, did I really say that as I pushed my finger into her ass? A surge of nausea burns my throat when I imagine what she must be thinking right now. She's shackled herself to a beast who has systematically dismantled her well-ordered life in the short time we've been together.

She's going to hate me before long if I'm not careful. As I soap up my chest, I realize I'm hard again, which has me swearing under my breath. I'm accustomed to indulging my stronger-than-average sex drive, not suppressing it. But I *will* suppress it before I'll do anything to scare a woman who has already known more than her share of fear when it comes to men and sex.

And for what it's worth, I don't even yet know the full extent of what was done to her, and I'm already pushing her for things even the most sexually seasoned of women often find off-putting. What if that monster Stone sodomized her? What if I brought back painful memories with what I just did?

I feel like I'm having a heart attack as that possibility settles on me. I have to know. Right now. I hastily rinse the soap from my body and grab a towel, drying off as I leave the bathroom.

Natalie is right where I left her, lying on her side, facing away from me. Her exposed shoulder bears a bright red mark from where I bit her in the throes of passion.

I'm horrified and gripped by paralyzing fear. I force myself to walk around the bed and sit next to her. "Are you okay?"

She doesn't look at me when she says, "Uh-huh. All done in the shower?"

"Yeah. Nat…"

"I'd better get in there before they're telling us to take our seats for landing." She gathers the sheet up around her naked body and takes it with her into the bathroom. The door closes, and the sound of the lock engaging is like a bullet through my heart.

I'm so fucked.

Natalie

Something is terribly wrong. Flynn is fairly vibrating with stress. I'm afraid to even ask because he looks like he's about to lose it as we get off the plane and into the SUV that awaits us on the tarmac. I'm carrying Fluff, and Flynn has his phone pressed to his ear, but he hasn't said a word that I could hear since he took the call. Addie has gone in a different car after saying she'll see us later.

"Fine," he finally says, "give me a couple of days and then we'll talk." After another pause, he says, "Sounds good." He ends the call and stashes the phone in his pocket.

"What's wrong?"

"What? Nothing. That was my partner Jasper. Oscar nominations are in the morning and he's wound up."

"I know you well enough by now to be able to tell when something is wrong, Flynn. You're so tightly wound, you're about to snap."

"I'm not tightly wound because of Jasper."

"Oh. How come, then? Is it the Oscars?"

"No." After a long moment of silence, he says, "Why can't you look at me?"

"What?"

"You haven't looked at me once since we got up."

I turn my head and deliberately look him dead in the eyes. "Like that?"

"Yeah, just like that."

"What's your point?"

"I'm sorry about before."

"What're you sorry about?"

"The stuff I did and said… It was too much too soon. I shouldn't have…"

"Flynn," I say on a huge exhale of relief, "stop it. I loved everything we did. And if I couldn't look at you, it's only because I was embarrassed by how much I loved it."

He stares at me. "You loved it."

"I loved it, and you would've heard as much if I'd been free to scream my head off. But with your assistant on the other side of a thin door, I felt it necessary to curb my desire to scream."

His fingers curl into the stiff muscles of his thighs. "You have to tell me what happened to you, Nat. I have to know so I won't do anything to trigger a flashback."

I look down at my hands, which are folded in my lap. "I don't know if I can."

"I'm so afraid of doing the wrong thing."

"Nothing you do is wrong, because you love me."

"I love you more than life itself. I'm obsessed with you. I want to hold you and kiss you and touch you and make you scream, but the thought of doing *anything* to make you afraid… I'm losing my mind over that, Nat."

I lean into him, and he puts his arm around me, drawing a low growl from Fluff that makes us laugh.

"At least she's not biting you anymore."

"I've been going crazy thinking about the things I did and said…"

"I loved it. I want more."

"*Natalie…*"

I giggle at the way he says my name, as if he's barely able to contain himself. Never in my wildest dreams did I think I'd find a man like him. We've known each other a matter of days, and yet I believe, deep in my bones, that he will love me for the rest of our lives. And I will love him just as much for just as long.

"Are you laughing at me?" he asks.

"Maybe a little."

"Do you know what happens to a naughty girl who laughs in her lover's face?"

"No," I say breathlessly, "what happens?"

He leans in to whisper in my ear. "She gets her sweet ass spanked until its red and rosy."

My mouth goes dry and my hands begin to sweat. "You wouldn't dare…" But I already know he would, and I'd probably love it as much as I've loved everything else we've done together.

"Try me." He kisses me, a soft, sweet caress that belies the intensity of our conversation. "But I'm not laying one finger on you again until I know what happened to you. I can't handle the fear of scaring you. I have to know, Nat."

He's right, and I know it. Just like he doesn't want me to be afraid, I don't want that for him either.

"We'll talk soon."

"Tomorrow."

"Okay."

He takes hold of my hand, laces his fingers between mine and holds on tight the rest of the way to Malibu.

Hayden's beach house is nothing like Marlowe Sloane's, which is somewhat of a disappointment. Whereas hers is a cozy cabana, his is all glass and blond wood and contemporary angles. It has none of the charm that I loved about Marlowe's place, but who am I to complain about a multimillion-dollar waterfront estate that has been made available to us on a moment's notice? I look forward to checking out the view when the sun comes up.

"Why don't you have a place out here?" I ask Flynn as we get ready for bed.

Fluff is making herself right at home, running around checking everything out.

"I did for a while, but I didn't get out here often enough to justify the cost of it. I sold it to Marlowe."

"Oh! That was your place? I *loved* it there."

"I did, too, but I was hardly ever there. She wanted it, so I sold it to her."

"That's a fantastic house."

"This one," he says, "not so much?"

"No, it's great!" The last thing I want him to think is that I'm ungrateful to him or his friends, who have stepped up so completely for me since my life blew up. Despite my rocky start with Hayden, he has proven himself a friend to both of us in the last couple of days.

Flynn laughs at my distress. "It's not what I would choose either."

"Thank goodness."

We share a warm smile.

"Are we setting the alarm to get up for the nomination announcement?" he asks.

"We sure are."

He sets the alarm on his phone and crawls into bed with me.

"Will you be able to sleep with the nominations coming?"

"Yeah. It's exciting, but certainly not the most important thing in my life right now." He gives me an extra squeeze and the next thing I know, the alarm is going off and Flynn is groaning in my ear.

"Come on," I say, tugging his arm, "let's go watch you be nominated for an Academy Award."

"Don't say it! You'll jinx me."

I love his superstitious side. It makes him so incredibly human. Even though he'll definitely be nominated, he doesn't take anything for granted.

"I'm starving," he says.

"I could eat."

We raid Hayden's fridge to make a big breakfast and enjoy coffee and mimosas as the sun begins to rise over the Pacific. Hayden's view is spectacular. At five twenty-five, we turn on the TV to watch the nominations, which come rolling in for *Camouflage*, culminating with a nomination for him as best actor and the movie as best picture.

Our screams of excitement make Fluff bark her head off, but we are too caught up in our celebration to chastise her.

I hug him so tightly and try not to cry all over him. I'm so proud and happy for him, and I love sharing this special moment with him.

Flynn's phone chirps with a text right before it rings. He puts the phone on speaker and takes the call from Hayden.

"Flynn! Wake up! You're an Oscar nominee and so am I, and so is Jasper and so is the film! We got the most nominations! Are you listening?"

"I'm awake and I'm listening." He winks at me, playing along with Hayden as if he doesn't already know the tally. "Wow, that's incredible. The most nominations, huh?"

"Twelve! They nominated us for everything—adapted screenplay, makeup, score, cinematography. Fucking A, Flynn! We kicked ass!"

"That's so cool. I can't even get my head around it."

"At long last, my friend. For the rest of our lives, we're Academy Award nominees and probably winners—"

"Hayden! *Stop!* Don't say it."

"Christ, Flynn, you and your superstitions! Go back to bed. I'm getting bombed."

"It's six in the morning, and you have the Critics' Choice awards tonight."

"I'll be sober by then. And I'll accept for you when you win. Oh—call your parents! They'll want to know."

"All right. Thanks for calling—and congratulations to you, too. *Camo* never would've happened without you."

"Without both of us. Go celebrate."

I hug him again. "I'm so *thrilled* for you and so proud!"

"Thanks. Wow. I had no idea it would feel this good."

"I've said it before and I'll say it again—you deserve every award in the world for the work you did in *Camouflage*."

"Thanks, sweetheart."

His phone rings nonstop with calls from his parents, sisters, friends and colleagues. Then his publicist, Liza, calls with requests for interviews that keep him tied up for the next couple of hours. While he spends most of the morning on the phone, I keep us both in champagne. We're giddy and more than a little buzzed by the time the phone finally stops ringing around eleven.

He puts his arms around me and holds me tight.

"How you feeling?" I ask.

"It's surreal. My parents were so excited. I love that."

"They're so proud."

"That's all that mattered to me for the longest time—making them proud. But now I want you to be, too."

"I'm so proud I could burst. And so are they."

He smiles and kisses me. "Thank you for that. Means a lot." He kisses me again. "Want to hit the beach?"

"Would it be okay if we hit the deck instead of the beach?" Despite the security people who met us at LAX and surround us at the house, I'm not ready to be seen in public quite yet.

"Whatever you want, sweetheart." He kisses my forehead. "Come on, let's go get changed."

"Flynn?"

"Hmm?"

"Thank you for bringing me here, for knowing what I need before I need it. For everything."

"I can't believe you're thanking me when I feel like the luckiest bastard who ever lived because I get to spend today and tonight and tomorrow and the next day with you."

"We're both lucky."

He wraps me up in his strong arms. "Yes, we are."

CHAPTER 5

Natalie

We pass a magical, relaxing day at Hayden's pool. The housekeeper, Connie, serves us a delicious lunch that includes a bottle of ice-cold chardonnay from the Quantum Vineyard in Napa. After she serves our lunch, Flynn tells Connie to take a paid vacation and that Hayden will call her when he needs her to come back to work.

"Thank you so much, Mr. Flynn. You enjoy yourselves."

"Who is paying for her vacation?" I ask when we are alone. "You or Hayden?"

"Hayden of course," he says cheekily, making me laugh.

"Does he know that?"

"What he doesn't know will never hurt him."

"Any connection between the vineyard and the production company?" I ask after Flynn opens a second bottle. We're sitting together on a double lounge chair next to the pool, which overlooks the ocean below. Between the stunning scenery and the gorgeous man snuggled up to me, I'm on sensory overload. Fluff is curled up between my feet, enjoying the warm sunshine.

"Yep. We own it."

"What else does Quantum own?"

"A lot of real estate, most of it in New York and LA, a couple of restaurants, four radio stations, six TV stations. I think that's everything."

"Wow. I figured you were all about making movies."

"For the most part, we are, but we believe in diversification."

"Your life is fascinating to me, and not because you're famous. It's the scope that's mind-boggling. Right when I think I've got the full picture, there's more."

A strange look crosses his face, but he quickly erases it with one of his trademark smiles. "We also believe in living life to the fullest."

"How did the five of you come together to form the company?"

"I've worked with Hayden from the beginning. We've made six films together and produced five others. Marlowe was in two of our early films and was interested in getting into producing. Jasper, who's a cinematographer, and Kristian, a producer who came along later, were a good fit for us because we share a similar vision about the kinds of films we want to make and produce. It sort of happened organically." He tops off both our glasses. "This is a tough business. It's nice to work with people I trust and who trust me."

"I'm looking forward to meeting Jasper and Kristian."

"You'll fall in love with Jasper's British accent. We call him the Panty Dropper."

"Dare I ask?"

"We joke that panties drop every time he opens his mouth."

"The British accent is extremely sexy."

"Oh jeez. Spare me. My sisters are positively smitten with him. Last year at Christmas, Ellie asked him to read 'The Night Before Christmas' and then made a flaming fool of herself panting and moaning over the accent. The kids thought she was having a stroke or something. It was mortifying."

I'm laughing so hard, I nearly choke on my wine.

"You know," he says, swirling the wine around in his glass, "I love talking about my friends and my business, but I'd much rather talk about you and your family."

Just that quickly, my stomach knots and my body tightens with tension.

"Nat?"

"Yeah?"

"Look at me, sweetheart."

I force myself to meet his intense gaze.

"I want to know you. I want to understand you. And more than anything, I want to protect you so nothing can ever hurt you again."

"Not even you are that powerful."

"You'd be surprised at what I can do when someone I love is hurting."

"You've already shown me what you're capable of."

"I've only shown you the start of it."

I can't put this off any longer, not if I hope to have a meaningful relationship with this amazing man who has repeatedly revealed his heart to me and shared his truth. He deserves nothing less than my truth in return.

"Tell me about who you were as a kid. I want to know everything."

"My name was April then. They named me that because I was born on the fifteenth of April, and the joke was that I was destined to work for the IRS because I was born on tax day."

"Ugh, nothing funny about taxes. The joke in my family is I single-handedly support the Pentagon with what I pay in taxes."

"Aww, poor baby."

"I know, right?"

"Back then, before everything happened, I was really into dance, gymnastics, cheerleading. All the usual stuff."

His eyes widen with interest. "You were a cheerleader?"

"Uh-huh."

"Will you, you know, sometime…"

I hadn't expected to laugh while talking about my past, but Flynn makes it easy. "If you're very good."

"I'm going to be so good."

"Anyway, growing up, Oren Stone and his family were a big part of our lives. My dad and Oren had been friends since they were kids. According to my mom, who grew up with them, Oren always had an odd influence over my dad. I didn't realize that when I was a kid, but with hindsight, I can see that their relationship was bizarre. My therapist said Oren was a classic narcissist. It was all about him, and my dad was his chief enabler. Whatever Oren wanted, Oren got… jobs, money, women, power. My dad helped make it all happen. Oren's wife, Stephanie… She was a really nice lady who had no idea what went on behind the scenes. My parents used to fight about the things my dad did for him. He always said he didn't have a choice if he wanted to keep his job. My mom would cry and beg him to get another job, but he'd say Oren needed him and he couldn't desert him."

"Were they into illegal stuff?" Flynn asked.

"They were into everything. It all came out during the trial. My charges were the tip of the iceberg. But I'm getting ahead of myself." I take a deep breath. "Even though my mother didn't think too much of Oren, she loved Stephanie. We kept up the pretense of our families being friends. When Oren became governor, they traveled a lot, and they asked me to travel with them during the summer and on vacations to help with their kids, who were much younger than me. I hadn't been able to find a summer job, so I took them up on their offer. My parents were thrilled. I remember my mom saying how happy she was that I'd be working for friends, people we knew and trusted."

When he strokes my face, I realize tears are spilling down my cheeks. Flynn takes my glass and puts it next to his on a nearby table. Then he gathers me close to him, holding me and caressing my back. "Take your time, sweetheart."

"I'm okay. It was a long time ago now. It's so long ago that sometimes it's like it didn't happen to me, like I saw it all in a movie or something." I take a deep breath, summoning the fortitude to get this over with so we can move forward together. "I spent a lot of weekends with them, helping with the kids while they attended events and other things he had to do as governor. So it wasn't unusual for them to call me to set up a weekend babysitting gig. It was unusual, however, for Oren to make the call. But I knew Stephanie had been sick with the flu and had lost her voice, so I didn't think anything of it."

My hands begin to tremble and my stomach aches. "My mom dropped me off at the governor's mansion after school on Friday. She said she'd see me Sunday and to keep a close eye on the kids. All the stuff she always said. We'd done this a hundred times before, so it was no big deal. Except… When I went into the house, the only one there was Oren. He said Stephanie and the kids would be home soon."

"Take a deep breath, sweetheart. That's it… If it's too much, you don't have to tell me."

That's when I notice there are tears in his eyes, too. This is killing him to hear as much as it's killing me to recount it. Knowing Flynn is right there beside me, that he feels this almost as deeply as I do, gives me the courage to continue.

"He was drinking when I got there. After about an hour, he told me Stephanie and the kids were in New York visiting her parents for the weekend. I was confused. I made the mistake of asking him why I was there. He... He slapped me hard across the face and said I knew exactly why I was there, that I'd been 'coming on to him' for years, that I was 'hot for it' and all sorts of other things I didn't understand at the time."

"Son of a bitch." Flynn's voice is a low growl. "It's a good thing he's already dead, or I'd kill him with my own hands."

"He tore my clothes off. I tried to fight him, but he was so much bigger and stronger than me. The whole time it was happening, I was in a state of disbelief. That this man I'd known all my life, my father's closest friend... I couldn't believe he would do this to me. He hit me and choked me and told me he'd kill me if I made so much as a sound."

"Motherfucker," Flynn whispered as he wiped away tears on my face and his own.

"The first time happened in the family room. It hurt so badly, I passed out from the pain. I think he drugged me at some point, because I was in and out of it for what I later discovered was two days. Every time I came to, he was inside me, hurting me."

"On the plane," he says haltingly, "when I woke you up that way, did it make you think of the attack?"

"No. You had me so turned on. I didn't think of it."

"It would kill me if I did anything to remind you of what happened then."

"I know." I squeeze his hand and take a deep breath before continuing my story. "When I tried to fight back, he would hit me. He restrained me, beat me with a belt... I thought it would never end. And when I thought it couldn't get worse, he shoved it down my throat, and I thought I was going to die because I couldn't breathe."

"That's enough, Nat." With his arms like bands of steel around me, his tears wet my face and neck. "You don't have to say another word."

"I'm okay, and I want to tell you the rest so we can never talk about it again."

He shudders and draws in a deep breath. I can feel his agony, and in that moment, I am absolutely certain he loves me every bit as much as he says he does.

"On Sunday afternoon, he told me to get up and take a shower. I hurt everywhere. He came into the shower and scrubbed me, violating me all over again as he washed himself off me. After, he grabbed a huge handful of my hair and brought his face down close to mine. He said if I told anyone what he'd done, he would fire my father. He said my dad would go to jail for the stuff he'd done and our family would be homeless. He said no one would believe a fifteen-year-old slut over the governor, and that if I breathed so much as a word to anyone, he'd kill me. I'm not sure what exactly came over me, but I had this vision of him doing the same thing to my sisters. When he told me to get my stuff and get out, I walked straight to the police station, which was half a mile from the governor's mansion. I was so scared because of the things he said he would do to me and my family if I told, but I knew I had to protect my sisters or he would do this to them, too. I couldn't let that happen."

"God, Nat. You're incredible. That you could be so clearheaded after what had been done to you."

"I stayed focused on Candace and Olivia when I told the cops what'd happened. I was afraid he'd go after them or other young girls, which is how I was able to report him. At first, I could tell the cops didn't believe me. I mean, when you think about it, here I was, this fifteen-year-old nobody accusing the governor of Nebraska of raping me—repeatedly. But he'd left bruises that forced them to take me seriously. They took me to the hospital… That was almost worse than what Oren had done. They gave me something in case I'd gotten pregnant, and the exam… It hurt so badly. I cried the whole time. I had to have stitches and… it was horrendous." I take the napkin he hands me and wipe my face and blow my nose. "Except when I saw Dr. Richmond the other night, I haven't been to a doctor again since."

"And here I am asking you to go on birth control. I never would've asked you to do that if I'd known."

I comb my fingers through his hair, needing to touch him, to comfort him. "You're hearing this story for the first time. Don't forget it's old news to me. I don't think about it every day anymore."

"It's going to be a very long time before I don't think about it every day."

"Is it going to change everything between us?"

He raises his head off my chest. "What? No, of course not."

"If you treat me differently now that you've heard the dirty details, that will hurt me."

"Nat... Christ... If anything, I love you more than I already did."

"There's more." I'm determined to get through this and be done with it, so I press on. "The cops called my parents. They came to the hospital, and with my permission, the detective in charge told them what'd happened. My father looked at me like I was insane. His exact words were, 'Are you out of your goddamned mind?' He absolutely refused to believe that his precious Oren could've done what I was accusing him of. He also looked really scared. I found out later why. He'd been up to his elbows in all sorts of shit for Oren, and he had to testify against him to keep from going to jail himself. Somehow, I can't imagine how, he managed to hang on to a job in state government."

"What about your mom?"

"She believed me. I could see it in her eyes, but she was completely under my father's control. He was in charge, and she did what he told her to. He said if I went forward with this, if I pressed charges, I was dead to them."

"How could he do such a thing to his own child, especially when you'd been so badly hurt?"

"I don't know. I've never understood the dynamics of his relationship with Oren. The cops told him it was no longer up to me. Oren had scrubbed me clean, but he hadn't removed every trace of himself from me. They had DNA evidence and were moving forward with charges. 'As we speak,' the lead detective said, 'Stone is being arrested.' Hearing that, my dad dragged my mother out of the ER, and I've never seen or talked to them or my sisters again."

"Good God, Natalie."

"The sad part is, I wasn't even surprised that he chose Oren over me. At least he was consistent."

"What did you do? Where did you go?"

"I got really lucky. One of the detectives took me into his family while we awaited trial. They were incredibly good to me. In many ways, they saved my life by getting me into therapy and helping me finish high school with tutors. The worst part was losing my sisters. I've always wondered what they were told and what they know. I wonder if they miss me or think about me, or if my dad poisoned them against me. Candace is in college now, I suppose, but I've never been able to work up the courage to reach out to her. If she hates me, I'd rather not know that."

The sadness is still so pervasive after all this time. "It was a really tough couple of years, but I got through it with the help of the family that took me in and the financial support that flooded in from anonymous donors who hated Stone and wanted to help me bring him down. That money paid for my new identity and my first two years of college. The other half… Well, I'm not sure what I'll do about that now that my contract has been voided."

"I'll take care of that. Don't worry about it."

"I will worry about it, and *I'll* take care of it, not you."

"Are you kidding me right now? Why are you in this mess to begin with?"

"I'm in this 'mess,' as you call it, because Oren Stone raped me when I was fifteen. I've been dealing with it on my own ever since, and I'll continue to deal with it."

"You're not alone anymore, baby," he says softly, so softly I almost don't hear him. "Everything is different now, and the last thing in the world I want you worried about is student loans that I could pay off for you tomorrow without even feeling it."

I'm shaking my head before he finishes speaking. "I don't want you to do that. I'll figure it out the way I always have. I'll get another job."

He starts to say something, but then shakes his head, pulling away from me. "What?"

"I'm going to take a shower."

"Okay."

He gets up and walks into the house without looking back. Watching him go, I'm fearful that despite his assurances to the contrary, hearing my story is going to change everything for us.

CHAPTER 6

Flynn

I want to punch something. I want to kick the shit out of Natalie's father and shake sense into her pathetic excuse for a mother. I want to dig up Oren Stone and kill him all over again for what he did to her.

The shower in Hayden's downstairs bathroom is big enough for six people. Standing under the pulsating water, I try to contain my rage, but there's no containing the despair I feel after having heard what happened to my precious Natalie. I slam my fist against the tile wall. When that doesn't make me feel better, I do it again.

And then she's there, pulling me back and wrapping her arms around me. I realize I'm sobbing. I can't remember the last time I cried before I met Natalie, but my heart is literally breaking for the girl Natalie once was and for the woman she is today, thanks to her own grit and determination.

"It's okay, Flynn." She runs her hand over my back in a soothing caress.

Why is she comforting me? I should be comforting her, but I'm reeling. I can't seem to get control of myself or my emotions, which is all new for me. I am always in control. Always.

"I'm okay. It was years ago, and I've put it behind me where it belongs."

I want to follow her lead, to put it behind me and move forward with her, but I don't know if I can. How will I not think of what happened to her, what was done to her, every time I touch her? What if I can't control myself? What if the overpowering desire I feel for her makes me forget, even for a moment, what she's endured in the past? I won't be able to live with myself if I harm her in any way.

Every sexual encounter we've already had runs through my mind with new context. Have I already pushed her too hard or too far? Have I frightened her with my desire? My entire body is trembling from the fear and the rage that pound through me like a jackhammer.

"God, you're bleeding." She raises my injured right hand to the water.

The sting of the hot water on my split knuckles snaps me out of the stupor. "It's fine."

"It's not fine. You're hurt."

I pull my hand free of her hold and shut off the water. "I need… I'm going to go for a run."

"Don't run away from me, Flynn. Please don't."

"I don't trust myself to be what you need right now."

"You *are* what I need. I had no idea how badly I needed you until you forced your way into my life and made me fall in love with you."

"Nat…" She slays me with her sweetness and her light. How can there be all that light when she's endured so much darkness? I admire her as much as I love her.

Her arms come around me, and she guides my head to her shoulder. "You're exactly what I need. Please don't run away. Stay with me. Be with me. Hold me."

I'm shaking like a tree in a hurricane. "I'm afraid to touch you."

She takes hold of my arms and wraps them around her waist.

We stand there in the lingering steam from the shower for long minutes. I have no idea how much time goes by, but I feel myself begin to relax ever so slightly. The trembling subsides, and in its place a deep, lingering ache settles in my bones.

Natalie leads me out of the shower and wraps a towel around me. I go through the motions of drying off. She ducks into the closet and emerges wearing an oversize "I♥NY" T-shirt that's another reminder of what she's lost thanks to me.

She takes me by the hand and leads me to the sink, where she rinses the blood off my knuckles. I'm so numb I can barely feel the throb of pain coming from my injured hand. She shuts off the faucet and takes me into the bedroom. "Sit." She points to the bed. "I'll be right back."

What the hell is wrong with me? I should be taking care of her, not the other way around. But I can't move. I can't think about anything other than the storm that rages inside me as I come to terms with what she told me.

Natalie returns with a first-aid kit and an ice pack. After she dabs antibiotic ointment on the wound, she wraps it in gauze that she seals with medical tape. She settles me against a pile of pillows and places the ice pack over my swollen knuckles.

"I'm sorry," I say when she joins me on the bed, curling up to me.

"Don't be."

"I've made this about me, when it's all about you."

"Not anymore. Isn't that what you said? It's about *us* now."

"Yes," I whisper fiercely.

"I've thought about this, you know."

"What do you mean?"

"About what it would be like to tell the man I've fallen in love with what happened to me. I knew I'd have to someday, and I thought about how it would feel."

"How does it feel?" I have to know.

"It's freeing, actually, to share it with you, to no longer be alone with it the way I was for so long. For the first time in longer than I can remember, I feel free." She adjusts the ice pack on my hand.

"You are free, Natalie, to have and be anything you want, but you have to let me help you. I need to help you. Let me pay off your loans so you don't have to worry about that anymore. Let me take care of you until you figure out what's next. You can't ask me to be someone I'm not. I have more money than I can spend in a lifetime. Let me use what I have to make your life easier. This is who I am. This is how I love you—I *need* to take care of you."

"You're so sweet to want to do that for me."

"I'm not being sweet," I say in a low growl that makes her laugh.

"Yes, you are."

"No, I'm not."

"We can agree to disagree on the sweetness. As for the loans… Let me think about it."

"Okay."

"Did we just have our first fight?"

"Fuck no. That wasn't a fight. That was me behaving badly. When we fight, you won't have to ask."

She smiles and hovers above me, her lips a heartbeat away from mine. "I love you even when you think you're behaving badly."

"I did behave badly."

"No, you showed me again how much you love me by making my pain yours, too."

"I love you more than I'll ever be able to show you."

"I love you just as much."

I bury my fingers in the damp mass of curls that frames her gorgeous face. "That makes me one lucky son of a bitch."

"We're both lucky. No matter what happens, no matter what's already happened, we have each other. And that's more than I've ever had before."

"Me, too, baby." I draw her into a soft, sweet kiss that's all about love and affection. But then she runs her tongue over my bottom lip, and the fire ignites inside me. As if I've touched something too hot, I withdraw from her.

"What's wrong?"

"I'm all wound up, sweetheart. It might be better if we just take a nap or something. If I touch you…"

"What? What would happen if you touch me?"

"I don't know, and I'm afraid of that. You're so incredibly precious to me. You have no idea how precious you are. I don't trust myself to be gentle with you, and that's what you need and deserve."

"I need and deserve *you*."

"Not like this." The ice pack slides off my hand and hits the floor.

"Flynn." She's on her knees next to me.

I'm afraid to look at her because I always want her more than I want my next breath, but now… Now I want her desperately. I want to right every wrong that's ever been done to her. I want to make every dream she's ever had come true. More than anything, I want to make her mine in every possible way.

Her fingers find the hem of her T-shirt, and then she lifts it up and over her head, leaving her bare except for a tiny pair of silk panties.

My mouth goes dry, and every thought that doesn't involve her exquisite beauty leaves my mind like water running down a drain. She's a fucking goddess, and for some reason that I may never fully understand, she loves me. She's given me the incredible gift of her trust, which fills me with guilt over the things I continue to keep from her. I don't deserve her. That's never been in doubt, but I want her anyway.

"Tell me what to do. What do you want?"

She looks at me like I hung the moon, waiting for me to tell her what I want. If I told her what I really want—her complete and total submission—I'd lose her and rightfully so. So I tamp down those needs and reach for her, arranging her on top of me with only the thin silk of her panties between us. She gasps as she comes down on my hard cock.

I grasp her hips, trying to summon the gentleness she needs from the first man she's allowed to touch her this way. She's given me the most precious gift of her love and trust, and I want to be worthy of her. "The other times… have I done anything that scared you?"

"No. I could never be scared of you."

I grit my teeth against the urge to tell her I could terrify her if I wanted to. But I don't. I don't want to, and I don't say it. Those needs and urges have no place in this bed or this relationship. "What I said earlier, about wanting you here…" I squeeze her bottom cheeks in both hands. "Did he do that to you?"

She shakes her head. "He talked about it, threatened me with it, but thankfully it didn't happen."

My eyes close as I exhale deeply. "I'm so sorry I said that, Nat. I wasn't thinking. I got carried away—"

She kisses the words off my lips. "I want everything with you, Flynn. I want you to show me and teach me. Make me yours in every possible way."

If she knew all the ways I want her, she'd never make such an offer. "You are mine. No matter what happens between us, that will never change. I knew, the first time you looked up at me with those amazing eyes that saw inside me from the very first glance… I knew you were mine."

"About that…"

"What?"

"My eyes aren't brown."

I have no idea what to say to that.

"I wear contacts that change my eye color from green. And my hair is naturally much lighter. I didn't want anyone to recognize me as April."

"Do you want to go back to being April now?"

"No. She's my past. Natalie is my present and future."

"You don't have to hide in plain sight anymore. You can be whatever you wish to be, whomever you wish to be."

"I'm very happy being Natalie with you."

I reach for her and bring her down for a deep, searing kiss. Our tongues tangle in an erotic dance that quickly has me on the edge of madness. She's like the finest of wines, the sweetest of chocolate, the most potent drug I've ever encountered. I want to turn her over and fuck her hard and fast until this craving inside me is satisfied.

But I don't do that. Rather, I force myself to remain still, to stroke her silky skin with reverence rather than greed, to kiss her with love rather than domination on my mind. I cup her breasts and tease her nipples. When her eyes close and her head falls back, I take advantage of the opportunity to sit up and suck a rosy red tip into my mouth.

She screams from the pleasure and pulls my hair so hard I may have a bald spot. It would be well worth the sacrifice of a little hair to know I pleased her.

"Let me hear you, sweetheart. Scream your head off. No one will hear you but me." I run the tip of my tongue around the edge of her nipple before drawing it into my mouth again, sucking hard as I bring my teeth down on it, taking her to the edge of pain but not going too far.

Her hips move rhythmically over my rock-hard cock. I reach between us to test her readiness and discover her panties are soaking wet. "*Fuck,*" I mutter, desperate to be surrounded by all that tight wet heat. I want to tear the fabric from her body, pin her arms over her head and take her. I want to possess her. But I can't do that.

"Nat." I slip my fingers under the elastic and into the flood of dampness between her legs.

"Mmm."

I move quickly to get rid of her panties and find a condom before I settle her back on top of me. "Is this okay?"

She bites her lip and nods.

If I'd had my way, I wouldn't have touched her today, not until I'd gotten myself together. But if I'd rejected her advance, I would've done more harm than good. "You're the boss, sweetheart." It goes against everything I believe in, everything I am as a dominant, to put my hands under my head, to yield the power to her, to remain passive while she takes charge, but I do it for her.

She lifts herself up, just high enough to position my cock where she wants it. Then she comes down slowly, exhaling as she takes me in, her eyes widening, her lips parting, her breasts heaving. So fucking sexy. "Is that right? Am I doing it right?"

"You're perfect. Feels so good." I have to bite my lip to keep my focus on the pain that sears my lip rather than what I'd like to do right now. I have to be calm for her, tender, gentle.

It takes a good five minutes, maybe longer, before she takes me all the way inside her. She is so tight and so hot around my cock, which gets harder from the effort it's taking to remain still and in control.

Natalie lays her hands on my chest and gazes down at me, the look of concentration on her face beyond adorable.

"Move your hips, honey. Like before. Ride me."

She pivots her hips, and I feel her tighten around me, her muscles rippling as she struggles to accommodate me. It's the most incredible feeling, but I can't help but think about the many ways I could make this even more incredible for both of us.

"Flynn... I want your hands. Touch me."

I sit up and wrap my arms around her, bringing her breasts in snug against my chest.

"Yes," she says with a sigh as she curls her arms around my neck. "That's so much better." The new position sends me deeper into her, allowing me to reach the spot that has her mewling with pleasure. We settle into an increasingly more frantic pace, her fingernails digging into my shoulders and her hips swiveling. I love the ways she feels, how she smells, the sounds she makes, the way she clings to me as we make love.

The love, I discover, makes all the difference. I can do this. I can be this regular guy with her, because I love her so damned much. I reach down to where we're joined, and the light touch of my fingers to her clit makes her scream as she comes. I could make this last for an hour or more if I wanted to, but she's not ready for that, so I give in and go with her, riding the waves of her release.

She shudders in my arms, and our mouths come together in a deep, searching kiss. I kiss her for a long time, until I feel her trembling begin to subside, and then I turn us so I'm on top, looking down at her.

Her eyes are wide and her cheeks rosy from the heat we've generated together. "So good," she says softly.

I nod in agreement.

"Was it good for you, too?"

"Nat, of course it was. It's amazing."

"You don't have to say that if it isn't true. I know you've had so many other women—"

I kiss her before she can finish that thought. "I've never had any woman that I love as much as I do you. That makes all the difference." I kiss her again and withdraw carefully from her. "Be right back." In the bathroom, I dispose of the condom and wince when my injured hand reminds me of the emotional breakdown earlier.

I'm on a tightrope with this relationship, moving carefully to avoid a disaster, but constantly off balance as I navigate this difficult situation. On the one hand, I've never been happier in my life than I've been since Natalie came into it, making me feel like I've finally found the other half of me. But on the other hand… The other hand is where the trouble lies. It's where the other half of my personality lives, the half I'm keeping hidden from her lest I scare her away.

Leaning over the sink, I splash cold water on my face. My injured hand has begun to hurt, but I can't take the time to care about that when Natalie is in the next room waiting for me. I have to stay focused on her and what she needs as we continue along this journey together.

She's the only thing that matters.

Natalie

After dinner, Flynn opens another bottle of wine, and we settle in to watch the Critics' Choice awards on TV.

"Do you wish you were there?" I ask an hour into the show.

"Nah. It's okay. I have the best possible excuse for missing it."

I smother a yawn. "Why does your category always have to be at the end?"

"Because it's the most important," he says with a wink.

I'm half-asleep by the time his name is called for Best Actor. Hayden goes up on the stage to accept the award.

"I'm happy to accept this award on behalf of my friend Flynn, who was unable to be here tonight." He doesn't say why. He doesn't have to. "Flynn asked me to pass along his thanks to the Broadcast Films Critics Association for this incredible honor. The making of *Camouflage* was an amazing experience for all of us at Quantum, and I have to say with complete objectivity, you got it right with this award. Flynn did the best work of his career in this film. Thank you for honoring his amazing performance with this award. I gratefully accept it on his behalf."

"That was really nice," I say softly, pleased and touched by Hayden's heartfelt words.

"Yeah, it was."

We watch long enough to see *Camouflage* win the award for Best Picture before Flynn shuts off the TV.

"So amazing," he says softly. "We worked so hard on that film, put everything we had into it. To see it recognized this way..." He stops when his voice seems to leave him.

"It deserves every award, every accolade. I could watch it a hundred times and still want more."

"You like it better than *The Sound of Music?*"

"Oh damn, that's a tough one…"

Laughing, he says, "I'm fucking wasted." I know he doesn't mean drunk, although we've had a lot of champagne and wine today. This has been a very long day for both of us.

"Let's get some sleep."

When we're cuddled up to each other with Fluff curled up in a ball between our feet, I release a sigh of contentment.

"What was that for?"

"It was a happy sigh. This was such an incredible day for you—"

"It was an incredible day for *us*."

"Yes, it was. I'm so glad you know everything now."

"I am, too, but I would give everything I have to rewrite history so you never had to go through all that."

"It means everything to me that you feel that way about me."

"I feel everything for you, Natalie."

I fall asleep listening to his sweet words of love.

CHAPTER 7

Natalie

We spend a late morning in bed and then pass a lazy afternoon by the pool. I had no idea it was possible to be this happy. I crave his touch, and he's always willing to indulge me. I feel as if I've awoken from a long nap to discover the woman I've always been meant to be. Flynn has unlocked the door to my self-imposed prison.

Tucked away in our own private paradise, it's easy to forget what's happening in the world around us. People are talking about me, about my painful past and about my new romance with Flynn. I can't believe that I don't care. Let them talk. They can't touch me if I don't let them. I refuse to sacrifice one second of my newfound happiness to those who would dissect the life of a rape survivor in an effort to gain ratings and clicks and to sell magazines. I have no time for them, and neither does Flynn.

However, his publicist, Liza, has again suggested we do one sit-down interview to tell my side of the story and then never speak of it again. Flynn is still adamantly opposed, but I think we ought to do it. He's promised me he'll think about it, but I'm not optimistic.

He's been very tense and broody since I told him my story. I can see him making an effort to keep things light with me and to treat me carefully in bed. As great as it is, it's different than it was before he knew everything. Believe me,

I'm not complaining. Making love to Flynn is amazing, even when he holds back. But it's different.

I keep hoping that he'll come to terms with what happened to me years ago and find a way to move on. In the meantime, I'm trying to be patient with him and to give him time to process it. I've had eight years. He's had one day.

While I eat a bowl of cereal on our second morning at Hayden's beach house, Flynn is on the phone with Addie. I'm not trying to listen, but it's hard not to when he's yelling. I can't imagine what has him so upset that he's talking to Addie that way.

"I don't want to talk about it. I'm not going." He runs his fingers through his hair as he paces on the deck. "Hayden can accept it for me if it comes to that." His head drops to his chest. "I know, Addie. I know it's my peers, and it's a big deal. But this is a bigger deal. That's all I'm going to say about it. I've got to go. I'll speak with you later."

The phone gets jammed into the back pocket of his cargo shorts as he comes inside to join me.

"What's wrong?"

"Nothing."

I tip my head in question. "That didn't sound like nothing."

With his hands flat against the counter, he sighs. "The SAG Awards are at the end of the month, and she's getting bombed with calls after I told them I'm not going."

"Why aren't you going?"

"You know why."

"No, Flynn. We're not going to hide out like we've done something wrong. We haven't."

"There's no way I'm exposing you to that madness. No fucking way. And I'm not going without you."

I put down my spoon and push the bowl away. Going to him, I put my arms around him from behind and lay my head on his back. "You worked so hard for this, Flynn. The film means so much to you. You can't miss out on the award shows."

"Yes, I can."

"You're not missing it. If you're worried about me, I'll stay home and cheer for you from the sofa."

"I'm not leaving you home, and I don't want to expose you to more bullshit."

"Will you look at me? Please?" I pull on his shoulder, compelling him to turn and face me.

He does so reluctantly.

"We can't hide out. That's not how I want to live."

"I can't protect you from what they'll say, the questions they'll ask. They'll violate you all over again."

"Then let me do the interview so I can put my story out there in my own words beforehand. There won't be anything left to say after that."

"I don't like it."

"I know, but I want to put an end to this story so we can get on with our lives."

"What if it has the opposite effect? What if it throws gas on the fire and makes things worse?"

"If we make it very clear that we'll never again discuss it, that should put an end to it for us. Others can say what they will, but it'll be a dead subject for us."

His cheek twitches with tension as he contemplates what I've said. After a long pause during which I have no idea what he's thinking, he says, "Carolyn Justice. She's the only one I trust to handle this properly."

Carolyn Justice is a goddess, and I've been a fan of her show for years. "Okay."

"You're sure, Nat? Please don't do this for me. My career and I will be just fine if we never say a word about this to anyone."

"I'm sure, and I'm doing it for us, so we can have some peace and put a stop to the frenzy. If we do the interview and answer all their questions, then maybe they'll move on to something else, and we can go to the SAG Awards without worrying about getting slammed with questions."

Another long silence ensues. "I'll have Liza set it up."

"Are you angry at me?"

His eyes widen with surprise. "Angry at *you*? Why in the hell would I ever be angry at you?"

"Because I'm pushing you to do something you don't want to do."

He places his hands on my shoulders and draws me into his embrace. "I am *not* angry at you. I could never be angry at you. I think you're fearless and fabulous and you amaze me every day with your strength and your courage and your fortitude. I'm angry that you've been put in this position in the first place. I'm angry at people who feed off the pain of others. I'll never understand how someone entrusted with your most personal business could sell you out to the highest bidder." He looks down at me and kisses my forehead. "I am *not* angry at you."

I snuggle up to him. "You've been so tense."

"A lot on my mind, sweetheart. This has been so nice, to have this time with you, relaxing and sleeping and stuff."

I laugh at the word "stuff."

"But I have to go back to work one of these days."

"I've sort of wondered when that would happen."

"We've got a meeting coming up for the foundation, and at some point I've got to be at the office with Hayden. He's into postproduction on the new film that has defied naming. I've got to make some decisions on future projects. A lot to do."

"I'm sorry if I've been keeping you from your work."

"You haven't been. I've enjoyed every second that we've spent together, and I'm looking forward to much more."

"I was wondering… About the foundation."

"What about it?"

"Would it be possible—and please feel free to say no if it's not a good idea…"

His smile makes his eyes twinkle, and I'm struck again by how gorgeous he is. That I get to hug him and kiss him and make love with him any time I want still amazes me all these days later. "What's your idea, sweetheart?"

"I'd like to be involved with the foundation." I swallow hard. "If it's okay with you."

"Yes, of course it's okay. I should've thought to ask you."

"I wouldn't have asked if I didn't think I could make a contribution."

"I'd love for you to be part of it in any role you wish to take."

I'm filled with the giddy sort of joy that reminds me of how I felt the night before my first day at school. "Thank you."

"I guess I'd better go call Liza and make her day—and Carolyn's. You're really sure about this?"

"I'm sure. While you're at it, call Addie, too. Tell her we're going to the SAG Awards because my boyfriend is expected to win, and I need her and her stylist pal Tenley to fix me up."

"You got it, sweetheart." He kisses me and squeezes my hand before he leaves the room to go make his calls.

Flynn

I have to do something. I can't bear sitting around waiting for things to happen. I'm a proactive kind of guy, and this situation is forcing me to be reactive. I'm on the verge of losing my mind.

Liza and Natalie have talked me into the interview with Carolyn against my better judgment. Though I've had nothing but positive dealings with Carolyn in the past, I fear the interview will make everything worse rather than better. I know it's irrational because Carolyn is a consummate professional, but I can't help the way I feel.

I go into the office and shut the door. Dropping into the chair, I put my feet up on the desk and try to get myself together. Losing my shit isn't going to make anything better for Natalie.

I need a shrink, but since I don't know one I can call out of the blue, I settle for the next best thing. I call my dad. I'm not worried about interrupting his day, because he always takes calls from his family, no matter what he's doing.

He answers on the second ring. "Hey there."

"Hi, Dad. Am I getting you at a bad time?"

"Not at all. What's wrong?"

"What makes you think there's something wrong?"

"You've been my son for thirty-three years. I knew with 'Hi, Dad' that something was wrong."

Despite the gravity of the situation, he makes me smile. I lean my elbows on the desk and run the fingers of my free hand through my hair, over and over.

"Flynn. Talk to me."

"I love her so much."

"I know you do, son. Your mother and I knew the first time we saw you with her that she is the one for you."

"I can't bear to see her going through all this because she made the mistake of getting involved with me."

"What does she have to say about that?"

"The more agitated I get, the calmer she seems to be, which is maddening."

Dad grunts out a laugh. "Why am I not surprised? Don't forget, she's been through this once before, unfortunately, and probably has a better grip on how to handle it than you do."

"Once was more than enough."

"Indeed, but it's happening, and she's handling it. That's what matters."

"She and Liza have convinced me that if we do one interview, with Carolyn Justice, it'll help the situation."

"You don't think it will?"

"I'm afraid that somehow it'll make everything worse."

"I know you like to be the one calling the shots, Flynn. But in this case, I'm afraid you're going to have to follow Natalie's lead. She knows what she can handle and what she can't. If she's intent on doing the interview, let her. It might help her to put the story in her own words rather than letting everyone else tell it for her."

I hadn't thought of it that way before. "What if it makes things worse?"

"How could it make things worse? What are you truly afraid of?"

"Her being hurt again in some way that I can't predict ahead of time."

"You know what the most difficult part of fatherhood has been?"

Taken aback by the change in direction, I say, "No, what?"

"Not being able to protect my kids from any kind of pain or suffering. We all wish we had a crystal ball so we could see the future and steer the people we love clear of any trouble. But short of that, all we can do is the best we can and then be there for them when things don't go according to plan."

"I'm not used to waiting for things to happen. I'm far more accustomed to *making* things happen."

"I know, son," he says with a low chuckle. "And I also know how painful it has to be for you to take your cues from someone else. But let me ask you this— are you doing everything you can to make this right for her?"

"Fuck, yes, I am."

"Are your lawyers all over it with the school that fired her and the guy who outed her?"

"Yes," I say through gritted teeth.

"Then tell me what else you could be doing that you're not doing?"

"I could go to Lincoln and beat the living shit out of the guy who exposed her."

"Please, don't do that. Don't jeopardize yourself or her or your sterling reputation by doing something stupid that'll only give you momentary reprieve and will definitely make everything worse than it already is."

He's right. I know it, but that doesn't mean I like it.

"Flynn? Tell me you're listening to me and won't do anything stupid."

"I won't."

"Natalie needs you to be strong for her, to guide her through her introduction to celebrity and managing everything that goes with it."

"I know. I'm trying."

"Remember it won't always be this way. Something else will happen, and they'll move on to the next big scandal."

"Any time now."

"I want you to keep in mind that as bad as this is, you've got her now, and she has you. That's the only thing that really matters."

"Thanks, Dad. You said what I needed to hear."

"I was hoping you'd call. I didn't want to bother you with everything you're dealing with."

"It was either you or a shrink."

He roars with laughter. "I'm glad you chose me."

"So am I."

"We'll see you soon?"

"Yeah, you will."

"Hang in there, son. We love you guys, and we're here if you need us."

"Thanks. Love you, too."

I end the call feeling much calmer than I was before I reached out to him. He's talked me through many a rough patch in my life, and was my rock as I navigated the perilous path into acting and producing. He's always the voice of reason, and I needed that today.

Now I just have to put his advice into practice and take my cues from Natalie. I can do that. At least I can try.

Natalie

It's amazing how quickly things happen when the biggest movie star in the world is involved. Carolyn Justice flew from New York to LA on a red-eye, and the interview is set to take place at the Quantum office at noon. I'm wearing my trusty black dress. My hair is long and curly, and because I'm tanned from the long days in the sun, I've gone with only mascara and lip gloss.

Hopefully I won't look like a country bumpkin on national TV.

Flynn is wearing a slate-colored suit with a white shirt and no tie. He, too, is tanned and looks fantastic, but then again he always does. He's been quiet and withdrawn since we made our decisions yesterday, and I'm hoping he'll be back to normal once we put this behind us.

When we arrive at the Quantum building, I finally meet Liza, who's younger than I expect her to be. She's petite with short glossy black hair, a killer power suit and teeters on four-inch heels. Despite her sharp, professional appearance, she's warm and funny, and I like her immediately.

Flynn introduces us, and she hugs me. "I'm so happy to meet you, Natalie."

"Thanks for your help with all this."

"It's my pleasure—and my job. Working for this guy is not exactly a hardship."

I hook my arm through Flynn's. "He is pretty great."

"I couldn't agree more. And I want you to know, I think you're doing the right thing today, and you've chosen the perfect person to talk to."

"Flynn chose her." We talk about him like he's not standing right next to me vibrating from the tension that has gripped him since I insisted on doing the interview.

"He chose well."

Flynn's sister Ellie, who works for Quantum, comes to say hello, greeting me with a hug like we're old friends. "This shit sucks," she says bluntly.

"Yeah, it does, but hopefully this will help."

"Our whole family is behind you, Natalie. I hope you know that."

"Thank you so much." Her sweetness nearly reduces me to tears. It's been so long since I've had a family behind me, and the Godfreys are one hell of a family to have on my side.

Carolyn swoops into the conference room at the stroke of noon with a team of producers, camera people, hair-and-makeup staff and an entire entourage of others who stand around talking on phones, barking out orders and generally trying to look important. The woman herself is a blonde with warm blue eyes that save her from being unapproachable. She's known for being a master interviewer who always asks the right questions and can make even the sturdiest of men break down into tears with probing inquiries about the most personal of matters.

One of the crewmembers outfits us with clip-on microphones. Flynn pushes the guy's hand aside and takes care of clipping mine onto my dress. The possessive action nearly makes me giggle, but he's not in the mood for silliness.

When the mikes are in place, Carolyn comes over to us and hugs Flynn. "So great to see you again."

"You, too, Carolyn. Thanks for doing this."

"Thank *you*. This is the interview of the year. Everyone wanted it. I'm so incredibly honored you chose me."

"I chose you because you've been fair to me in the past. I hope you'll do the same for Natalie." He's friendly and charming as always, but he puts her on notice nonetheless.

"Of course." She turns to me and extends her hand. "It's a pleasure to meet you, Natalie."

"Likewise." I'm totally starstruck. I've watched Carolyn Justice's daily talk show since college. "I'm a big fan."

"Thank you so much! That's so nice to hear. Before we begin, is there anything completely off-limits?"

I glance at Flynn. The pulsing muscle in his cheek tells me he's tightly wound and apt to get more so in the next hour.

"Nothing is off-limits, but I won't speak in detail about the assault."

"I understand, and I'd never ask you to."

I reach for Flynn's injured hand and hold it between both of mine as we're directed toward chairs under the bright lights Carolyn's people have set up. The wires and cords on the floor remind me of the day we met, a thought I share with Flynn.

His lips curl up into a smile that doesn't reach his eyes. I want to get this over with for his sake as much as mine.

When we're seated across from Carolyn, I continue to hold his hand, needing his comfort as much as I want to offer mine to him.

Carolyn has an intro prepared in which she summarizes the events of the last week and introduces us, making note that this exclusive interview is the only one Flynn and I plan to give.

"I want to start by asking you, Natalie, how your life has changed since you met Flynn."

The question takes me by surprise because I'd think the changes to my life would be rather obvious. I glance at Flynn, who's staring straight ahead, his face expressionless.

"My life has changed completely," I tell her. "With a few exceptions, it's changed for the better. I feel extremely fortunate to have met Flynn, to be part of his life and to have him in mine."

He gives my hand a gentle squeeze.

"We're all very curious as to how you two met. Care to share that story?"

We exchange glances, and he nods for me to go ahead. I relay the story of Fluff escaping from me in Greenwich Village and how I chased her right into Flynn's shoot. "I smashed into him and ended up on the ground with the wind knocked out of me while Fluff took a bite out of Flynn."

"The dog *bit* you?"

"Yep." He lifts his arm where the marks have faded but remain visible. "The old girl's still got game at fourteen."

"And with only about ten teeth left in her cute little head," I add.

Carolyn loses it laughing. "So what did you think when you realized your dog had bitten *Flynn Godfrey*?"

"She was afraid I'd sue her and Fluff for all their worldly goods," Flynn says with the trademark humor I've come to expect from him. It's good to have that back after living with tense, stressed-out Flynn.

"Which doesn't amount to much," I add. "Of course I was mortified. Fluff has never bitten anyone, and she makes her debut with *Flynn Godfrey*?"

"The whole thing was pretty funny," Flynn says.

"I have to ask how you go from her dog biting you to walking the red carpet together at the Golden Globes a week later."

Flynn glances at me. "I took one look at Natalie and knew I wanted her in my life."

Carolyn fans her face. "Whoa. I need a drink—and a cigarette."

We laugh at that.

"You don't smoke," Flynn reminds her.

"Today would be a good day to start! And you, Natalie... How do you go about dating someone like Flynn?"

"Carefully," I say, making them laugh.

"She made me work for it."

"When did you know this could be something special?"

The question is directed at me. "Flynn showed me who he really is several times in the first few days we were together. He's hard not to like, especially when he brings out the Godfrey charm."

"I imagine that can be quite formidable."

"You know it." By now I feel like I'm chatting with an old girlfriend, which is why Carolyn is so good at what she does and so well regarded in the business.

"Can you describe for us what it was like to learn that your painful past had been made public after you appeared with Flynn at the Golden Globes?"

I'm ready for this one, because Liza warned me to be prepared. "Naturally, it's terribly painful to relive a time in my life I'd much sooner forget, but in some ways it's been freeing, too. I no longer have to worry about someone finding out who I used to be. The whole world knows now, and shockingly, life has gone on."

"You did lose your job at the Emerson charter school in New York, though. Is that correct?"

"Yes." A spark of pain registers in my chest at the reminder of what's been lost.

"Do you have any recourse there?"

"We're looking at all our options," Flynn says. "Up to and including litigation."

That's the first I've heard of that possibility. I clear my throat. "The parents of my students have petitioned the school's board of directors, asking them to reinstate me. We're waiting to hear if the board will overturn the principal's decision."

"If you're offered your job back, would you take it?"

"I'm… I'm not sure. It would depend on a number of factors."

"Can you talk about what recourse you have against the lawyer who sold your story to the media?"

Flynn takes that one. "We're hoping for everything from disbarment to criminal and civil charges. I won't be satisfied until he suffers at least half as much as Natalie has."

"Even to those of us who were appalled by how your story came to be public, it's been hard not to be moved by your courage and fortitude. Can you talk about the decisions you made in the aftermath of the assault? Is it true that your attacker threatened your family's safety and livelihood?"

"He did, but there really was no decision. I had—or I guess I still have—younger sisters. I was absolutely certain that if I didn't pursue charges, he would turn his attention on them at some point. I couldn't let that happen, so going to the police was the only thing I could do."

"I understand you've had no contact with your family since you made that decision?"

"That's correct. My father worked for the governor and chose his lifelong friend over his own kid." Despite my matter-of-fact delivery, it still hurts, even all these years later, to think about my father dragging my mother out of the hospital and out of my life, leaving me traumatized, brutalized and alone.

"And how old were you, Natalie?" Carolyn's voice has softened, and her eyes are bright with unshed tears.

"Fifteen."

"What did you do? How did you cope? Did you ever consider not bringing charges against Oren Stone? Wow, sorry that's three questions."

I laugh at her befuddled expression. "I was lucky to be taken in by the family of one of the detectives who'd worked on my case. They were very good to me. I also relied on financial support from Stone's detractors who wanted to help me bring him down. And I never once considered not bringing charges or not supporting the case against him. What he did to me... Well, no one should get away with that."

"I'm curious as to how your name became public. You were a minor, and usually the names of assault victims are kept out of the media."

"We believe that Stone's team leaked my name, hoping I'd back down from testifying, and by the time of the trial, it was no longer a secret. I was also the daughter of one of his top aides, so it didn't take long for that connection to be part of the story."

"And when you heard he'd died in prison after being raped... What did you think?"

"Karma. People get what's coming to them in this life. I honestly believe if you're a good person, good things will happen to you. If you're evil... Well, you get what you deserve."

"I couldn't agree more," Carolyn says forcefully. That's when I know she's genuinely moved by my story. "I have to ask... Well, let's go back to the week before the Golden Globes. You've just met Flynn and begun a whirlwind romance. He asks you to attend a very public event with him. Were you at all fearful of being exposed when you'd gone to such tremendous lengths to change your name and appearance and build a new life for yourself?"

"To be completely honest... Maybe I was naïve to think the lawyer to whom I'd paid many thousands of dollars I couldn't afford to waste would protect me because that was his job. He was ethically required to keep my secrets. It never occurred to me for one second that he wouldn't."

"Flynn, before the story was made public, did you know about Natalie's past?"

I feel his entire body stiffen next to me. He doesn't want to be here. He doesn't want to talk about this, but he's doing it because I asked him to, and I love him for that.

"I knew she'd been assaulted. I didn't know the full story until the rest of the world heard it. Our relationship was still very new at that time, and we hadn't gotten that far yet."

"Natalie, would you have told Flynn your story eventually?"

"I don't know. At some point I probably would've had to explain why my family isn't part of my life anymore. My closest friends didn't know, so it's not something I talk about—or *talked* about—before the whole world knew. The family who took me in after the attack still knows me as April. I haven't seen them in years, though. They moved to Seattle after I was in college."

"The point," Flynn says in a low growl, "is that it should've been up to *Natalie* to decide when and what she told me. That was taken out of her hands by someone she trusted, and that never should've happened."

"I can only imagine how you must've felt, Flynn, when the story went public."

"I've never thought I was capable of murder, but in this case…"

"We could hardly blame you for feeling that way," Carolyn says. "Anyone would. So what're your plans now, Natalie?"

"I haven't really made plans, other than to spend some time here in LA with Flynn. We're looking forward to the upcoming SAG Awards."

"You're planning to attend? I'd heard you weren't going."

"You heard wrong," I say before he can reply. "We'll be there, and I'll be cheering for Flynn. His performance in *Camouflage* was amazing, and he deserves all the acclaim he's receiving."

"I couldn't agree more," Carolyn says. "Best movie of the year, far and away."

"Thank you," Flynn says gruffly.

"And congratulations on all the Oscar nominations for *Camouflage*, Flynn. Any predictions?"

"Nope," Flynn says, making us both laugh.

Carolyn props her chin on the upturned arm she's rested against her knee and leans in. "I have to ask… What's it like to date the biggest movie star in the universe?"

I laugh at the fangirl question and because that's how I've thought of him, too. "It's... When I first started seeing Flynn, my roommate in New York asked if I thought I'd ever see him as anything other than Flynn Godfrey, biggest movie star in the universe. To me... He's just Flynn, the sweetest, kindest, sexiest, most thoughtful man I've ever met, and I'm beyond blessed to be spending time with him, especially these last few days. He's been incredibly supportive through all of this."

"That's quite an endorsement," Carolyn says. "What do you think, Flynn?"

"I'm the lucky one." He brings my hand to his lips, and I imagine every woman in America swooning at the way he looks at me as he brushes his lips over my knuckles.

"Flynn, you've repeatedly said you'd never marry again. Have you changed your mind about that since you met Natalie?"

"Absolutely."

Carolyn clearly wasn't expecting him to be so definite. "Do I hear wedding bells ringing for you two?"

He never takes his eyes off me when he says, "As soon as we possibly can."

"Is that a proposal we just heard?" Carolyn nearly levitates out of her seat with excitement. He's handed her a huge scoop on a silver platter.

"No, it wasn't." Flynn laughs at her reaction. "*When* I ask Natalie to be my wife, it'll be a very private and personal moment between the two of us and no one else."

"And I'll be the first to know afterward?" Carolyn asks with a hopeful smile.

"Maybe after I tell my folks."

"Fair enough. Speaking of your parents, Natalie, have you met Max and Estelle?"

"I have, and they're every bit as wonderful as they seem, as are Flynn's sisters, brothers-in-law, nieces and nephews. They're an incredible family, and they've made me feel very welcome."

"One final question before I let you go. After all these years, if you could say anything to your family back home in Nebraska, what would it be?"

Without hesitation, I say, "I would tell my sisters that I love and miss them so much. And I'd love to hear from them any time."

"They can contact Natalie through my company, Quantum Productions, in LA," Flynn adds. "They'll always be welcome anywhere we are."

Carolyn reaches across the space between our chairs and puts her hand on top of ours, which are joined. "Thank you so much for talking to me today. I hope you know how awed we are by your courage and strength. I'll be pulling for the two of you and rooting for you, Flynn, as award season continues."

"Thanks, Carolyn," he says.

"Yes, thank you for having us."

"Entirely my pleasure."

"And we're out," the director announces.

"That was great, you guys," Carolyn says, rising to hug us both after we're relieved of the microphones. She holds me for a second longer than expected. "I'm in awe of you, Natalie. Truly."

"Thank you."

"You've got one of the good guys here."

"I'm well aware of that," I say with a smile for Flynn.

He puts his arm around me and kisses my temple. "Are we good to go, Carolyn?"

"Yes, you are. This'll air next week. We'll let you know when. Thank you again, and good luck at the Oscars. Not that you'll need it."

"Don't jinx him," I say. "He's very superstitious."

"No jinx intended. Just stating the truth."

Flynn kisses Carolyn's cheek. "You were spot-on today. I won't forget that." He guides me from the conference room. "You wanna see my office?"

"Sure."

It's located at the end of a long hallway and looks out over the sprawling city of Los Angeles. "Look," he says, pointing to the Hollywood sign in the distance. Farther to the west, I can see the Pacific.

His office is huge and modern, with three glass walls that make the most of his exceptional view. Like his home offices, the desk is stacked with piles on top of piles. "Let me guess, Addie isn't allowed in here either."

"That's right. A man's office is sacred."

"And messy. I'd love to get my hands on all three of your so-called offices. I'd have you whipped into shape in no time."

The look he gives me is filled with horror. "Don't you dare!"

I'm relieved by the return of his playful side, which I've missed. "You'd better be nice to me, or I might be tempted."

His arms come around me from behind. "Baby, I'm always nice to you."

I relax into his embrace. "Yes, you are."

He nuzzles my neck, setting off a chain reaction that has all my most important parts standing up to take notice of his nearness. "What're you thinking about, sweetheart?"

"What you said in there... To Carolyn."

"I said a lot of things."

"You certainly did."

"Do you mean about us getting married?" he asks.

"Um... yeah..."

"That surprised you?"

"Just a little."

With his hands on my shoulders, he turns me to face him. "Where do you think this is heading? I'd marry you today if I didn't think it was too soon for you."

"Oh. You would?"

He frames my face in his big hands and kisses me. "You bet your ass I would. I want you to be mine, forever and always. I want to know that we're going to spend the rest of our lives together. I don't think I'll be able to truly relax where you're concerned until my ring is on your finger."

"Flynn... You take my breath away."

"Is that a yes?"

"So wait, that was a *proposal*?" My heart is beating so fast, I place my hand over it, hoping to calm it.

"It was more of a fishing expedition. The actual proposal will be much more romantic than that and will include an absolutely stunning ring—a ring that will do justice to the woman I love and want to spend my life with. So no, that wasn't an official proposal. But if it had been, hypothetically... What might your answer be?"

I love him so much when he shows me his vulnerability and that he takes nothing for granted where I'm concerned. "My answer would be…"

"*Fuck*, Nat! You're killing me here."

"Yes. I would say yes a thousand times over."

He lifts me into a kiss. "Only a thousand?"

"A hundred million."

After another kiss, he says, "That's a good number, and it's about what you'll be worth once you say 'I do.'"

"I don't care about that. I hope you know—"

Another kiss. "I do, sweetheart. I know." He returns me to terra firma and holds me close. "Did we just talk about what I think we talked about?"

"I think we did. And despite what you think, I'd marry you today, too."

"I love you, Nat. I was so fucking proud of you during that interview. You amaze me every day, and all I can think about is keeping you forever, right here in my arms where you belong."

"There's nowhere else in the world I'd rather be."

"Not even in New York with your class?"

I think about that for a second, but it doesn't take even that long for me to decide. "Not even there."

His arms tighten around me until I can barely breathe. But who needs air when Flynn Godfrey is professing his eternal love?

A knock on the door interrupts the moment, but he only releases me partially, keeping an arm around my shoulders. "Come in."

Addie ducks her head in. "Sorry to interrupt."

"Were you able to get it?" Flynn asks.

"Please… Of course I was."

"I apologize for doubting you."

I have no idea what they're talking about.

Addie comes in and hands a package and a piece of paper to Flynn.

I do a double take when I see my photo on the page. "What is that?"

"That, my love, is your newly issued State of California driving permit. Today you're learning how to drive."

CHAPTER 8

Flynn

She's so nervous her hands are shaking as she takes the wheel in the silver Mercedes sedan she admired when we were here for the Globes. I told her it was hers to use whenever we were in LA, and that's when she said she didn't know how to drive.

My poor sweet Natalie missed so many of the rites of passage the rest of us take for granted, and I want to make it all up to her, starting with teaching her how to drive.

"What if I hit something or damage the car? You love your cars."

From the passenger seat, I take hold of her hand and wait for her to look at me. "I don't love my cars anywhere near as much as I love you."

Raising a brow, she says, "Even the Bugatti?"

She's bringing out the big guns. I swallow hard. "Even the Bugatti."

She loses it laughing. "You lie. You love that car more than anything."

"No, sweetheart, I love *you* more than anything. The cars are things. They can all be replaced. And they're insured. *Fully* insured."

"If you're sure."

"I'm positive. I want you to know how much fun it is to drive and to be able to go anywhere you want whenever you want."

In a nearby SUV is the security detail that's sticking close to us until the story about Natalie's past gets knocked out of the headlines by someone else's scandal.

We're in the Quantum parking lot, where there's plenty of extra room to practice the basics.

I go over all the features of the car and tell her where everything is. "Driving is all about being predictable. Whatever you do, it should be what the guy behind you expects you to do. Does that make sense? In other words, you don't stop at a green light or in the middle of a turn or anything that's going to get you hit from behind."

"Okay… What else?"

"Go slow at first, until you get a feel for the car and what it's capable of."

"I can't believe the first car I'm ever going to drive is a Mercedes."

"Mine was a Jaguar. My dad was a freaking mess the whole time. I accused him of being far more concerned about the car than he was about me. He didn't deny it."

The story makes her laugh, as I hoped it would.

"Let's give it a whirl." I point to the key, and she turns it, starting the car. "Now put it in Drive."

"You're sure about this?"

"Positive. Take me for a ride, sweetheart." I add a wink and a smile to remind her of the last time I said those words to her, and she blushes adorably.

We do a hundred laps around the parking lot, and as expected, she's a cautious, conscientious driver. I suppose that's the benefit of learning at twenty-three rather than at sixteen when you're too stupid to know how many ways this activity can get you killed. Natalie has been an adult since she was fifteen, and comes at driving with adult sensibilities.

"What do you think?" I ask her after an hour of driving in circles. "Want to take to the road?"

"Like the *actual* road with other cars? I don't think I'm ready for that."

"Sure you are. You'll do great." I signal to the SUV to let the security guys know we're leaving.

"Flynn, seriously, this is not a good idea."

I lean over to kiss her cheek. "It's a great idea. My parents are expecting us for a late lunch, and we need to get going." I point to the parking lot exit.

She grits her teeth and aims the car in the direction I've indicated. What should be a twenty-minute ride to Beverly Hills takes forty minutes as Natalie drives so slowly that it's all I can do not to lose it laughing as one car after another goes by us with angry drivers flashing the bird at my girl.

"People here are mean," she says, breaking a long silence.

"I think it's more that they expect the other cars on the road to at least drive the speed limit."

"I can *hear* you mocking me, and don't think I won't remember that later when you're wanting to get your hands on me."

"I would never mock you, sweetheart."

"Said the man who wants to get lucky later."

I love her madly. I love the way she bickers with me and puts me in my place and doesn't care who I am or what I have. For the first time in my adult life, I've found a woman who genuinely cares about *me* rather than the crap that comes with me. She's a miracle. My own living, breathing miracle, and watching her intense concentration as she follows my directions to Beverly Hills only makes me love her more than I already did.

"Stop staring at me."

"I don't want to. You're cute when you concentrate."

"Don't you mean I'm cute when I'm terrified?"

"No need to be terrified, and you're cute all the time."

"Right… Whatever you say."

"You're doing great. What do you think of it so far?"

"It's scary."

"It's fun. Wait till you get to drive a *real* car."

"This isn't a real car?"

"This, my love, is a *sedan*. We can do better."

"This is as real as I plan to get."

"We'll see…" I look over at her, drinking in the sight of her beautiful face, her lips set in an adorable pucker. "Is it okay that I did this?"

"Did what? Force me to drive through LA traffic when I've never driven a car in my life?"

"That," I say, laughing at her indignant retort, "the permit, all of it."

"I am wondering how you managed to enter me into a legally binding agreement with the State of California without my participation."

I scoff at that. "Anything is possible if you know who to ask."

"I suppose you must have a staff member devoted to the DMV since you own sixty cars."

"I do have my connections."

We're stopped at a light waiting to take a left turn into Beverly Hills when she looks over at me with that sweet, loving smile that stops my heart every fucking time she directs it my way. "Thank you."

"For?"

"Pulling strings to get me a permit, letting me drive this very expensive and beautiful car, taking me to lunch at your parents' home and, most of all, sitting next to me during that interview when it was the last place in the world you wanted to be."

The light turns green, and she makes the turn, her face a study in concentration. I direct her through the neighborhood to my parents' house. We pull up to the security gate, and I give her a code to punch in that will open the gates.

"I can't believe the way you just give me this kind of info."

"Why wouldn't I? I trust you with my life." The nagging voice in the back of my mind reminds me that while I may trust her with my life, I haven't trusted her with my truth. When the big wrought-iron gates swing open, Natalie pulls into the driveway.

"Where should I park?"

"Right there is fine."

We come to a stop and Natalie turns off the car, releasing a huge sigh of relief as she leans her head on the steering wheel.

I give her a second to recover. "Hey, Nat."

She raises her head and looks over at me.

"What you said before about the interview…"

"What about it?"

I reach over to tuck a strand of her hair behind her ear and take full advantage of the opportunity to run my fingertip over her cheek. "I didn't want to do the interview, but that wasn't the last place in the world I wanted to be. I want to be wherever you are, and if that means doing things I don't want to do, so be it."

She stares at me, seeming to take inventory of my face. "Are you real? Is this real? You're not going to suddenly turn into a raging bastard at some point, are you?"

There it was again, that pang of guilt over what I'm keeping from her. "No plans for that."

"Promise?"

"Yeah, baby, I promise." I'm about to kiss her when someone knocks on the window behind me. I growl with frustration and turn to find my father grinning like a loon as he stares into the car. Amused, I push the button to lower the window. "Hello, Dad."

"Hello, son. Natalie."

"Hi, Max."

"Whatcha up to?" Max asks.

"Well, I was about to kiss my girl before I was very rudely interrupted."

Natalie giggles like the girl she once was, before her innocence was stolen from her. The sound is music to my soul.

"Don't let me stop you," Max says.

"The moment is lost," I say, winking at Natalie. "Rain check?"

"You got it."

"So you're letting your lady drive you around, son?" Dad asks when we're out of the car and following him inside. "That's not like you."

"Natalie is learning how to drive and doing a fine job of it."

I can see by the way my dad's face softens that he immediately understands that learning to drive was something she missed out on. "That's wonderful." He hugs and kisses her and welcomes her into his home like she's his long-lost best friend. I love him so much. He's the best man I know, and my whole life I've strived to make him proud of me.

Natalie is blown away by the house. She tries to be surreptitious about taking it all in as my dad whisks her through the big airy rooms to the back patio, where my mom and the housekeeper, Ada, are laying out a spread of food.

"Look who's here, Stel," Max says.

My mom stops what she's doing and comes right over to hug Natalie. "Oh, my sweet girl. I've been so worried about you." She pulls back so she can see Nat's face but keeps her hands on Natalie's shoulders. "How're you doing?"

"I'm okay." Natalie glances at me. "Flynn has been taking good care of me."

"He'd better be." Mom reaches out to me, and I kiss her cheek. "This whole thing is just beyond outrageous. I hope you're going to sue the ass off that guy in Nebraska."

"We're on it, Mom. Don't worry."

"I've been sick with worry. I'm just... I'm beside myself over it. If I spend another fifty years in this business, I'll never understand how *any* media outlet could pay *money* for a story like this."

Dad puts his arm around Mom. "Take it easy, Stel."

Mom takes a deep breath. "I'm sorry. I don't mean to ruin our time together by dwelling on things that are outside our control."

"I want you to know that it means the world to me to have your support," Natalie says, addressing both of them. "It's been a long time since I've had parents to lean on, and your outrage is actually rather comforting."

"You have parents now, love," Mom says firmly. "We'll be your parents. We're actually rather good at it. Ask our kids."

Natalie blinks repeatedly, which is how I know Mom's kindness has touched her deeply. She hugs my mom. "Thank you so much."

"How did the interview with Carolyn go?" Mom asks after they embrace for a long moment that has all of us dabbing at our eyes afterward.

"It was good," Natalie says. "She was very nice and respectful."

"I'm just glad it's over," I add.

"When is it scheduled to air?" Dad asks.

"Sometime next week. They're going to let us know."

"What can we get you to drink?" Dad asks, his jovial tone lightening the mood considerably.

We pass a relaxing hour with my parents, during which my dad tells me he heard there's an underground plan afoot for celebrities on the red carpet at the SAG Awards to boycott the *Hollywood Starz* TV news magazine that broke the story about Natalie.

I tell her this on the way back to the beach house in Malibu. I'm driving so Natalie doesn't have to take on LA's notorious rush-hour traffic.

"Wow, so they'll blow off those reporters because of what they did to me?"

"Yep, and when they do that on live TV, it'll send a big message to the others that if you cross the line, you pay the price."

She doesn't reply, so I glance over to find her worrying her bottom lip.

"What's wrong, Nat?"

"You'll think it's silly after I pitched such a fit about going to the SAGs."

"What will I think is silly?"

"It's just… You worked so hard on *Camouflage*, and everyone's saying you're going to win again."

"Ack, don't jinx me!"

She smiles, but I can tell she's still troubled. "I don't want that night to be about me. It needs to be about you and your amazing accomplishments."

God, she's so sweet and so perfect. I want to take her to bed and not let her up until I've managed to slake the burning need she inspires in me. "It's about *us*, sweetheart. Everything is about us now. Whatever happens with the rest of the awards, all I care about is I get to go home with you after. The awards are a distant second place to that."

"Do you ever wonder how something like this could've happened as fast as it did?"

"Something like this? You mean me falling flat on my ass in love with you and hopefully vice versa?"

"Yes," she says, laughing, "that's what I mean, and there's no hopefully about it. I'm right there on my ass next to you."

"I don't wonder how it happened. I know exactly how it happened. You came barreling into me, your crazy dog bit me and infected me with love potion number something. The rest, as they say, is history."

"Poor Fluff. She gets such a bad rap in all this."

"She deserves every bit of bad publicity she gets."

Her ringing cell phone interrupts our "argument."

"Make sure you check the caller ID before you answer it." I'm always on guard against the relentless paparazzi. I wouldn't put it past them to have hunted down her phone number.

"It's Leah. Hey, how's it going?"

I can't hear Leah's side of the conversation, but Natalie is rapt, listening to whatever her roommate in New York is saying. "When do you think they'll decide?" she asks. "Wow, well, keep me posted and tell Sue thanks for the info." After another pause, "It's great. Sunny and warm every day. Today, I've been learning to drive—and we did an interview with Carolyn Justice."

I can hear Leah's screaming reply to that, which makes me laugh.

They talk for another couple of minutes before they say their good-byes.

"What's up?" I ask the second she ends the call.

"According to our friend Sue, who works in the main office, the board is seriously considering overturning Mrs. Heffernan's decision to fire me. Aileen and the other parents apparently presented one hell of an argument."

"That's great, Nat." It is great, and I'm happy for her, but the thought of her returning to New York is thoroughly depressing.

"Yeah."

"They should reinstate you. It's the right thing to do."

"I know." She runs her fingers through her long hair as she stares out the window at the scenery on the way into Malibu.

I want to know what she'll do if she gets her job back, but I don't ask. I'm afraid of her reply.

"How about a walk on the beach?" I ask when we're back at the house. We've been sticking close to the house since we've been here, but I recall how much Natalie loved the beach the first time she experienced it. And since Addie handed me the package I've been waiting for, I can move forward with my plans. My stomach is full of butterflies, but they're the happy excited kind.

"Can we do that? You don't have your Russian mafia hat with you."

"That would draw too much attention here. I do have a Dodgers ball cap and dark sunglasses. And we've got them." I gesture to the security guys who pulled into the driveway behind us.

"Sure, if you think it's okay."

After we change into shorts and T-shirts, we head out with Fluff, who's thrilled to have us back at home. Well, she's thrilled to have Natalie. She's tolerating me. The beach is largely deserted this late in the day, so we have the place to ourselves, other than the security team that trails at a decent distance. I've asked them to give us some privacy for what I have planned for this walk of ours.

We hold hands as we stroll along the edge of the cold water that sloshes over our feet.

"Does the water ever get warm?" she asks.

"In the summer, it gets tolerably cold."

"It's so pretty here. If I lived here, all I'd do is stare at the ocean all day."

"Do you want to live here?"

"I don't know," she says with a nervous laugh. "I have no idea where I belong anymore."

She's handed me the perfect opening for the conversation I wish to have with her. "I do."

"You do what?" She's staring out at the ocean, so she doesn't see me staring down at her, captivated by the way the breeze flutters through her hair. I will never get tired of looking at her, of talking to her, of holding her hand, of making love to her or anything else I get to do with her. "I know where you belong."

"And where's that?"

"With me." I stop walking and turn to face her, dropping to one knee before her.

She gasps, and Fluff barks. "Flynn! What're you doing?"

I push my sunglasses to the top of my head. "Natalie, I love you more than I ever imagined it was possible to love anyone. When I heard the other day what the press was doing to you, I felt like my own heart had been ripped from my chest. I couldn't think or breathe or do anything until I got to you."

Natalie wipes tears from her face. "I don't expect you to do this because of what happened with the press."

"You think I'm doing this because of that? My darling love, this is because of what happened in a park when you and that vicious wildebeest of yours mowed me over and changed my life forever with one look into the most amazingly beautiful eyes I've ever seen in my life. I'm doing this because every second I spend away from you feels like the most painful form of torture I've ever endured. And I'm doing it because I quite simply can't live without you. So do you think maybe you could help me out here and have some mercy on me? Will you marry me, Natalie?"

"Your parents… Are you sure they want all the crap that comes with me?"

"You heard them today. They're thrilled to welcome you into our family. And besides, they'll be busy celebrating the fact that a woman they too fell in love with at first sight has finally brought me up to scratch."

"Yes, Flynn," she says, laughing as she wipes away her tears. "I'll marry you."

"Why?"

She tips her head to look at me inquisitively. "Why?"

"Tell me why you want to marry me."

"Because I love you desperately—" She never gets to finish that thought because I stand up to kiss her.

"That's all I needed to hear."

"Let me finish." With her hands on my face, she stares into my eyes, and I feel as if she's showing me her very soul. "I don't love you for all the reasons the rest of the world does. I love you for all the other things about you that no one but me will ever get to see. I love you for your kindness, your generosity, your humor, the way you don't take yourself too seriously but take your work very seriously. I love you for the way you take care of your Great-Aunt Sally—"

"How do you know about that?"

"You're not going to tell me the press got that wrong, are you?"

"No," I say with a laugh, "that's one thing they got right."

"I love you for who you are, not what you have. That'll never matter to me as much as you do."

"And that, my love, is why, for you, I've broken all my earlier vows to never marry again and exactly why I'm willing to take all new ones with you."

I pick her up and twirl her around, bringing her down for a kiss that's far more chaste than I'd like it to be, but I'm mindful of the security detail watching us.

"I can't believe this is happening. Are we really getting married?"

"We really are. What're you doing tomorrow?"

"*As in the day after today?* You want to get married *tomorrow?*"

I love her so much. I don't have the slightest doubt that this is the right thing for both of us. "Yes, I do. We're checking on what we can pull together for tomorrow or Monday."

"We? Who is we?"

"Addie and me, of course."

"I think I'm hyperventilating. Am I hyperventilating?"

Laughing, I put my arms around her and kiss her. "Oh my God! I forgot the most important part of this whole proposal thing." I reach into my pants pocket for the ring I stashed there before we left the house. I've checked at least twenty times to make sure it's still there. Reaching for her left hand, I slide the ring I had made for her onto her finger.

"Flynn! Oh my God! It's gorgeous." She's crying freely now as she stares at the four-carat one-of-a-kind diamond in the platinum setting I chose for her. At times like this, it helps to have a brother-in-law in the jewelry business. Hugh and I have been in cahoots for days now, and the ring is perfect on her.

"So tomorrow or Monday? Unless you want the big white wedding. In that case, I suppose I could be convinced to wait a month or two, but absolutely no longer than two months."

"I don't care about a big wedding."

"I've already had one, and it was a lot of headaches for one day of partying." I hold her close to me with my chin resting on the top of her head as I watch the sun dip toward the horizon. "You don't care about the big wedding. I certainly don't want to go down that road again if you don't. We really ought to take advantage of this break in the action to take care of business."

"What about your parents? And your sisters. The kids…"

"This isn't about them. This is about you and me. We can have a big party later to celebrate. I don't need anyone else there. Do you?"

"Other than Leah and Aileen, I really don't have anyone else."

"You do now, sweetheart. You have me and an entire family that will love and protect you always. You are not alone anymore."

"This has to be a dream. Nothing this amazing could possibly be real."

"It's very real, and I've gone from publicly swearing I'd never get married again to needing to be married to you so badly, I can't bear the idea of waiting even two more days to make you my wife."

"Flynn… God. This is crazy."

"Is that a yes?"

"Yes!" She laughs even as she cries. "It's a yes."

I pick her up again and swing her around, making her scream with laughter, which of course makes Fluff bark and snap at my legs. The sound of Natalie's laughter is the sweetest music I've ever heard. I put her down, make sure she's steady on her feet and withdraw my phone from my pocket. I keep an arm around Natalie as we start back toward the house.

"Well?" Addie says when she answers.

"Green light for ASAP."

"Flynn… That's fantastic. Congratulations to both of you. The soonest they could do it was Monday, so I'll set everything up and call you tomorrow with the details."

I know she'll work nonstop to make it happen, but I also know she doesn't mind. She's a sucker for romance. "You're the best, Addie."

"I know! Congratulations again. I'm so excited for you."

"Thanks. Me, too." I stash the phone in my pocket and return my full attention to Natalie. We walk slowly, taking our time returning to the house.

"Are you happy, Nat?"

"I'm so happy. I had no idea it was possible to be this happy."

"That's all that matters to me. That's all that will ever matter." Before I marry Natalie, though, I need to talk to Hayden and quit the club. I need to deal with the playroom in the basement of my house as well, although I can do that later. It's under lock and key, so there's no chance she'll discover it. There's no place for the club and what goes on there or the playroom at home in my new life with Natalie.

CHAPTER 9

Natalie

We return to the house to find Marlowe sitting on the back deck waiting for us. She jumps up when she sees us coming. "There you are!"

"Hey, Mo." Flynn greets his close friend and business partner with a kiss. "What's up?"

"I brought dinner. I've been thinking about you guys and wanted to check in to see how you're doing."

He pushes his sunglasses to the top of his head. "How're we doing, Nat?" His eyes dance with the kind of glee I haven't seen since before my story was made public.

I hold up my left hand so she can see the ring I still can't believe he just put on my finger.

Marlowe lets out a scream and gets up to hug us both. "Oh my God! Flynn Godfrey is *engaged*! This is going to be the story of the century!"

"Shhhhh." He's amused by her reaction. "We're not telling the world yet."

"We need to have a party! Can we have a party? Please? Or do you guys want to be alone? Because if you do, I'll invite the boys over and have a party on your behalf at my house."

Flynn glances at me. I can tell just by looking at him that he'd rather be alone, but these are his closest friends and business partners—two of whom I haven't met yet. "A party sounds fun."

"Yay!" Marlowe claps her hands in delight. "I left my phone inside. I'll go make the calls."

When we're alone, Flynn puts his arm around me and steals a kiss. "You're sure this is all right?"

"It's perfect. Look at this night and this ring and this view and my gorgeous fiancé. So much to celebrate."

"I love to see you glowing with happiness."

"I'm glowing because of you. Because you love me."

"I love you so fucking much."

"And you wonder why I'm glowing."

We stand there like that, wrapped up in each other, until Marlowe returns. "Everyone is coming, and they're bringing booze and more food. I love a party that comes together without me having to do anything other than decide to have it."

Her excitement is contagious. What am I doing at Hayden Roth's Malibu beach house about to party with Marlowe Sloane and my new fiancé, Flynn Godfrey? It's beyond surreal, but it's also my life now. My new life. With a pang of regret, I think of my kids in New York and hope they're getting by without me.

"You okay, sweetheart?" he asks, tuned in to me as always.

"Yeah, I'm great." I'm better than I've been in eight long years.

"Hey, Mo, what'd you make for dinner?"

"Enchiladas, baby! Is there anything else?"

Flynn laughs. "Marlowe can't cook anything other than Mexican. We think she might've been kidnapped from a Mexican family at some point."

"What can I say? I've got tamales in my blood. Margaritas for everyone, coming right up!" She goes back inside to make the drinks.

Flynn's phone rings, and when he checks it, he grimaces. "I've got to take this."

"I'll go help Marlowe." I start to walk away, but he brings me back for a kiss.

"I'm good now. You can go."

He makes me light-headed with the way he loves me. It's all-consuming and overwhelming in the best possible way. Inside, I find Marlowe in the kitchen running the blender as she mixes the drinks.

"Anything I can do to help?"

"Crack open that bottle of tequila."

"Got it." I twist the top off the bottle and hand it to her. "Hey, Marlowe?"

"What's up?"

"Can you recommend a good doctor here? A female preferably."

"Are you sick?"

"I'm fine. I just need, you know…" I realize I'm about to share something rather personal with a superstar I haven't known that long. But I like her, and I'd like to think of her as a friend. "Birth control."

"Ahhh. Gotcha. I have the best doctor *ever*." She pulls out her phone, and before I can say a word, she's making a call, explaining who I am and what I need and setting me up with an appointment at seven thirty Monday morning—all of this while continuing to run the blender.

I'm slightly astonished by her multitasking capabilities, and absolutely terrified about that appointment.

Marlowe ends the call and returns her focus to the blender, adding more tequila until she's satisfied. "Doctor Breslow will see you at seven thirty before they open to other patients. That'll get you in and out before anyone else is there. You'll love her."

"It must be nice to make a call on a Saturday night and get an appointment first thing on a Monday morning."

"Celebrity does have its perks," she says with a wink. "Breslow's admin is a fan, and I get her tickets to premieres and stuff. We take care of each other."

"Thank you."

"Sure thing. Breslow will fix you right up." She pours a margarita, takes a sip and declares it perfect so she pours one for me and then writes down the doctor's address for me.

"I've never had a margarita." The second the words are out of my mouth, I feel like an unsophisticated hick next to her.

"Well, you've been missing out. Give it a try."

I love that she doesn't blink an eye at my confession. I take a sip of the tart drink. "Mmm, that's so good."

"Right? Just go easy. You know what they say about tequila…"

"What's that?"

"Makes you take your clothes off, not that Flynn would object."

"Object to what?" he asks when he joins us and accepts the drink Marlowe hands him.

"Natalie finding out about the power of tequila."

"You're right." He winks at me. "I won't object."

The doorbell rings, and Marlowe runs to get it.

Flynn notices the slip of paper in my hand. "What's that?"

"Marlowe got me an appointment with her doctor for Monday morning at seven thirty. Is that doable?"

"Sure, I don't have anything until the foundation meeting at nine."

"I'm kind of scared. Will you come with me?"

He puts his arm around me and kisses my forehead. "Of course I will, sweetheart."

I immediately feel less anxious about it, knowing he'll be there to hold my hand.

Marlowe returns with two incredibly handsome men, both of them carrying twelve-packs of beer and bottles of wine that they stash on the counter.

Flynn greets them both with bro hugs. "Jasper, Kristian, I want you to meet Natalie."

Jasper is tall and blond with a lean, muscular build. He hugs me like we're old friends. "Natalie," he says in the crisp British accent Flynn warned me about. "It's a pleasure to meet the woman who's finally brought our boy up to snuff."

I wave a hand in front of my face in deference to the accent, and Flynn rolls his eyes.

"Nice to meet you, too, Jasper. I've heard a lot about you."

"What's he said about me?" Kristian asks. He's got dark hair and piercing blue eyes.

I desperately try to think of something. "The Lamborghini."

"Yeah." He laughs as he hugs me. "He hates it."

"I don't think he said 'hate.'"

"Yes, I did," Flynn says. "Now get your hands off my fiancée."

"*Your what?*" Jasper and Kristian say in stereo.

"You heard him right, boys," Marlowe says. "Pigs are now flying in hell!"

"I'm sorry," Jasper says, staggering dramatically. "I need a moment."

"Shut the fuck up," Flynn says, laughing as he gives his friend a playful shove.

The doorbell rings again, and Marlowe returns with yet another stunningly gorgeous man. This one has chestnut brown hair and golden eyes. He's dressed in a dark suit that fits his muscular frame like it was cut just for him. It probably was.

"Emmett!" Jasper cries. "You aren't going to believe it. Our boy Flynn is *engaged!*"

Emmett stops short on his way into the kitchen. "What'd you say? He's *what*?"

"Show him, Natalie," Kristian says.

I hold up the ring for Emmett to see.

He takes a close look at the ring, then at Flynn and then at the ring again.

"Get the poor guy a drink, Mo," Jasper says. "He's been shocked speechless."

"You're seriously engaged," Emmett says.

"As serious as it gets. Emmett, meet my fiancée, Natalie Bryant. Natalie, our chief counsel, Emmett Burke."

He shakes my hand. "So nice to meet you."

"You, too. Thanks for all your help this week."

"Believe me, I've enjoyed sticking it to that bastard David Rogers. We've made his life a living hell, and we're just getting started."

"Thank you."

Addie arrives with Flynn's sister Ellie, and then Hayden comes in a short time later, bearing grocery bags and another twelve-pack of beer.

"You let a guy borrow your beach house and how does he thank you? By throwing a rager."

"You're lucky we decided to invite you." Flynn gives Hayden one of those side-handed handshakes guys do these days.

"There's big news afoot," Jasper says.

Hayden cracks open a beer and drinks half of it. "What's that?"

"Our boy Flynn? *Engaged.*"

Hayden chokes on the beer, coughing profusely while Jasper laughs and pounds on his back.

I have no idea how to take Hayden's reaction. Once the coughing stops, he stares at Flynn for a long, uncomfortably quiet moment.

"Well," he finally says, "it appears congratulations are in order."

"Thanks," Flynn says tightly. I can tell he's less than pleased with his best friend's reaction.

Like the first time I met him, I can't help but notice that Hayden is incredibly handsome in a rugged sort of way. I muster the courage to speak directly to him. "Hayden, I wanted to thank you for your support on Twitter this week. It meant a lot to me."

"Sure. We're all on your side in this thing. I still can't believe it happened."

"Neither can we, but the outpouring of support has made it more bearable."

"Glad to hear that."

"How'd the interview with Carolyn go?" Kristian asks.

"It was good," Flynn replies. "Natalie is a natural, and Carolyn asked all the right questions. We're hoping it'll put an end to the insanity."

Hayden laughs at that.

"What's so funny?" Flynn asks.

"Wait till they hear you're engaged. You haven't seen insanity yet."

"They aren't going to hear that."

"What do you mean?"

"We're getting married Monday night in Vegas. By the time they hear about it, it'll be a done deal."

The announcement is met with stunned silence.

"Monday," Marlowe says after at least a minute has passed. "That's like two days from now."

"Yep."

"What's the rush?" Hayden asks.

I can feel the tension coming off Flynn in waves. "No rush. It's just what we want." He puts his arm around me. "Where are those enchiladas, Mo? I'm starving."

With that, he sends the message that he's done talking about our plans.

Flynn

I'm fucking furious at Hayden. I don't expect him to jump for joy over my announcement, but I certainly didn't expect him to question me that way in front of Natalie. Hours later, I'm still fuming. I'm with the guys outside on the deck, playing poker and enjoying some Cuban cigars Kristian brought. The girls are inside laughing and talking and drinking. I've been keeping an eye on Natalie, and she seems to be enjoying herself with my friends and my sister.

"I'm out," Emmett says, folding.

Jasper tosses his cards on the table. "Me, too."

Kristian follows suit. "Me, three."

It's down to Hayden and me. I glare at him, letting my fury drive my desire to not only beat him at poker but to have it out with him before this night is over. He studies his cards for a long time before he drops them on the table. "Fold."

"Seriously?" Though he's handed me an easy victory, it's all I can do not to leap across the table and go for his throat.

He shrugs. "My heart's not in it." Then, in a low tone, he says, "What the fuck are you doing, Flynn?"

"What am I doing? I thought I was playing poker."

"You know what I'm talking about. You're getting *married*? To a girl you met two weeks ago? Who knows nothing about your true lifestyle?"

"Shut the fuck up, Hayden. It's none of your fucking business what I do."

"Oh, is that how it is now? I see."

"You don't see anything."

"I see you about to make a massive mistake, and you don't want to hear it from anyone."

"You're right. I don't." It's all I can do to remain in my seat and not act on my earlier urge to jump over the table and beat the shit out of him.

Emmett clears his throat.

"You got something to say?" I ask him.

"Just wondering… And don't get pissed at me, too… But have you considered a prenup?"

"No, I have not considered a prenup. I love her. She loves me. This isn't about money."

"*Flynn…*" The single word from Jasper is full of something I don't want to hear.

"You're really prepared to give her half of what you've worked so hard for when this goes bad?" Hayden asks.

"*When* it goes bad? Gee, thanks for the vote of confidence. I really appreciate it."

"You know he's only looking out for you," Kristian says quietly. "All of us are."

"I don't need him to look out for me. I don't need any of you to do that. I guess it was too much to hope for a little support from my closest friends."

"That's incredibly unfair," Hayden says. "We've always got your back. You know that. But when you *turn* your back on everything you are and everything you believe in for a woman, you'll have to pardon us if we call foul on that."

"I haven't done that," I say, even if Hayden's words score a direct hit to my deepest worries where Natalie and I are concerned.

"Have you told her about Club Quantum?" Hayden asks.

I glance toward the house, where I can see Natalie with Marlowe, Addie and Ellie. "No need to. I'm quitting the club."

The announcement is met with dead silence.

"I gotta go," Hayden says as he gets up from the table.

"You've been drinking, dude," Kristian says. "You should crash here."

"I'm not crashing here."

"Then come to my place, but don't drive back to town."

"Fine, but I want to go. Now. Oh, and Flynn, any time you want to come back to work, I could sure use some help on that film we're supposed to be finishing."

"Next week," I reply tersely.

"Great."

Jasper stands. "I drove Kris, so I guess I'm going, too. Good time tonight, everyone. Flynn, congratulations. I'm happy for you both."

"Thanks."

Hayden heads into the house without another word to me.

The three of them take their leave, but Emmett remains. The dustup with Hayden has left me unsettled, not that I'm entirely surprised by his reaction. He's been wary of my relationship with Natalie since the first minute I met her.

"You know he's just looking out for you," Emmett says after a long silence.

"I wish he was a little less concerned."

"Unfortunately, we all remember the aftermath of your divorce a little too well."

"This is different, Emmett. I already love Natalie more than I ever loved Val. It's nothing like that."

"*Nothing?*" Emmett asks, his brow raised in query. "The thing that caused you problems with Val is not something you can turn on and off like a switch. It's who you are. Who *we* are. You've tried to live outside the lifestyle before with disastrous results for you and for Val. None of us want to see you there again."

"I know that, and I appreciate the concern. But this is different."

"So you've said. Look, Flynn, it's none of my business. It's none of Hayden's business. You're our friend, and we care about you. That's it. One thing you've never been is a fool. But if you marry this woman—or any woman—without protecting yourself and your considerable assets, you're a fool."

He's right. I know he is, and if one of my closest friends was considering marrying a woman he'd known two weeks without a prenup, I'd be freaking out all over them. But I can't imagine broaching that subject with Natalie. She isn't after my money. I know that in the deepest corners of my soul, and it's one of the reasons I love her so damned much.

"She couldn't care less about the money, Em."

"Everyone cares about money, Flynn. Especially people who don't have any of their own."

I hate this conversation and the way it makes me feel with a fiery passion.

"There's a way around it, you know," Emmett says tentatively.

"What's that?"

"Set her up with a big account and have her sign something that says that's all she'll get if the marriage ends."

I'm shaking my head before he finishes speaking. "I'm not going into this marriage like it's a business deal. That would be disrespectful to her and to what we are to each other."

"I hear you, and I'll even confess to being envious that you've found someone you feel that way about. But as your friend and your attorney, I'd be negligent if I didn't urge you to reconsider."

"I appreciate your concern, your friendship and your legal advice."

"But you're telling me to fuck off anyway, right?" he asks with a laugh.

"In the nicest way possible."

"Fair enough. I've done my due diligence. If you change your mind, give me a call. I can put something together for you in the morning."

"I'm not going to change my mind."

"Then I'll be on my way." He gets up, and I shake the hand he offers me. "Thanks for a great time tonight."

"It was fun. Just what the doctor ordered after the week we've had."

"You know I wish you all the best, Flynn. Natalie seems like a really great person."

"You have no idea how amazing she is." I look up at him. "Keep me posted on the situation with Rogers and Natalie's school."

"I will. Congratulations again."

"Thanks."

After he leaves, I sit for a long time staring out at the dark ocean, where a half moon leaves a glowing trail over the surface. My friends have left me with doubts, which are infuriating in light of the certainty I feel where Natalie is concerned. I wasn't lying when I said that I know, in the deepest part of me, that our relationship has nothing to do with my money or my fame or my celebrity or any of the other bullshit reasons women in the past have been interested in me.

No, with Natalie, it's all about the two of us and what we've found together.

"What're you doing out here all by yourself?" she asks as she comes out to join me.

"Enjoying the view, which just got exponentially better. Did everyone leave?"

"Yeah, they said thanks for a fun night."

I hold out a hand to her and guide her onto my lap. When she's settled in my arms, her familiar scent filling my senses, I feel like I can breathe again. Nothing about this could ever be wrong. It is the most genuinely *right* thing I've ever known in my life.

"Why so quiet?"

"No reason."

"Did you have fun with your friends?"

"I did. How about you?"

"They're so nice. I love them all."

"They loved you, too."

"Even Hayden?"

"Of course. He thinks you're great."

"Sure he does. He ran out of here awfully quickly, leading me to wonder if the two of you had words over our plans for Monday. And just in case you're interested, Addie went after him."

She's incredibly astute and insightful, which is part of why I love her as much as I do. "He's a little concerned about the haste but not about you. You have to know you've earned the undying admiration of everyone in my life this week."

She drops her head onto my shoulder. "I would much rather have earned it the old-fashioned way."

"And how would that be?"

"By loving you the way you deserve to be loved for the rest of my life."

And that, right there, is why there'll be no prenup ahead of this wedding. "You know what we haven't done yet?"

"What's that?"

"Properly celebrated our engagement."

"And how does one properly celebrate an engagement? I've never been engaged before, so I have no idea."

With her in my arms, I get up to head inside. "Come with me, love, and I'll show you."

Natalie

Flynn carries me into the house, past Fluff curled up in a ball on the sofa, and straight into the first-floor bedroom we've been using. He puts me down beside the bed.

"Get naked, sweetheart."

Lifting his own T-shirt up and over his head, he watches me remove my top and shorts.

His shorts fall into pile at his feet, and he reaches for me.

"Wait, I'm not done getting naked yet."

"I'll do the good parts myself." He quickly removes my bra and panties and then stands back to admire me, which invokes a full-body blush. "Mmm, look what I get to love for the rest of my life. The sexiest woman in the world."

I don't know if I'd go that far, but he makes me feel as if it's true by the way he touches and caresses me until I'm ready to beg him to move things along.

With his hands on my ribs, he bends his head to kiss my neck. His lips are soft and gentle and utterly persuasive. I'd give him anything he wants as long as he doesn't stop touching me. He's promised me a lifetime of pleasure and love and laughter and all the amazing things we've found together, and I'm more than ready to collect.

"Flynn…"

"Hmm?"

"I just want to say…" It's hard to talk when he's got my earlobe clamped between his teeth and my breasts in his hands.

"What do you want to say, sweetheart?"

"I'm so excited to marry you. To be with you. To have everything with you."

"I am, too. You've made me crave things I said I'd never want again."

"I want to make you happy."

"I've never been happier."

"I mean in here, too." I gesture to the bed and then glance up at him to gauge his reaction.

"You know how to fire me up, sweetheart."

"Teach me something new. Something we haven't done before."

His low groan is followed by a devouring kiss.

I loop my arms around his neck, pressing my body into his and opening my mouth to his tongue. His hands are everywhere, stroking me into a frenzy of need. And then he's lifting me, his hands on my bottom.

With my legs wrapped around his hips and his tongue invading my mouth, I lose all sense of time and space and anything other than what's happening right here and now with the love of my life.

He breaks the kiss, his breathing heavy and labored. "You want something new?"

I nod. "I want to know everything. Teach me."

"You're officially killing me. You're so fucking sweet."

I should hate when he's crude, but I don't. I love it. I love everything he says and does.

He seats me on the bed. "Turn around."

I move tentatively to turn so my back is to him. "Like this?"

"Uh-huh. Now slide your butt forward and lie back, so your head is hanging off the bed."

Thought I can't quite figure out what he's got planned, I move into the position he's requested.

He bends over me to tug my nipple into the heat of his mouth.

I run my hands up his legs, needing to touch him while he drives me mad with the slow, steady tug of his lips on my nipples.

"Open your mouth," he says, his voice a hoarse rasp.

When I comply with his request, he takes himself in hand and sinks into my open mouth in small increments. In this position I can take more of him than I have before.

"Easy, baby, nice and easy. Take as much of me as you can."

My lips sting from stretching around his wide shaft. I stroke him with my tongue, making him gasp.

"God, yes, Nat… Just like that. If you need to stop, just pat my leg." He takes my hand and raises it to his leg to demonstrate. "Right there. Like that. Okay?"

I pat his leg to tell him I understand. I'm so caught up in trying to take more of him that I barely notice when he bends over me, puts his hands under my thighs and pulls my legs up and apart. Only when he opens me to his tongue do I understand his intentions.

How am I supposed to concentrate on breathing and taking him deeper into my mouth and throat when he's doing that to me? God, it's amazing. I raise my hips, wanting more. His fingers slide through the flood of dampness between my legs, stroking into me and back out as he begins to move his hips, ever so slightly, withdrawing from my mouth and then returning.

I lash him with my tongue, which makes him tremble. Then I reach up to touch his balls and feel him get harder and wider in my mouth.

His tongue is relentless against my clit, his fingers stroking in and out of me. Then one of them is pressed against my back entrance, demanding entry. I'm on sensory overload, the orgasm that's been brewing breaks free, and I'm thrashing under the weight of him, my moans against his shaft making him cry out.

I come down from the incredible high to his finger fully seated in my ass and his tongue stroking my clit.

When my body finally stops contracting, he withdraws his finger, stands upright and slides his penis out of my mouth. It's shiny from my saliva and so hard it's standing up straight against his belly button as he reaches for a condom. I'm still rippling and throbbing with the aftereffects of my release when he climbs onto the bed, gathers me up against him and slams into me, triggering another orgasm. He's so hard and so big, my body struggles to accommodate and adjust.

"I love you so much, Nat. So fucking much." His low growl against my ear is like an electrical current, setting of a new wave of desire that I feel in every part of my body. Gone is the cautious, tentative lover who'd worried about scaring me. In his place is Flynn Godfrey unleashed, and I love him this way. I love that I drove him to this by asking for something new. I love knowing he's mine forever and no one else will ever know him the way I do.

He drives deep into me and freezes, his head thrown back and his eyes closed. "I've never felt anything better than this, Nat. Ever."

"Me either."

"Do you love it? You really love it?"

"I can't get enough of you."

"God, you make me crazy when you say things like that." He bends over me, takes my nipple into his mouth and reaches down to where we're joined to stroke my clit.

And just that fast, I feel the tension begin to build again. I squirm under him, trying to get him to move, but he won't be coaxed. "Flynn…"

"What, honey?"

"I need you to move."

"I will."

"Now."

He's smiling when he kisses me.

I tug on his hair, hoping to get his attention so he'll quit torturing me, but that only seems to make him harder inside me. Groaning, I close my eyes and try to breathe, wondering how it's possible he can get any bigger than he already is. I feel like I've been impaled by him.

"I'm not moving until you come again."

"I don't know if I can again."

"Then it's going to be a long night."

"*Flynn…*"

He pushes his hips against me, setting off waves of sensation that fall just short of a full-on release. "I can stay here all night."

"Help me. Make me come."

He lets loose with another of those low growls I love so much. "I love when you say shit like that."

"I can tell. You just got even bigger."

Hooking his arms under my legs, he opens me wider and slides in deeper. Then he bends over me and draws on my nipple, clamping down on it with his teeth. I discover a direct connection between my nipple and the place where we're joined. I explode. I absolutely detonate. I come so hard that I scream from the sheer pleasure that rocks through me.

He releases my legs and starts to move again, until he's coming, too. Pressing into me repeatedly until he lands on top of me, big and heavy and sweaty and all mine.

"You wiped me out," he says after a long period of silence.

"You demolished me."

"What do you think of engaged sex?"

"I'm a little afraid of what married sex might entail."

He raises his head and smiles down at me. "You'll find out soon enough."

"I can't wait."

CHAPTER 10

Natalie

Early on Monday morning, Flynn drives me into town for my appointment. I told him I'm too nervous about seeing a doctor to drive, and thankfully he didn't push me. Despite the travel mug of coffee he made for me, I can't stop yawning. We were up really late "celebrating" some more and then the alarm went off super early so I'd have time to shower and mentally prepare for this appointment.

We spent the whole day in bed yesterday, getting up only to shower and eat before going back for more. So in addition to being tired, I'm rather sore, too, which has me dreading the appointment that much more. I can't even think about our exciting plans for later until the trip to the doctor is completed.

"You don't have to do this if you don't want to," he says. "I know it's traumatic for you, and I hate the idea of you doing something for me that makes you so stressed out."

"It's not just for you. It's for me, too. It'll give us the kind of freedom all newlyweds should have."

He shifts in his seat as if he's uncomfortable or something.

I glance down to notice he's hard. "That's all it takes?" I ask with a laugh.

"All you have to do is look at me, and I'm hard. But when you talk about our sexual freedom… Well, I'm only human."

"I'm surprised you didn't wear *him* out completely yesterday."

"He's amazingly resilient. Can't keep a good man down."

I'm giggling madly by now as I engage in verbal foreplay for the first time in my life—and quickly realize I'm dealing with a master.

He brings our joined hands to his lips and nibbles on my fingers. "Yesterday was so much fun."

"Yes, it was."

"Tonight will be even more so."

"I can't imagine more."

He has nothing to say to that, which leads me to wonder what he's imagining. I know I'm a neophyte at all things sex, but I kept up with him pretty well until we finally fell asleep around four a.m. I worry about keeping him happy in bed. Will I be enough for him for the rest of our lives? God, I hope so. If he ever cheats on me, I'll die.

My stomach aches when I recall the story he told me about infidelity on both sides when his marriage ended. He said then that giving his now ex-wife a taste of her own medicine hadn't been his finest hour.

"What's going on over there?"

I force a smile for him. "Nothing. Doctor jitters."

"Are you sure that's all it is?"

"Yeah." I tell him what he needs to hear, but the worries weigh on me and stay with me when we go into a big brick building. The office staff greets us with utmost professionalism, even if they stare at Flynn like starstruck girls. We've agreed that I should remove my ring while we're there, so the news of our engagement doesn't leak before we're prepared to go public. My hand already feels naked without the gorgeous ring I've zipped into a pocket in my purse.

After I complete a medical history form, get weighed and have my blood pressure taken, I'm shown to a room and asked to take a seat. The doctor will be in momentarily.

I sit in one of the chairs, and Flynn sits next to me, holding my hand.

Thankfully, she doesn't make us wait long. A knock on the door precedes the doctor entering the room. She is younger than I expected her to be, a true Southern California girl with blonde hair and blue eyes.

"It's so nice to meet you both," she says, shaking our hands.

"Doc," Flynn says, "you and the rest of the world know what Natalie's been through in the past, but you should also be aware that this is the first time she's been to a doctor since the night of her rape exam. She's extremely nervous, which is why she asked me to be here."

"Of course, I completely understand. Natalie, what brings you here today, other than the fact that you're long overdue for an exam?"

"I... I'm interested in birth control."

"Is this your first sexual relationship?"

I nod. "Yes."

"And you've been using protection?"

"We have," he says for me.

"Okay, that's good to know." She asks about my periods and if I've had any health issues, which, thankfully, I haven't. "All right, then." She retrieves a gown from a cabinet and places it on the table. "We'll need everything off, okay?"

Though I'm already trembling, I nod and she heads for the door. "I'll be back in a minute."

For a long time after she leaves the room, I stare at the gown, remembering the last time I wore one as a broken, traumatized girl. The sight of a doctor's gown takes me right back to that long-ago night.

"Sweetheart?"

I almost forgot he's there.

"The table, the gown... Brings it all back."

"Let's not do this, Nat. Not today anyway."

"No, I want to get it over with. I'll have to do it eventually if we're going to have babies." I turn to him. "We are going to have babies, aren't we?"

He smiles sweetly at me. "As many as you want, sweetheart."

My heart soars from the way he looks at me when he says that. "Then I guess I need to get over my doctor phobia." I reach for the hem of the dress I wore in deference to the foundation meeting we're attending afterward.

"Let me." Starting with my dress, he removes my clothing one item at a time and then wraps the cotton gown around me, tying it at my waist. "You're sure you want me in here for this?"

"I'm very sure. I just hope you'll still want to have sex with me afterward."

He puts his arms around me and brings me in close to him, propping his chin on the top of my head. "I'll always want to have sex with you."

We're still standing there when the doctor knocks and enters the room.

"If you'll have a seat on the table for me." She goes over to the sink to wash her hands and prepare for the exam.

As I sit on the table, I begin to tremble violently. I'm not sure I can go through with this.

"Mr. Godfrey, you can have a seat here." She refers to a stool that she positions at the head of the table.

"Come here, sweetheart."

I lie back into his welcoming arms, and he cradles my head so that neither of us can see what's happening elsewhere.

"Is this okay?"

I breathe in the sexy scent of his cologne, which calms and centers me. "Yeah."

The doctor is good about telling me everything she's doing before she does it, beginning with a breast exam that would've mortified me if Flynn hadn't kept his head down, resting against mine. I get the sense he doesn't want to look any more than I do. She talks to me about breast self-examination and how important it is to be diligent about prevention.

I hear her and I'm listening, but my eyes are tightly shut and I'm willing my way through it, wanting it to be over as fast as possible. She settles between my legs, drops the end of the table and guides my feet into stirrups.

Flashbacks of the last time my feet were in stirrups come rushing back, stealing the breath from my lungs. I'm sobbing, and nothing has even happened yet.

"Take it easy, sweetheart." Flynn strokes my face and hair as he talks softly to me.

"Shall we continue?" the doctor asks.

"Yes," I say. "Please."

She explains the Pap procedure in detail and asks if it's okay to proceed.

"Yes." I close my eyes and grit my teeth.

Flynn holds my hand and whispers to me about the fun we're going to have in Vegas, how we'll be married by this time tomorrow, how much he loves me.

I'm sore from yesterday's lovemaking, so I flinch when the speculum enters me, but she moves quickly and efficiently to take the samples. It's over before I can give in to the hysteria that's hovering just below the surface.

"How're you doing, Natalie?"

"Okay," I manage to say, though my jaw is locked.

"Now just two fingers to examine your uterus and ovaries." Like before, she is quick but thorough. "Everything looks good, Natalie. You can sit up now."

I'm still shaking, but the relief is profound. I did it. I got through it. She goes over my options for birth control, and after Flynn and I discuss it, we agree on a three-month injection, which will be fully effective in a week. Her nurse enters the room and gives me the shot.

The doctor surprises me when she hands me a written prescription. "Take this the next time you need to see a doctor. It'll help to settle your nerves."

"Thank you so much for your patience."

"You're very welcome. I hope you know it's very common for sexual assault survivors to have doctor phobias after withstanding the assault and the rape exam. It's not just you, honey." She hands me her business card. "Please call if there's anything I can do for you. My cell number is on the back. Call any time."

"Thank you so much."

"Yes, thank you," Flynn says. "We appreciate your sensitivity."

"It was a pleasure to meet you both." She starts to leave the room but turns back. "What happened to you this week, Natalie… That kind of thing can be a trigger that reopens old wounds. Take good care of yourself, and please call if I can be of any assistance."

"I will. Thank you again."

"Take all the time you need in here," she says before she leaves the room, closing the door behind her.

My hands are shaking so badly, I have to rely on Flynn to help me into my clothes. He works with silent determination to get me dressed. The dress comes over my head, and he adjusts it until it's where it's supposed to be. With a hand on either side of me on the exam table, he drops his head onto my shoulder as if he needs a moment to collect himself.

I run my fingers through his hair.

"I'm so sorry, Nat. I never should've let you go through this."

"I would've had to do it eventually."

"But you didn't have to do it today."

"I'm glad I did. I got the first time over with, and now we'll soon be protected, too."

He withdraws a piece of paper from his pocket, unfolds it and hands it to me. "What's this?"

"Proof that I'm clean. My doctor sent it over this morning. I had the testing done in New York."

"A fresh, *clean* start for our married life."

"Yes, exactly."

"You said you did this in New York, but you only asked me to marry you yesterday."

"I knew by the third time I saw you that there was no going back. You're it for me." He bends his knees so he can look directly into my eyes. "Are you okay? I would totally understand if you wanted to postpone our plans for today because you don't feel up to it."

"I'm okay now that it's over, and you're not getting out of marrying me today."

He breathes a sigh of relief as he hugs me. "Thank God."

Flynn

Watching Natalie endure that exam was about the most torturous thing I've ever been through in my life. I can't begin to know what it must've been like for her. We're on our way to the Quantum offices for a meeting with the group that will soon make up the board of directors for my hunger foundation.

After Natalie's emotional reaction to the doctor's appointment, I thought about postponing the meeting, but it was too late to cancel with so many busy people already en route.

She's quiet on the drive to the office, and I don't push her to talk. I know she's dealing with yet another reopened wound, which makes me want to start punching things again.

Bringing her to the office—again—leaves me unsettled in light of the secrets we're hiding in the basement of the Quantum building. Like in New York, our secret BDSM club is housed there, not that Natalie will ever know about that. It's not a part of my life that I can share with her, so I'll put it in the past where it belongs.

After witnessing the trauma the medical exam caused her, I'm further convinced that my now-former lifestyle will never play a part in our relationship, so why would I ever tell her about it? She won't understand it unless she experiences it, and after what she's been through, there's no way I'm bringing dominance or submission into our bed. I'll find a way to live without it, because living without her isn't an option.

When we arrive on the top floor of the Quantum building where our executive offices are housed, everyone is thrilled about the Oscar nominations. The receptionist tells me my parents are waiting for me in my office. I'm glad I'll get a chance to talk to them about our wedding plans before the meeting.

We're holding hands when we enter my office, where my parents are enjoying cups of coffee and sitting together on one of the sofas. I've asked them and my sisters to be on the board of directors for the foundation, and they were all thrilled to accept. My parents jump up to greet us. Both of them hug and kiss Natalie. I love their easy familiarity with her and the way they've welcomed her into our family. She needs that right now, and they seem to know it.

"I'm glad you guys were able to get here a few minutes early."

"You said you had some news for us that has nothing to do with the meeting," Dad says, his eyes dancing. "That's going to get our attention every time."

I glance at Natalie before I return my gaze to them. "Natalie and I are getting married tonight."

I've rarely seen my parents speechless, but they are truly stunned by my announcement.

And then my mom begins to tear up, and I know it's going to be okay.

"That's wonderful news, son," Dad says. "Congratulations to both of you."

"Yes," Mom adds, "we're thrilled for you."

Beside me, I feel Natalie relax ever so slightly when it becomes clear that they don't object to our news.

"What a whirlwind," Dad says, which is his way of asking if we're being hasty. He would never use that word with us. It's just not how he rolls.

"Could I see your ring, Natalie?" Mom asks.

"We agreed I shouldn't wear it this morning so our news doesn't get out before we want it to." Natalie unzips the ring from her purse, slides it back into place and extends her hand to Mom.

"It's beautiful." To me, she says, "Well done, honey."

"All thanks to Hugh. He was instrumental."

"Where do you plan to get married?" Dad asks.

"We're going to Vegas for the night."

"This is so exciting," Mom says. "Natalie, your head must be spinning."

"In the best possible way," she says, looking up at me with a smile.

"We'll have a party," Mom declares. "We'll have it at our house. You have to let us celebrate with you. Sometime in the next couple of weeks."

I look at Natalie, who seems pleased by the idea. "Sure, Mom, that'd be nice. Nothing too crazy. Just immediate family." In our case, immediate family includes a couple hundred of our closest friends.

"Of course." She claps her hands. "I'd given up hope that you'd ever get married again, but after we met you, Natalie, I told Max our boy is going to marry that lovely girl."

"And you know how much your mother loves to be right."

"I do enjoy my ability to predict the future," Mom says, "and I predict you two will be very happy together. Welcome to our family, Natalie, and thank you for making Flynn happier than we've ever seen him."

"He's made me very happy, too, and thank you for your warm welcome. I can't tell you how much it means to me to be part of a family again."

"You may be wishing for simpler times after you spend more time with the Godfreys," I tell her.

"No, I won't. Show me your worst."

"We won't tell the girls she said that," Mom says, making us all laugh.

We chat with them for a few more minutes until one of the admins tells us the others are here for the meeting. I send my parents along and take a minute alone with Natalie.

"That went well, huh?" I ask her.

"They're wonderful. They never batted an eye."

"They never would. They know me, and they understand that, more than anything, I know myself and what I want." Once again, my conscience rears its ugly head to remind me of the part of myself I'm denying as I enter into marriage with Natalie. "Are you okay with waiting to tell everyone else until after the fact? Although I trust my family and your friends, I'd hate for the word to get out before we're ready to let it out."

"That's fine with me. Whatever you think is best. You certainly know better than I do how to handle that kind of announcement."

"I wanted to tell you, in the meeting, I'm going to name you chair of the foundation board."

Her face goes slack with shock. "You're going to do *what?*"

"I want you to oversee the entire thing. Everyone will answer to you."

"You're serious."

"Dead serious."

"But I know nothing about running a foundation."

"Neither do I. We'll figure it out together. You know far more than I do about the problem we're hoping to solve, having worked as a teacher in the city. You're better qualified than I'll ever be to head up this effort."

"You've been close to this issue for years, and your name will be on the door. It should be you."

"*Our* names will be on the door, and I haven't been as close to the issue as I'm going to be."

"Our names?"

"It will be called the Flynn and Natalie Godfrey Foundation."

"Flynn... I don't know what to say. Your faith in me is..."

"I've found the very best possible person to lead this effort that's as near and dear to my heart as you are. I think you can make a real difference, Nat. But if you don't want to take it on, I'd totally understand."

"I'd love to try, as long as you know I might mess things up before I find my footing."

"You won't mess up anything. We've got a great staff here at Quantum who will be at your disposal."

"What if..."

"What if what?"

She looks up at me, her expression filled with uncertainty. "I get my job back in New York?"

"I guess we'll have a decision to make if that happens. Either way, I want you involved in the foundation, and I feel very comfortable putting you in charge and putting you on salary beginning today. But only if it's what you want, too."

"I'm honored by your faith in me, and I'd love to try. Thank you."

"Then let's go meet with our new board of directors."

CHAPTER 11

Natalie

This will surely go down as one of the most surreal days of my life. We're on another private plane heading for Vegas as the sun drops toward the horizon. With Fluff sleeping in my lap, I'm curled up next to Flynn on the sofa.

He shocked the hell out of me by asking me to head up the foundation, but once the shock wore off, I began to feel excited about the challenge. I left the meeting with a three-page to-do list that will keep me busy for the first half of the year.

I have to give Flynn credit for recognizing that I need something to pour my energy into since losing my job. The work we plan to do helping to feed hungry children is an extremely worthwhile cause that needs this kind of attention.

I saw it with my own class, most of them from good families with hardworking parents, and yet from time to time, some of them came to school without having had breakfast and with no money for lunch.

They broke my heart with the kind of quiet shame that no child should ever experience.

"What're you thinking about, sweetheart?"

"My to-do list from the meeting."

"I knew I hired the right person for this job. You're already all over it."

"So it's a job, huh?"

"Of course it is. I told you I was putting you on the Quantum payroll. And your first-year salary is the exact amount of your student loans plus fifty percent."

Laughter bursts from my chest, spontaneous and free. "You're a smooth operator, Flynn Godfrey."

"Why thank you, sweetheart. I'm glad you think so."

"I decline your generous salary and *volunteer* my time to the foundation. You see, my soon-to-be husband is *filthy* rich, so I don't technically *need* to work."

"Ohhh, well-played, my love."

"Why thank you." I love every second I get to spend in the presence of this extraordinary man. It doesn't matter what we're doing, he makes me happier than I've ever been or had ever hoped to be.

"But that's not happening. You do a job, you get paid. That's how it works. And speaking of your filthy-rich husband…"

"You probably want me to sign something. Whatever you need, I'll sign."

"No, I don't want you to sign anything."

"Flynn, be serious. Anyone with half a brain who has what you have would expect his girlfriend of two weeks to sign a prenup before they say I do."

"Well, I guess I have less than half a brain, because there isn't going to be any prenup."

He's so emphatic that I begin to question whether he's already had this argument with someone else. "Is this why Hayden left the way he did other night?"

"What way did he leave?"

"Pissed off. I assumed it had something to do with me, as I have that effect on him."

Flynn seems to be deciding how much he wishes to say.

"Did your friends tell you you're a fool to not have a prenup?"

"I don't know that *fool* was the word they used."

I roll my eyes at him. "For what it's worth, I agree with them. I'd actually be more comfortable if there was something that protects you. Just in case."

"In case of what?"

I throw him a look that lets him know I'm on to him. "Don't be obtuse."

"I do so love your vocabulary, Ms. Bryant, and just for your edification, this marriage is forever, so I refuse to go into it making plans for it to end."

"While I appreciate your complete and utter faith in me and in us, it would be prudent for you to ask me to sign something that says I don't want your money. I only want you."

"Which is exactly why you're not being asked to sign anything. I believe you when you say you only want me. You're the only woman I've ever been with who's with me for the right reasons. Everything I have is yours."

Tears fill my eyes. How can this be really happening? "I love you so much. Who you are to the rest of the world and what you have... None of that matters to me as much as who you are to me, what you give to me every day, by loving me."

He leans in to kiss me.

I reach up to keep him from getting away, which disturbs Fluff.

She comes to with a growl and a bark that make us laugh once again.

Caressing his cheek, I say, "I live in mortal fear of her biting this world-famous face."

"A scar or two would add some character."

"You're perfect exactly the way you are."

A short time later, we land in Vegas, where we're met by a limo that whisks us into town. I'm dazzled by the Vegas Strip—the lights, the gaudy grandeur and the palpable energy. Flynn, who has been here a million times, enjoys watching me see it for the first time.

We end up at the Bellagio, where we're taken in through a special entrance and escorted to an elevator that deposits us directly into a palatial suite with floor-to-ceiling windows that overlook the Strip and the elaborate fountains the hotel is famous for. I walk over to the window to take it all in.

Flynn joins me there and slides his arms around me from behind. "What do you think, sweetheart?"

"It's amazing. I'm not sure where to look first because there's so much to see."

"I wish we were normal people, and I could take you for a walk to get closer to the fountains or show you the casino, where you could try your luck at the tables."

I turn to face him. "I wouldn't want us to be anyone other than who we are. I'm perfectly satisfied with this beautiful suite and to have you all to myself."

"You'll have me all to yourself after we take care of a little business."

"What kind of business?" I ask with a coy smile, though I know perfectly well.

The doorbell rings. "Hold that thought." He kisses me before he goes to answer a door that I hadn't noticed.

I'm still staring out the window when there's a flurry of activity behind me reflected in the glass. I turn to find four people and a rack of dresses. "What's all this?"

"I couldn't ask you to get married without a fabulous dress and, at the very least, having your hair done however you want it. Oh, and flowers. They're on the way up."

"Let me guess. Addie?"

"With a little help from me." He looks adorably uncertain all of a sudden. "I hope this is okay."

I go up on tiptoes to kiss him. "It's perfect. Everything about this is perfect."

"I'll leave you to get ready, then. See you soon?"

"Yes, you will."

An hour later, I'm wearing a gorgeous white silk dress by a designer I've never heard of. It fits me like it was made just for me, which is why I chose it. It's also subtly sexy with a deep V neckline that I'm quite certain my future husband will appreciate. The bodice is beaded with crystals and pearls, but the rest is exquisitely simple, which suits me perfectly.

I've brought the diamond earrings and necklace Flynn gave me before the Golden Globes, and my hands tremble ever so slightly as I put them on. I'm still terrified of losing them, even though he's told me not to worry. They're insured. Still, I'd die if I ever misplaced the priceless gems.

I've chosen to wear my hair down because that's more "me" than an elaborate updo will ever be. It's long and curly, the way I like it best. I never feel more "me," the new and improved me, than when I'm with Flynn, so I want to be beautiful for him tonight.

I wonder about the people who help me get ready and what sort of threats they must be under to keep our secrets. I hope none of them buckles to the pressure to spill the beans. I'm certain Flynn's team has a plan for how they will release this news to the world.

That, however, is not my concern right now. At the moment, all I can think about is that I'm about to marry the most wonderful man I've ever known, and I can't wait to commit the rest of my life to him.

Everyone else leaves, and I take a last look in the mirror before I declare myself ready. I'm not sure if I should wait in the bedroom or go out to see if Flynn is ready, too.

A soft knock on the door ends my debate. My belly flutters with excitement as I cross the room to answer. Flynn is there in a sexy black suit with a thin tie. His hair has been combed into submission, and he's freshly shaven. He's absolutely stunning, and the way he looks at me takes my breath away.

"Natalie… God, you're beautiful. Come out here and let me see you." He takes me by the hand and leads me into the enormous living room that's bigger than my entire apartment in New York. Still holding my hand, he places his other hand over his heart. "I have to be the luckiest guy who ever lived to have found you. And that you love me…"

"I love you so much. I can't wait to be your wife."

"Then let's make it official, shall we?" He hands me a bouquet of white roses and snapdragons and other flowers I don't recognize. Then he places a call on the house phone, and a few minutes later, the doorbell rings again. This time he admits a man in a suit who gestures for the woman who is with him to enter ahead of him. They both have gray hair and warm, friendly smiles.

"Natalie, this is Judge Henry Gallagher and his wife, Teresa. He'll marry us, and they'll serve as our witnesses."

I shake hands with them. "Nice to meet you both."

"Likewise," he says. "We're both huge fans of your work, Mr. Godfrey."

"Please, call me Flynn."

"I have a few things for you both to sign," Judge Gallagher says.

We take care of the paperwork and decide to stand before the fireplace for the ceremony. When Flynn reaches for my hands and flashes a giddy smile, I set the flowers on a nearby table and take hold of his hands.

All of a sudden, it registers with me that we're actually doing this. We're getting married, and I'm not even slightly nervous. That's because I know without a shadow of a doubt that I'm doing the right thing. The smile that stretches across Flynn's handsome face lets me know he feels the same way. I squeeze his hands.

"Flynn and Natalie, you have come here tonight to be married. Are you both taking these vows of your own free will?"

"I am," we say together.

Flynn squeezes my hands.

"Natalie, if you'll repeat after me."

I recite my vows, listen to Flynn recite his and become teary when he slides a platinum band on my finger that matches my engagement ring. I panic for a second when I realize I don't have a ring for him, but of course that's been taken care of as well.

He produces a matching ring and drops it into my hand with a wink and a smile.

As I slide it onto his finger, the magnitude of what we're doing seems to hit me all at once, leaving me light-headed and joyful. It's been so long since I've felt anything that could be described as joy, but standing here in a luxurious suite in Las Vegas, marrying the man of my dreams—hell, the man of everyone's dreams—I know real, true joy for the first time in longer than I can remember.

And then he's kissing me and the judge is declaring us husband and wife. I'm Flynn Godfrey's wife.

Flynn produces his phone and asks Mrs. Gallagher to take a picture for us. She takes a dozen and then asks if it would be too much to get one of her with Flynn. Naturally, he obliges and produces an envelope that he hands to them. "A little something to thank you for your time."

As we're seeing them off, two tuxedoed waiters arrive, one pushing a table that's been set for two and the other carrying an ice bucket containing two bottles of champagne. The older of the two says, "When you're ready, Mr. Godfrey."

"Give us ten minutes, please."

"Of course."

They depart, closing the door behind them and leaving me alone with my husband. My *husband*. Someone pinch me, please. He wraps his arms around me and buries his face in my hair. "Hello, Mrs. Godfrey."

I slip my arms inside his suit coat to return the embrace. "Hello, Mr. Godfrey."

"How does it feel?"

"Unreal. Amazing. Perfect."

"For me, too."

"I'll never forget this, Flynn. Any of it. The whirlwind has been…"

"Life changing."

I nod in agreement. "Incredible." It's my favorite word to describe him and our relationship.

Without breaking the intense eye contact, he kisses me softly. I can tell he's holding back because he has other plans before we consummate this marriage.

"We have one piece of business to attend to."

"What's that?"

He pulls his phone from his pocket. "Help me pick the best one." We scroll through the photos Mrs. Gallagher took.

"That one."

"That's a good one." He sets up a text message and fires it off to Liza with the words "green light."

"What's going to happen?"

"She's going to release the photo with a single sentence that says 'Flynn Godfrey married Natalie Bryant in Las Vegas tonight.' That's all we plan to say about it."

"That's all there is to say."

"Oh, sweetheart, there's so much more I could say, but I'll save all of that for you. No one else needs to know."

"Would it be okay if I text the photo to Leah and Aileen so they don't hear about it on Twitter?"

"Of course. I'll send it to your phone."

When I have the photo, I fire off a quick group text to my friends in New York, who reply immediately.

Leah: *WHHHAAAAATTTT??? SHUT THE FUCK UP! OMG! So happy for you guys! You both look beautiful—and happy. Congrats, Nat. I can't even tell you how thrilled I am for you.*

Aileen: *I'm in tears for two beautiful people who deserve a lifetime of happiness. xoxo from me, Logan and Maddie*

I share the replies with Flynn. "You should probably tell your friends—and your family."

"You're right. I should." He sends off a group message, and his phone starts dinging frantically with replies.

His sister Aimee: *Never say never! Way to go. Welcome to the family, Natalie!*

Marlowe: *Fantastic! Congrats, guys! Looking forward to celebrating at the SAGs. Love you!*

Kristian: *Congrats! Great pic. Happiness always.*

His sister Annie: *Shut the front door! Have you been hacked? Abducted by aliens? Laid low by love? Happy for you, bro. Welcome to the Godfrey family madness, Natalie!*

Emmett: *Mazel tov! My best wishes for a long and happy life together.*

Stella: *Congratulations, my darlings. Thrilled and delighted to welcome Natalie to our family. Dad and I love you both! xoxo*

Jasper: *Well done, chap! Natalie, you've got one of the good ones. All my best always.*

His sister Ellie: *Welcome to our family, Natalie! Anyone who can put up with Flynn full time has my undying respect and admiration. Happy for you both! Love you.*

Addie: *Thrilled and delighted for you both. Enjoy every minute!*

"Very good advice from Addie," I say. Neither of us mentions that the only one who didn't reply is his closest friend, Hayden.

"Enough with the phones." He powers his down and tosses it on a table. "I don't know about you, but I'm starving."

"I could eat."

He goes to the door to let in the waiters, who deliver a beautiful meal that consists of Caesar salad, grilled shrimp, tender beef, asparagus and mouthwatering risotto. They uncork the champagne and fill crystal flutes.

Flynn raises his in toast to me, and I touch my glass to his. "To my wife."

"To my husband."

He leans over to kiss me. "I like the sound of that."

"So do I."

I try some of everything, even though my stomach is alive with nerves and excitement for the night ahead of us. I can't wait to be completely alone with him, my husband. Seeing that ring on his finger and recognizing all it stands for is truly humbling.

"Do you like your wedding ring?" he asks, tuning in to my thoughts.

"I love it. It's beautiful. Everything is. I can't believe what you and your magician Addie managed to put together with two days' notice."

"She's good at what she does."

"Your stamp is all over this, Flynn. Take your share of the credit."

"I'll take this much." He pinches his thumb and index finger together. "I chose the rings and said yay or nay to a bunch of dresses, hoping there'd be one you liked."

"I love this dress. I never want to take it off."

He raises a brow. "It's coming off. Very soon."

I laugh at the thinly veiled yet playful threat I hear in his tone. "Thanks for the warning."

We share a chocolate dessert that's the most sinfully delicious thing I've ever tasted. Coupled with the champagne and the strawberries that came with the dessert, I'm bordering on sensory overload. When we're finished eating, the waiters return to remove the dishes and then the table, leaving us with yet another bottle of champagne in a fresh bucket of ice.

"We need a song," Flynn says.

"A song?"

"For our first dance as husband and wife. What shall it be? Lady's choice."

"Hmmm, this is a huge decision and not one to be taken lightly. For the rest of our lives, whatever song we choose will be the song we danced to on our wedding night."

"Which is why I left that decision up to you."

"I'm feeling a tremendous amount of pressure to get it right."

"I have faith in you, sweetheart."

"May I consult my iTunes library?"

"By all means."

As I scroll through the songs on my phone, dismissing one after the other as not right for us, he turns the lights way down. "What song did your parents dance to at their wedding?" I ask him.

"'Moon River.' They love that song."

"That's a good one."

He looks over my shoulder as I consult my song list. "Wait, what was that one? 'Love, Laugh, Fuck.' That works."

"We are not having a wedding song with that word in it."

With his arms around me, he presses his erection against my back. "Why not?"

"Because we're not, and that's it."

"Buzz killer."

"Maybe so, but you're stuck with me now."

"Never been so happy to be stuck with anyone in my life."

I smile at his sweet words. The kisses he's leaving on my neck set off goose bumps that cover my entire body. "I can't concentrate when you're doing that."

"My apologies," he says but doesn't stop.

"How about this?" I choose "I Won't Give Up" by Jason Mraz and play it for him.

"That sounds sort of perfect for us in light of everything."

"So we have a winner?"

"Yes, we do." He takes my phone from me and plugs it into the suite's sound system. Then he turns and extends his hand. "May I have this dance, Mrs. Godfrey?"

"Absolutely, Mr. Godfrey." I go to him and let him wrap me up in his love. My hands find their way inside his coat, and I lay my face on his chest. "Flynn…"

"What, honey?"

"I just want you to know that for the first time since everything happened to me, I feel like I've found my way home again. The whirling inside my head has finally stopped, and I'm… I'm calm, at peace. And it's all because of you and what we've found together."

"Nat… There's nothing you could say that would make me happier, especially in light of everything that's happened since you met me."

"There's relief in having nothing left to hide, so while I wouldn't have wanted it to happen the way it did, I'm glad there're no secrets between us."

He tightens his arms around me as we sway to the music. "I won't give up on us, Nat. Ever. No matter what happens."

"Neither will I."

CHAPTER 12

Flynn

I die inside when she says there're no secrets between us. I've kept something huge from her, something that might've changed her mind about marrying me if she knew. I tell myself it doesn't matter because I've put that in the past to focus on my future with Natalie.

She's the only thing that matters now. Neither my past nor hers has any bearing on the future we're going to create for ourselves. I've made my choices, and now I'm going to make this marriage work or die trying.

She's warm and soft and pliant in my arms as the song comes to an end and another begins. I don't want this moment to ever end, the first time we dance together as a married couple. It may be the first time, but it won't be the last. We've got everything to look forward to, and I refuse to spend any portion of this night looking back.

Nuzzling through her silky hair, I focus my attention on the long column of her neck, kissing her until I feel her begin to tremble in my arms. I love the way she responds to me, how even the most innocent of caresses gets a reaction from her. I love that no one else but me will ever get to touch her again. I love that she has trusted me to be the first man to touch her after she was so brutally attacked as a teenager.

She has given me a priceless gift, and every day of my life, I will aim to be worthy of her. Her hands encircle my neck and she gazes up at me, her eyes full of love and trust and desire. I've tried to be patient tonight, to give her romance and memories that will last a lifetime, but now I want her with a desperation that can't be contained.

"Natalie…"

"Hmm?"

"I want to make love to my wife."

"Your wife approves of that plan."

"I love you so much."

"I love you, too."

With my hands on her face, I kiss her softly, reverently. Before things can spin out of control, I take her by the hand and lead her into the bedroom, which was transformed by the hotel staff while we were eating. The room is bathed in candlelight, the bed covered in red rose petals. There's yet another bottle of champagne in an ice bucket on a table.

"Wow," she says with a sigh. "You thought of everything."

"This is why I wanted to come here. No one does it up like they do in Vegas."

"I can see that." She worries her bottom lip, which tells me there's something on her mind.

"What're you thinking?"

"I didn't bring anything special to wear tonight. I don't really have anything that would be worthy—"

I kiss her again because I can't stand to see her worried about anything. "Natalie, honey, all I need is you. May I help you out of your dress?"

"Yes, please." She gathers up her hair and pulls it to the front, leaving her back bare to my hungry gaze. The zipper is hidden by a row of buttons that, thankfully, are just for decoration. If I had to take the time to undo a hundred tiny buttons, I'd lose my mind. I draw the zipper down, and the dress falls open to reveal the enticing curve of her back. Since she hasn't worn a bra, the dress slides off her shoulders and down her arms, leaving her covered only from the waist down.

"What's the trick to getting it off?"

She smiles at me over her shoulder and shimmies her hips, letting the dress drop. That's when I see that she's wearing a white silk thong, a garter belt and thigh-high stockings.

"I'm going to need you to turn around. Like immediately."

Still wearing her fuck-me heels, she turns, hands on hips, breasts jutting out proudly, and my heart literally stops for a brief second. "Holy mother of God. You almost gave me a heart attack. And you said you didn't bring anything to wear."

Her smile is coy and full of satisfaction. "I lied."

I place my hands on her ribs, trying to control the overwhelming need to toss her on the bed and take what I want so fiercely. "Where in the name of hell did this getup come from?"

"It was one of several choices that came with the dresses. Your assistant is nothing if not thorough."

"God, I love her."

Natalie tosses her head back to laugh, and I take advantage of the opportunity to cup her breasts and suck her nipple into my mouth. My inner dominant hovers on the razor's edge, wanting to break free and take what's mine. I want to own her, possess her, rule her. I want every part of her, and I want her to surrender to me in every possible way.

But more than all that, I want her to never be afraid of me, so I suppress my driving natural inclinations and give her the softness, the sweetness and the love she needs and deserves.

She's a more than willing participant, shoving the suit coat off my shoulders, pulling off my tie and attacking the buttons on my shirt without missing a beat in the tongue-twisting kiss. Her hands flatten against my bare chest, ratcheting up the desperation for more. We work together, our hands colliding as we both reach for the clasp on my pants at the same time.

My pants fall to the floor. I shrug off the dress shirt and practically tear the sleeve off when one of the cuff links refuses to cooperate. "Fucking shit," I mutter, making her laugh.

"Allow me." She takes my arm, gently works the cuff link free and drops it into my hand.

Only because they were my grandfather's do I take the time to put them both on the bedside table before I return my attention to my gorgeous, sexy wife. "I want a picture of you like this."

"An actual picture?"

"Yeah. Can I?"

"I don't know…"

"It would be just for us. If you think I'd ever share you with anyone…" I've shared women in the past, but not this one. No fucking way could I ever stand to see another man's hands on her.

"Okay…" She's tentative, but I can see that the request has turned her on. Her eyes have gotten very bright, and her cheeks are flushed with color. Even her breasts are rosy with heat.

"Stay right there." I dash into the other room to grab my phone, powering it up as I make my way back to where I left her.

"How do you want me?"

I groan, loudly. "Fuck, sweetheart, you might want to think twice before you ask me such a leading question."

"Why?" The innocence, the overpowering sweetness… She destroys me and then puts me back together every fucking time.

"There're a lot of ways I could have you."

"Will you tell me about them? All of them?"

I swallow hard, summoning control that's hard to come by right now. "We've got the rest of our lives to try everything once, twice if we like it. For right now, move your hair to the front so your nipples are peeking out and put your hands on your hips. Strike a pose."

I'm hard as concrete as I snap a few photos. "Now gather your hair up with your hands and hold it over your head. Fuck, that's sexy. Just like that. Oh my God, Nat." I throw the phone aside and take her down with me onto the bed, our lips and tongues coming together in an urgent kiss that drives my need so deep into the red zone, I can't think of anything other than being inside her. Right now.

Motherfucking hell. I'm never going to survive this.

Natalie

I've never seen him quite like this before. His kiss is so fierce, so out of control that all I can do is go along on the ride with him. His tongue is everywhere, teasing and tempting and making me want to beg for whatever comes next. I want him to touch me and take me and make me his.

I've never wanted anything quite like I want him inside me, right now.

"Flynn," I gasp when he finally comes up for air.

"What, honey? Talk to me."

It's all I can do to breathe when he attacks my neck, finding the place that I didn't know made me wild until he discovered it.

"I want you now."

"I'm here."

It hasn't taken me long to become brave where he's concerned, so I run my hand down the front of him and push his boxers out of the way in my quest to get to what I want. When I wrap my hand around his thick erection, he moans. I stroke him the way he taught me to, hard and tight.

"This is what I want. Make love to me. Please, Flynn. Right now."

He literally tears the thong right off my body in a move that leaves me dazzled by the sheer power of his desire. "I don't want to hurt you. Tell me if it hurts."

"It won't." I don't care if it does.

He takes himself in hand, rolls on a condom and drives into me in one deep thrust that makes me scream from the impact, the pleasure and the heat that come together in the place where we are joined and ripple out to every other corner of my body. I can feel him trembling from the effort it takes to remain completely still, until he's certain I'm ready for more.

"I've never felt anything that's better than this, Natalie."

"Move, Flynn. Please…"

He doesn't have to be told twice. Rising up to his knees, he begins slowly, thrusting deeply and then withdrawing to pound into me again, over and over.

I throw my arms over my head, seeking purchase, something to hold on to as he takes me on the wildest ride of my life.

Then he's over me, reaching for my hands to grip them together while his other hand grasps my ass, holding me in place for his fierce possession. When I realize I can't move my hands, or any other part of me, for that matter, a slow drumbeat of panic begins in my chest.

He's kissing me as he makes love to me, and all of a sudden I can't breathe. I can't move. I can't do this. I wrench my head to the left, breaking the kiss and let out a scream as the memories come flooding back to remind me that while I might be determined to outrun my past, it always catches up to me eventually.

I fight him like a wild animal, thrashing and kicking and screaming.

He stops immediately, pulls out and lets go of me. "Natalie."

I'm hysterical, screaming and crying and fighting the demons with everything I have inside me. In the far recesses of my mind, I hear Fluff freaking out right along with me, barking and snarling.

"Sweetheart, oh my God, it's me, baby. Please… Natalie. It's just me, and I love you more than anything."

His words permeate the hysteria, and I deflate like a balloon that's been stuck with a pin. Fluff plops down next to me, licking my face and offering her own sort of comfort.

Dear God, I just totally lost my mind while making love to my husband for the first time. The sobs shake my body, and I'm afraid to open my eyes, to see how he must be looking at this broken, damaged shell of a woman he's shackled himself to for a lifetime.

"Natalie…" He lays his hand on my heaving abdomen.

I flinch and Fluff growls, but Flynn doesn't remove his hand. "Sweetheart, look at me. Open your eyes."

I shake my head. I can't. I'll never be able to look at him again after ruining what should've been the most special moment of our lives.

He replaces his hand with his lips, kissing my belly, my hipbones, between my breasts, my neck, my jaw, my face and finally my lips. Each kiss is like a bandage on the wound I carry with me. Each kiss is about love and devotion and has nothing at all to do with what happened to me so long ago.

I tell myself that, but will he ever forgive me for losing it while he was inside me? Will he ever again touch me without thinking about what might happen if he makes the slightest wrong move?

"It was the hands," I tell him, keeping my eyes closed.

"I held down your hands, and that triggered a memory."

I nod. "I'm so sorry." Tears soaking through my closed eyes leave hot tracks as they slide down my face.

He kisses them away and strokes my hair, my face, my body, which soothes and calms me. "Could I hold you?"

I turn into his arms and hold on to him for dear life as sobs shake my body and my newfound resolve. What other repressed memories are waiting to resurface to remind me of all the many ways I'm broken? How will my beloved husband ever know if what he's about to do is the wrong thing?

"I'm sorry."

"Do not apologize to me, Natalie."

His sharp tone makes me whimper like the wounded animal I am.

"I'm sorry," he says in a softer tone. "I didn't mean to say it so harshly. You're perfect just the way you are, and if it takes the whole rest of our lives, we'll figure out what works for us—and what doesn't. No matter what happens, I'll never, ever blame you for any of it. Ever."

"I hate that I ruined our wedding night."

"You haven't ruined anything. Our wedding night is far from over. It's just getting started."

He holds me for a long time, making soothing circles on my back and kissing my forehead over and over again until I begin to settle.

"Do you feel better?"

I nod. "Are you okay?"

"I'm great as long as I'm here with you."

"Do you think… we could… can we…"

"What honey?"

"Can we try again?"

"We don't have to. We've got all the time in the world."

"I know we don't have to, but I want to. If you're willing. I wouldn't blame you if you weren't."

He props himself up on one elbow and looks down at me. "I am always willing to make love to you. There will never be a time when I don't want you, Natalie. But you are always free to say no."

"I'm saying yes. I'm saying yes to everything."

"We'll take it nice and slow." He kisses me. "But we need a word, something you'll say if it's ever too much or something scares you. It needs to be a word that we both know means stop. No matter what's happening, if you say that word, it's game off."

"Okay…"

"What word do you want to use?"

I finally open my eyes, look up at his handsome, earnest face and offer a faint smile. "How about Fluff?" My little dog lets out a yip when she hears her name.

He smiles back at me. "That's perfect."

I reach up to bring him down to me. "I love you. Nothing you could do will ever be wrong. It's not you. Please tell me you know that."

"I do. I know."

"I loved the way we were before."

"How were we?"

"Wild and uninhibited. I want to be that person. I want to be her with you."

"We'll get there."

I run a finger over the pulse in his cheek that lets me know how difficult this is for him. "Having sex with me is like playing with dynamite without knowing where the fuse is."

"Having sex with you is like the closest thing to heaven I've experienced on this earth, Natalie. There's nothing that could happen that would change that."

"Can we try again?"

"Only if we go slow this time. We'll save wild and uninhibited for another day."

Fluff lets out a snore that makes us both laugh, and I watch the tension leave his body in a deep exhale. He begins anew with deep, soft, undemanding kisses that make my head spin. My body reawakens one kiss at a time.

He's in no rush as one kiss becomes two and two become three. His touch is careful rather than unrestrained the way it was before. I can feel him holding back, and I ache with the knowledge that it's costing him to give me what I need. He showed me earlier what he really wants, and I freaked out.

"I can *hear* you thinking."

"I can't help it."

"Shhh. Just relax and don't worry about anything. Everything is all right. It's just you and me here, Nat. No one else. I love you more with every passing minute.

I want you any way I can have you. You're absolutely perfect to me. I wouldn't change a thing about you, except to take away any pain you ever experienced and replace it with beautiful new memories." As he speaks, he's kissing my face and returning to my lips for brief caresses before moving on to my neck and chest.

"You're the only one I want, the only one I'll ever want." He cups my breasts and runs his tongue over my nipples, which clears my mind of every thought that isn't about the sublime pleasure I've found in his arms. Long before I've had enough, he moves on, leaving a path of kisses over my ribs and belly before moving lower. "So soft and so sweet. I love how you smell and how you taste. I could die happy right here." He nuzzles the hair between my legs, taking a tentative swipe with his tongue over my most sensitive area before moving down to run his hands over the silky stockings that cover my legs.

I'm carried away on a sea of sensation. His words, kisses and gentle caresses start a new drumbeat of desire that lives between my legs. I want him there, but he's still in no particular rush.

"So hot and so sexy. My wife is beautiful. Every guy in the world will be envious of the woman I get to sleep with every night." His lips find a spot on the back of my knee that makes me moan. "They'll look at you, and they'll wish they were half as lucky as I am." My legs end up propped on his broad shoulders. His hands are flat against my inner thighs, and his head is bent above me. "I've never tasted a sweeter pussy," he whispers before he dips his head and opens me to his tongue. In keeping with the slow, undemanding theme, he drives me to the edge of insanity by kissing me everywhere but where I need him most.

I grasp a handful of his hair to direct him, but he resists.

He laughs. "Are you trying to take over my show?"

"Just trying to move it along."

"Is this what you want?" He sucks my clit into his mouth and runs his tongue back and forth as he eases his fingers inside me. The combination triggers an orgasm that rolls through me in slow waves, one right after the other, until Flynn brings me down slowly, carefully.

I reach for him. I need him to hold me, and he understands. He reaches for another condom before he comes to me, kissing me with lips that taste like me but feel like him. He's more insistent now, his tongue demanding entry as he settles between my legs, his erection pulsing against me.

With my hands on his back, I arch my hips, asking him to take me away, to make me his. He's still kissing me when he begins to enter me, slowly and with far more patience than I have after this slow seduction.

"Easy, baby," he whispers. "Nice and easy."

It will be, I realize, a very long time before I see fast or frantic Flynn again, and that saddens me profoundly. I love him that way, but I love him this way, too.

He pushes into me in slow increments, watching me intently for any signs of distress. "You feel so good, sweetheart. So hot and tight and wet." He throws his head back. "Ah, God, you just got wetter. I love that."

"I love when you talk to me when we do this."

"Do you love when I talk dirty to you?"

"I love it all."

His hips pivot, and he's finally fully seated inside me, throbbing and hot as my body adapts to his size.

"Are all men as big as you are? Down there?"

"*Fuck*," he growls, and I swear he gets even bigger. "You know how to make a guy feel good, baby."

"You know how to make me feel good."

"Does it feel good?"

"It feels amazing. And tight. Very, very tight."

"We're a perfect fit." He pulls back ever so slightly before pressing forward again. "I'm right on the edge. Is it okay if I move a little?"

"*Please* move."

"I want you to keep your eyes open and on me, okay?"

I bite my lip and nod. My inner thighs are trembling from the pressure of keeping my legs so far apart.

"What's your safe word?"

"Fluff."

The dog lets out an indignant snort and begins to snore again.

Flynn smiles down at me. "I'm surprised she's allowing such scandalous behavior in her bed."

I'm on the verge of a witty reply when he begins to move faster. He's propped up on his hands, watching me carefully as his hips pivot with increasingly urgent movements in and out of me. It feels so good. My eyes want to close, but I keep them open and fixed on him so there can be no chance of panic.

I move with him, picking up his rhythm and experiencing a profound sense of belonging to him.

"I'm going to look away, sweetheart. You stop me if you don't feel right. Okay?"

"Okay," I say on a long exhale.

His right hand holds him up while he bends to capture my right nipple in his mouth, and his left hand reaches down to where we're joined, touching me exactly where I need him. I'm hovering at the edge of release when his teeth tighten on my nipple and he pinches my clit, triggering my orgasm and his.

"Ah, God," he says when he comes down on top of me, capturing my lips in a deep kiss.

He kisses between my breasts, his forehead resting against my chest.

I comb my fingers through sweat-dampened hair, massaging his scalp, which makes him sigh with what sounds like contentment. I hope it is.

I'm going to make him happy. No matter what I have to do, I will make him happy. Despite my determination, a niggle of doubt begins to take hold. What if I can't do it? What if I just can't be what he needs?

CHAPTER 13

Flynn

Her panic attack has left me totally undone. I don't want to be afraid to touch her, but I am. I'm terrified of doing something to bring that fear back to her eyes. If I never see that again, it will be too soon. It's like navigating a minefield, not knowing what will set off the panic.

Her fear was loud and scary. Mine was silent but no less terrifying.

The most pervasive thought in my head is thank God I didn't give in to the guilt and tell her about the club. That would've been a fatal error. She never would've married me if she knew about that.

When my racing heart finally returns to a normal beat, I kiss her and withdraw to go into the bathroom to get a towel to clean her up. Then I use it myself and drop it to the floor before I crawl back into bed with her.

She curls up to me, her hand on my belly. "Thank you for what you did."

"What did I do?"

"You gave me exactly what I needed when I needed it. Most guys would've run screaming for a lawyer after that show I put on."

"I'm not most guys, sweetheart, and I will never leave you. Ever."

"I wouldn't blame you if this is too much for you."

It pains me that she's worried about me right now. "I'm going to pretend like you didn't say that. I knew exactly what I was getting when I said 'I do' earlier, and nothing has changed since then except now you can't get an annulment."

I feel her lips curve against my chest. "That's the last thing I want."

"It's the last thing I want, too." I hug her in closer to me. "I've got everything I want right here."

Now if only I could figure out what to do about my fear of triggering another flashback for her. I'd rather die than do anything to cause her pain, and it's going to be a long time before I forget the terrified look on her face, the screaming, the crying…

It's unbearable.

I finally fall into restless sleep hours later. The next thing I know, we're in the dungeon in New York, she's facedown on the spanking bench, her arms and legs propped on the pads, her bottom raised for my pleasure. I'm aware that I'm dreaming and should put a stop to this while I still can, but I can't bring myself to do that. I want to see how this plays out. I need to know.

Her ass is red from my paddle, and the largest of my plugs peeks out from between her cheeks. It's still not as big as I am, as she's about to find out. We've been building up to this moment for weeks now, but something is holding me back.

I'm afraid to scare her, to push her too far. She's trembling, her legs shaking violently.

"Nat." I run my hands up the backs of her legs to cup her heated cheeks. "We don't have to do this. You can still say no. Let me hear your safe word if you're not ready."

"I'm not saying no, and I'm not saying my safe word either."

"You're trembling."

"I'm excited."

"You're not scared?"

"Only a little. You said it will hurt."

"It will. At first, but if you stay with me, I can make it so good for you. You'll come so hard, harder than you ever have before."

A huge shudder overtakes her. "Do it." She's so wet that her inner thighs are glistening.

I bend to lap up that moisture with my tongue, licking her from front to back where she's stretched by the plug. She's as ready as she'll ever be, and I can't wait any longer. I have to have her sweet ass. I need to know that every part of her is mine.

Grasping the base of the plug, I begin to withdraw it, removing it in slow, steady increments that make her whimper from the pressure. Withdrawal is every bit as grueling as insertion was, and I take my own sweet time, drawing out the pleasurable pain until she's a trembling, vibrating mess of sensation. As the plug pops free, I move quickly to stroke a handful of lube onto my hard cock. I apply more lube to my fingers and press them into her, making sure she's as ready as she can be.

I remove my fingers and replace them with my cock, pressing against her insistently.

She cries out. "It's too big, Flynn. I can't."

I spank her ass, hard, and gain an inch. She's so tight and hot that I worry I'll come before I make it all the way inside her. "Who am I here?"

"Sir." She's sobbing, but she's not using her safe word.

"Don't forget it." I soothe the place where I spanked, wanting to calm and comfort her now. "Press back against me, sweetheart. You can do it. You can take me."

"I *can't*."

"Yes, you can. I know you can." I reach around her to stroke her clit, and her entire body seems to clamp down on my cock, making me grit my teeth from the powerful need to come. That's not happening until she takes all of me.

I stay where I am, about two inches inside her, giving her time to adjust. "Ready for more?"

"There's *more*?"

I can't believe she makes me laugh at a moment like this. "A lot more." Bending over her, I kiss her back, which is covered in goose bumps. I slide my hands under her, tweaking her nipples, trying to give her something else to think about other than the cock that's breaching her ass.

Rolling her nipples between my fingers, I give each of them a hard pinch that makes her scream and allows me to gain another inch.

"Holy fuck," she whispers. I've never heard her use that word before, and it's hotter than hell coming from her.

"Does it still hurt?"

"It's… Not like it did. It doesn't feel good yet, though."

"Give it a chance, sweetheart. Try to relax and let yourself go. I promise it'll be amazing."

She grunts, and I'm not sure, but she might be laughing. "Relax… Right. You try to relax when you've got a gigantic cock jammed up your ass." She gasps. "Oh God, it just got *bigger*."

"That's what you get for talking dirty to me." I pull back, ever so slightly, drawing a keening moan from her, and then push back, deeper than I was before. She's now taken more than half of me, grunting and moaning all the way. I repeat the in and out movements several times, adding more lube to ease the entry. "That's it, sweetheart. Just a little more."

She moans—loudly—and then screams when I give her the wide base. Her muscles spasm so hard I have to bite the inside of my cheek to give myself something else to think about other than the desperate need to come. "You did it, sweetheart. You took all of me."

Her grunt is her only reply.

I stay there, buried in her ass for a long, amazing moment, and then I begin to move, fucking her in gentle strokes intended to make this as good for her as it can possibly be. "That's it, baby. I love you like this. So hot and tight. I've never felt anything as good as this. Your ass is on fire."

I pick up the pace, moving in and out of her incredibly tight passage until I feel the telltale signs of impending climax as her muscles ripple. No way am I letting go until she does. Reaching around to the front of her, I find her clit standing up hard and tight. I use the flood of wetness between her legs to make my finger slick and then run it in circles over her clit until she's screaming out her release and clamping down so hard on me that I can't hold back any longer.

I come with a roar of hot, liquid pleasure that seems to come from my very soul. It goes on for what feels like an hour.

Natalie is like a rag doll under me, kept upright only by the pressure of my body against hers.

I withdraw from her as slowly as I went in. Reaching for a towel, I clean us both and then pick her right up from the bench and cradle her in my arms. Her eyes are closed, her face is flushed and her lips are swollen from the blow job she gave me earlier.

I kiss her face, her lips, her nose. "Nat."

"Hmm."

"Open your eyes."

"Can't."

"Try."

They flutter open to meet mine, and what I see there amazes me—she's absolutely glowing.

"Talk to me. Tell me how you feel."

"I feel… I… You were right. Once it stopped hurting, it was incredible. When can we do it again?"

"Natalie…" I'm stunned and humbled by her acceptance of me and the needs that drive me. "Baby, I love you."

"Mmm, love you, too. Now when can we do it again?"

Laughing, I kiss her sweet lips. "Talk to me about that tomorrow when you know what the day after is like."

She draws me into another kiss and bites my lip. The sharp stab of pain wakes me from the dream to discover it's happened again. I've dreamed my way to orgasm while Natalie sleeps next to me, unsuspecting.

The dream comes back to me in increments, torturing me with scenes of things I can only dream about. I feel betrayed by my own subconscious mind. It's punishing me for my deception by showing me things I'll never have with the woman I love more than life itself.

Natalie turns toward me, her hand landing on my chest, above the mess I've made on my belly.

I lift her hand and get out of bed, leaving her to sleep while I go into the bathroom to clean up.

I'm disgusted with myself and afraid, deeply afraid that I may not be able to live without the things I've given up for her.

I wake to daylight and my ringing cellphone. Addie's ring tone. Natalie is curled up to me, sleeping soundly. Moving carefully, I get up without disturbing her and take the phone to the other room to answer.

"Hey." My voice is scratchy and my head is pounding from the goddamned champagne, the lack of sleep and yet another disturbingly erotic dream starring the woman who is now my wife. "What's up?"

"You know I'd never, ever bother you this morning unless I really had to."

"Yeah, I know, which is why you're making me nervous."

"The whole world is going *mad* over you getting married. It's the lead story *everywhere*."

"Everywhere meaning..."

"The whole fucking world, Flynn. The paparazzi have descended upon Vegas. They have every street in the city covered. I've been in touch with the security firm this morning, and they're worried about getting you guys out of there today."

I can't help it. I start to laugh.

"Are you *laughing*? What the hell is wrong with you?"

"It's just so ridiculous, Addie. So I got married. Why does anyone care?"

"Umm, is that a rhetorical question?"

"It is in the sense that I don't expect you to answer it."

"Well, that's a relief. It's your own fault for saying you'd never get married again and then marrying someone you met a few weeks ago."

"You have to admit it's a cool story."

"Precisely why the whole world is interested, especially in light of everything that's come out about her in the last week."

"I have an idea of how we can get out of here. Let me make a couple of calls, and I'll get back to you."

"I'll be here."

I place a call to Gordon Yates, the owner of the security firm we work with for all of Quantum's needs in LA. He answers my call on the first ring.

"There's the man of the hour."

"So I hear."

"I understand congratulations are in order."

"Thanks, Gordon."

"We're trying to figure out the best way to get you out of there. I've been in touch with security at the hotel, and we're working on a few ideas."

"What about a chopper from the roof?"

"That's on our short list."

"Let's do that. I'd like to get Natalie out of here and back to LA with minimal fuss and no screaming paps."

"Give me two hours to set it up."

"Take three. I got married last night. I want to wake my new wife properly."

Gordon laughs. "You got it. I'll call you in three hours with the details."

"Thanks, Gord."

I call Addie back to tell her the plan and ask her to have my Ducati taken to the LA airport along with two helmets.

"I'm on it."

"Thanks, Addie. One of these days, you'll get a day off. I promise."

"I'm not holding my breath, but that's okay. I happen to love my job."

"Thanks again for everything these last couple of weeks. We both appreciate it so much."

"The picture from last night was awesome. I hope you guys had the best day ever."

"It was a good one. Talk to you when we get back to LA."

"Sounds good."

I leave my phone on a table in the main room and return to the bedroom, where Natalie is still asleep. I use the bathroom and brush my teeth before getting back into bed with her. She murmurs in her sleep and snuggles up to me, her arm wrapping around me like she's been sleeping with me for years rather than days.

It's so natural between us, the attraction, the banter, the desire. It's all there. Her body is warm and soft against mine, and my reaction to her is swift and predictable. If she's in the same ZIP code as me, I want her. When she's naked in bed with me, I'm helpless.

I lay there holding her for a while before she stirs, looking up at me with those big eyes. "Why are you awake so early?"

"Already dealing with logistics to get out of here. Apparently, we're the story of the day around the world."

"Yay," she says with a nervous laugh.

"How do you feel about becoming famous practically overnight?"

"About the same as I feel about becoming married practically overnight. It's all good."

"Yes, it is."

"So what happens the morning after one marries the most famous actor in the world?"

"You have a number of choices as the wife of the most famous actor in the world. A, you can order anything you want for breakfast. B, you can make love to your famous actor husband, and C, you can do all of the above."

"C," she says with a warm, sexy smile. "All of the above."

Natalie

After Flynn outlines our escape plan, I'm curious and nervous about my first ride in a helicopter. It'll be another first in a long line of them since I met him. I'm worried about Fluff panicking about the helicopter, so Flynn has a tight hold on her leash as we are escorted to the roof by hotel security.

The helicopter is huge, and apparently it will be taking us all the way to Los Angeles because both airports are under siege with reporters hoping to catch sight of us today. We're loaded into the helicopter, and Flynn straps me in, handing over custody of Fluff, who's put out by the whole thing.

Then the engines fire up and she goes ballistic, barking and snarling. Once again she makes us laugh when we need it most.

I gather her into my arms and stroke her, hoping to settle her. "We used to live such a quiet boring life, Fluff-o-Nutter." We're sitting very close to Flynn so we can hear each other over the roar of the engine.

"I think she preferred that life to the one you're leading now."

"She'll adapt. She has before."

"How did you get her after everything happened?"

"The detective who was nice to me? He went to my house and got her for me."

"They just handed her over?"

"He never said, and I didn't ask. I didn't care how it went down. All I cared about was having her with me. She was always my dog. She was literally the only thing I took with me from my old life into my new life. The clothes I was wearing when I left Stone's house and the items in my backpack were considered evidence."

He shakes his head in disbelief. "I hope I never cross paths with your parents. I won't be held responsible for my actions."

"We won't see them. For years, I half-expected them to show up out of the blue to say it had all been a huge mistake. After about two years, I stopped waiting for that to happen."

"People are funny when it comes to money. Now that you have a lot of it, they may become interested in you again."

"Wouldn't that be something?"

"Don't spend one minute worrying about that. They won't get anywhere near you. Not as long as I've got a breath left in me."

I drop my head to his shoulder. "What you must think… growing up with a family like yours to hear about one like mine."

"It makes me feel even more exceptionally lucky than I already felt to have been born to Max and Estelle. Until I met you, the greatest stroke of luck in my life was having them as my parents." He cups my cheek and runs his thumb over my face. "I don't want you to spend one second worrying about me thinking less of you because of who you come from. I think the world of you. You have to know that."

"I do, but thank you for reminding me."

"Any time you need a reminder, you let me know."

"I keep thinking about my sisters and what we said at the end of the interview. Do you think they'll try to get in touch with me? What if they don't even see it or if they haven't heard the news about me?"

"They've heard, and they'll see it, and they'll call. Of course they will."

"I can't get my hopes up."

"If you don't hear from them, I'll put someone on finding them."

"You will? Really?"

"Yes, I will. What happened between you and your parents had nothing to do with them. We'll find them and we'll set the record straight with them. You want your sisters in your life, you'll have your sisters in your life. Damn it."

I smile at him, loving him for loving me so fiercely.

Our first morning as husband and wife was as sweet and tender as our first night. Like last night, he went out of his way to keep from doing anything that could possibly trigger a flashback. He was a perfect gentleman in every possible way. Despite the satisfying conclusion for both of us, I was left wanting more.

After seeing him unhinged and lost in the passion we generate together, I'm saddened to know that he'll be holding that back every time he touches me from now on.

I think about the therapist who was so instrumental in helping me put my life back together after the assault. I spent two years seeing him three times a week before I changed my name and left for college. I haven't spoken to him again since then, but I'm tempted to call him to help me navigate this new relationship with Flynn.

The first chance I get, I'll reach out to him. I need all the help I can get in trying to be the wife Flynn needs and deserves.

Our arrival back in LA is uneventful. We land in a secure area of the airport, and after handing Fluff over to the security detail, we take off on Flynn's motorcycle with helmets covering our faces and concealing our identities. As we fly down the freeway, I begin to understand why he feels so free when he's driving and even more so on the bike. Pressed up against him, holding on tight to the man I love, I'm able to let go of a lot of the worries that have occupied my mind in recent days. It's hard to think about anything else when you're on the "four-oh-five," as they call it here, with your legs wrapped around the biggest movie star in the world, who also happens to be your gorgeous new husband.

My life today might bear no resemblance whatsoever to the unassuming life I was leading two short weeks ago, but if I had it to do over again, I wouldn't change a single thing about it. I've reinvented myself before and survived. This time, I'm not alone. This time, I have the love of the most exceptional man to hold my hand as I navigate my way through these uncharted waters.

Because Flynn's house in the Hollywood Hills is overrun by reporters, we return to Hayden's Malibu beach house. We pass a relaxing afternoon by the pool with Fluff. That evening, we throw together dinner on the grill and down a bottle of chardonnay before we settle in to watch the broadcast of the interview with Carolyn.

She has evidently filmed a new lead-in that includes the photo we released last night and the news of our marriage. "The Internet is literally on fire today with the news that the world's most eligible bachelor is officially off the market as of last night. The word that Flynn Godfrey married Natalie Bryant in Las Vegas took Twitter by storm last night after his publicist released the news with a single sentence and a single photograph. I had the distinct honor and privilege to talk with Flynn and the amazing woman who is now his wife. After hearing her story, I think you'll see why Flynn changed his mind about getting married again."

Flynn holds my hand, and Fluff is curled up in her favorite place in my lap as I watch myself with a detached sense of disbelief. Is that really me on national television, being interviewed by none other than Carolyn Justice?

"You sound great, sweetheart," he says. "The whole country will be as in love with you as I am after this."

"I'm not sure how I feel about that," I reply with a nervous laugh.

"You know, the upside is you can do anything you want, be anyone you want to be. The door will swing open to you in ways you can't begin to imagine."

"I'm not sure how I feel about that either."

"You don't have to decide now. The word 'no' becomes your best friend. You say yes to the things that interest you and no to the things that don't. You can take full advantage of your newfound fame to promote the foundation. The bottom line is with fame comes opportunity. I'm sure my management team will be hit with a slew of calls about you."

"Wow, seriously?"

"Yep. But don't worry about it. They'll screen it all and bring only the most interesting stuff to us."

"I'm having trouble wrapping my mind around this."

"I didn't tell you to stress you out. Just to make you aware of what to expect."

"I signed on to be with you, not to be part of your business."

"You don't have to be part of it. Like I said, you pick and choose, and you have the power to say no to all of it."

"Just over two weeks ago, I was a teacher in New York, and now I'm married to you and hearing I might be the hot new thing in Hollywood. It's a lot to take in all at once."

"You don't have to take it in all at once. As long as you take *me* in once in a while…"

Laughing, I push my elbow into his ribs.

When the interview ends, Flynn's phone begins to ring. He takes the call from his parents, putting it on speaker so we can both hear it.

"You were brilliant," Max says. "Absolutely spot-on."

"Everyone in Hollywood is going to want to meet you," Stella says.

"I was just telling her that. She's not sure how she feels about it."

"Don't you worry about that, honey," Stella says. "You're surrounded by people who can handle all that nonsense for you."

"I told her that, too."

"We don't want to intrude on the newlyweds," Max says. "We just wanted you to know we loved the interview. You did great, Natalie. You're a natural."

"That's what I'm afraid of," I say, making them laugh. "Thanks for calling. I'm so glad you thought it went well."

"Better than well, honey," Stella says. "I just have to say… After hearing your story, I'm so proud to know you and to welcome you into our family. Our son couldn't have chosen a more worthy woman to spend his life with."

I'm so touched by her kind words that I can't find the words to tell her so.

"She's trying not to cry right now, Mom."

"Thank you so much for that, Stella. That's so very sweet of you to say."

"We'll let you go," Max says.

"Thanks for calling, guys."

"We love you both," Stella says.

"Love you, too." He ends the call and puts the phone on the coffee table. It immediately starts ringing. "Do you want to hear from your adoring public?"

"Tomorrow is soon enough."

"Do you want to know what people are saying about the interview?"

"Not so much. Do you want to know what they're saying?"

"Not so much." He bestows a suggestive smile on me. "What do you want to do?"

"I'd like to make out with my sexy husband."

"You'll need to relocate the wildebeest if you want to do that."

I get up slowly and carefully to place Fluff on a blanket on a different part of the sectional sofa. Other than a grunt of irritation, she settles back to her snoring. I can tell that I surprise Flynn when I slide onto his lap, straddling him.

"Well, well, what's this?"

"This is your wife, who loves you desperately, who doesn't want you to be afraid to touch me, to make love to me the way you want to. She doesn't want you to hold back or treat her like she might break."

"Nat…"

"I know that what happened last night upset you far more than you let on. It upset me, too, but we worked through it. It's apt to happen again, maybe even more than once, and we'll work through it then, too. But I can't bear to watch you try to control yourself because you're so afraid to scare me or to do something wrong."

"I am afraid of scaring you. I never again want to see you frightened like that, especially because of the way I'm touching you."

"You got swept up in what we were doing, and you weren't thinking about what you *shouldn't* do, and that's okay. I need you to know…"

"What?" he asks softly.

"I loved what we were doing and how we were doing it before it went bad last night. I loved you like that, knowing I made you crazy."

"You make me so crazy. I'm afraid that if I show you even a fraction of how crazy you make me, I'll lose you."

I shake my head. "It'd be unbearable to me if I thought you were thinking about what happened last night every time you come near me." With my hands on his face, I kiss him, teasing him with my tongue until his mouth opens to let me in.

A groan rumbles through him as he takes hold of my ass and pulls me in tight against his erection. We kiss for a long time, his tongue rubbing against mine in a sensuous dance that has me wanting more. It's always that way with him. He kisses me, and I'm lost. He touches me, and I need more. He looks at me, and I see everything he feels for me.

His arms tighten around me as he brings me down on the sofa. "Is this okay?"

I nod and reach for him, wanting to feel his weight on me, his hands touching me, his lips kissing me. I want it all. "Don't be afraid, Flynn. Please don't be afraid of me."

"I could never be afraid of you. Do you remember your safe word?"

"Yes."

"And you'll use it if you need it?"

"I promise."

He lifts my shirt up and over my head, undressing me with an urgency that gives me hope. Clothes fly, and another pair of underwear is lost to his haste.

"I'll buy you more. A hundred pairs."

I'm actually relieved that the panties ripped again. I take it as a good sign that we might get past this early speed bump in what I hope will be a very long road together.

He applies a condom and then takes me hard and fast, watching me all the while for signs of trouble. He's rougher than he was last night and this morning, and though he's not quite as unleashed as he was before I freaked out, I'll take it.

I'll take him—any way I can have him.

Sliding his hands under me, he lifts me and settles us so I'm sitting on top of him, impaled by that huge erection that stretches me almost to the point of discomfort.

"How does it feel?" he asks.

"Big. Tight. Hot." I groan when those three little words make him bigger.

"I love when you talk dirty, baby. Tell me more."

"I can't."

"Yes, you can. Give me the words. I want them from you. Tell me more about how it feels."

"I'm stretched, so tight, it almost hurts."

"*Almost* hurts?"

"Almost but not quite. The pinch of pain is part of the pleasure." I gasp when the fit gets even tighter. "I refuse to say another word if that's going to happen every time."

"Can't help it, baby. That's what you do to me."

"There's no more room, so it can't get any bigger." And yet it does, and I can't believe he *laughs*. He actually laughs. "That's it. I'm done with you."

His arms around me keep me from escaping. "You can't ever be done with me. I'd die without you." He nuzzles my neck and presses deeper into me. "Hold on tight."

"For what?"

"This." Grasping my hips, he turns us again so he's on top.

"Smooth."

"You like that?"

"I like it all."

The statement seems to throw gas on his fire, and he lets loose. Still holding my hips, he drives into me, over and over again, until I'm screaming from the pleasure that seers me.

"That's it, baby. God, you feel so good. So, so good." He keeps up the pace until he's coming, too, groaning as he heats me from within with his release. Opening his eyes, he studies me, looking for signs of trouble. "You okay?"

"I'm great. You?"

"Never better." Still buried deep inside me, he brings his lips down on mine as he gazes into my eyes. "I can't believe we get to do this any time we want to for the rest of our lives."

"Not *any* time."

He kisses me again. "Any. Freaking. Time." Another kiss. "All. The. Freaking. Time."

"Yes, dear," I reply with a sigh of utter contentment.

"Now that's what I'm talking about."

I hold on tight to him, my heart full of love for the man who is now my husband.

CHAPTER 14

Natalie

It's almost noon when I drag myself to the shower the next day. I'm washing the conditioner out of my hair when Flynn comes into the bathroom, holding his phone and smiling widely.

"Natalie. Hurry."

I nearly end up with conditioner in my eyes before I make it out of the shower. "What is it?"

He hands me a towel and the phone. "It's Candace."

I'm frozen in place. I can't seem to do a single thing but stand there and stare at him.

He dries me and helps me into a robe and leads me to the bedroom, sitting next to me on the bed and nodding at me to go ahead and talk to her.

"H-hello?"

"April." Her voice is more mature, but it's her. It's my little sister.

I'm immediately reduced to tears. "Candace."

"Is it really you?"

"Yes, it's me." Flynn puts his arm around me, and I lean into him.

"And you're really married to *Flynn Godfrey?*"

I laugh at the way she squeals even as I hear her sobs through the phone.

Flynn chuckles next to me and kisses my forehead.

"It seems that I am. Tell me everything. Where are you? Where's Livvy? I've missed you guys so much."

"We had no idea where you were. We've looked for you for years."

"I had to disappear so I could have a chance at a normal life."

"And how's that working for you?"

I laugh even as I contend with a flood of tears. "It was working pretty well until I was waylaid by a sexy movie star and my well-ordered life was turned completely upside down in the best possible way."

"I saw you last night on Carolyn. You look so different, but I knew it was you. Liv called, and she was screaming because you said you wanted to hear from us. I was dying waiting for it to be nine o'clock out there so I could try to call Flynn's office... Oh, April, is it really you?"

"It's me, I'm here, and I'm so happy to hear your voice." I use the sleeve of the robe to wipe away more tears. "Tell me about you. Where are you?"

"I'm a sophomore at Colorado State, majoring in business. Liv is a senior in high school. She lives with Mom in Omaha now."

"Wait, what? She lives with *Mom*? Where's Dad?"

"I'm not really sure. They split about a year after the trial ended. We don't see him anymore."

"Wow... God, Mom actually left him?"

"She did. We couldn't believe it either, but things are so much better now, April. She's so different without him telling her what to do every second of her life."

This news sends me reeling. I never for the life of me imagined her leaving him.

"Should I not call you that? You're not April anymore."

"No, I changed my name, but you can call me whatever you want. I'm just so happy to hear your voice. You can't possibly know how happy I am."

"I think I know," she says, laughing. "What you said... In the interview, about how you went to the cops because of us... Liv and I, we couldn't believe it. What you did... What you sacrificed for us..."

"I'd do it again in a minute. He was a predator, Candace. He wouldn't have stopped with me."

"A lot of pieces have fallen into place for us in the last week. I'm sorry it was at your expense. You've been through so much."

"Yes, but I'm happy now. So truly happy with Flynn and this amazing new life with him."

"Can we see you? We want to see you so badly. And we'd *really* like to meet our new brother-in-law," she adds with a laugh.

Flynn is nodding. "Tell her we'll set it up."

"Flynn is telling me to give you my number—and I wouldn't have let you go without doing that. He and his awesome assistant, Addie, who is a magician, will figure out the details."

"I can't believe I'm actually talking to you. We were so afraid we'd never see you again."

"I was afraid of the same thing. We'll work out something so we can see each other soon."

"I can't wait."

"Neither can I. I never stopped loving you. Both of you."

"Us, too. We talked about you all the time."

"I'm glad to know you didn't forget about me or hate me. I was worried about what you'd been told."

"He tried, but we refused to believe him. We knew *you*, and we knew Oren. We *believed* you. He always gave me the creeps."

"Well, you were smarter than I was, then, because I never suspected he was capable of what he did to me."

"I don't want to hang up. You won't disappear again, will you?"

"I think I'll be easy to find after the events of the last few days." We exchange phone numbers before reluctantly ending the call, promising to talk again soon and text each other every day. For a long time after, Flynn holds me while I cry tears of unmitigated joy.

"I'm so happy for you all, sweetheart. We'll get them out here as soon as we can—and as soon as they can do it."

"I can't believe I just talked to Candace. I've fantasized about how it might be to talk to them again, but I was always afraid to reach out to them because I didn't know if they'd been turned against me. It would've killed me to find them and to hear they hate me."

"She sounded just as happy to talk to you."

"I know! Thank you so much."

"For what? I didn't do anything."

"Yes, you did. You dragged me into your life, refusing to take no for an answer, and now I have my sisters back."

"I hate to point out that you skipped a rather traumatic portion of the story."

"Don't you see? It was all worth it because not only did I get you, but them, too."

His smile lights up his eyes. "You're so beautiful when you're happy."

"Then I must be the most beautiful woman in the world right now."

"You won't hear me arguing."

We pass an absolutely blissful couple of days in which we don't see anyone but each other and the security personnel who are nearby if we need them, but mostly out of sight. I exchange texts with both my sisters nonstop, and finally get to talk to Olivia when she gets a chance to call without our mother around to hear her. We're not ready to tell her we're back in touch. They're both really busy with school and work, so we're trying to find a time to get together in the next few weeks.

Every day, Flynn takes me out to practice my driving. He says it's the perfect opportunity to show me Southern California. One day we drive north to Santa Barbara. Another day we drive down the Pacific Coast Highway, from Long Beach almost to San Diego and back again. We find out-of-the-way places to stop for lunch, and the security detail that follows us helps to ensure our safety and privacy.

Other than a few speechless waitresses and waiters, for whom Flynn signs autographs and poses for pictures, we get away with these outings. As I become more confident, I discover that I *love* to drive.

On Thursday evening, Flynn arranges a special trip to Disneyland in Anaheim. We have the place mostly to ourselves after it closes to the public. We go on every ride, a few of them twice, and have the time of our lives. As it's my first time visiting a Disney park, I feel like a little kid again, and Flynn, who has been here many times before, says it's like the first time all over again for him, too, because he's here with me.

We check out Palm Springs and the Palm Desert, San Bernardino and Big Bear. One city and town at a time, I fall in love with Southern California. I'm not even all that bothered by the tremors from a small earthquake that shake the house on Friday morning. Flynn says the tremors are a fact of life in California, and as long as you know what to do, they're nothing to be afraid of.

He takes the time to teach me everything I need to know about surviving a major earthquake, and then we don't talk about it again, which is fine with me.

We spend hours—in the car, in bed, on the sofa, by the pool—discussing our plans for the foundation, trading ideas and making lists. With his extensive contacts, Flynn isn't worried about raising the money we'll need to get the foundation up and running. He's far more concerned about making sure the money gets to those in need in the form of programs that make a real difference. That's where the major brainstorming is needed.

I'm thrilled to be part of such an important project. It fills the void created by the loss of my job and gives me a sense of purpose. We talk about goals for the foundation, and Flynn says he won't be happy until every kid in America gets three nourishing meals a day. Anything less than that won't be enough for him—or me. We're in complete agreement on that point.

When we're not out driving around Southern California or talking about the foundation, we're making love—in bed, on the sofa, in the pool, in the shower and once on the floor of the kitchen. We can't get enough of each other, and I dread the day when he'll have to go back to work. This little cocoon we're living in can't last forever, but I'm determined to enjoy every second of it for as long as I can.

On Sunday evening, we take a limo into the city for the Screen Actors Guild Awards at the Shrine Auditorium. Earlier, Flynn explained to me that these awards are particularly significant as they are decided on by peers, which makes them that much more special. The "Actor" is a coveted award. Unlike the Golden Globe he won for acting for the first time two weeks ago, he already has two Actors for earlier roles.

Because of his superstitious nature, he won't admit to wanting to win for his performance in *Camouflage*, but I know he's excited to see this particular role recognized by his peers. He poured his heart and soul into the role of a returning Special Forces officer who has to fight to regain his life after being grievously injured in Afghanistan.

"You look positively radiant tonight, Nat."

In deference to my newlywed status, I chose a white dress for the event. Flynn says me wearing white is a bit of a "fuck you" to the media that are still freaking out about us getting married. My husband does have a unique way of phrasing things.

The dress is subtly sexy and highlights the tan I've acquired during my afternoons at the pool. It also looks great with the jewelry he bought me to wear to the Globes. I told him not to buy me something new for the SAGs. I'm perfectly happy with what I already have.

I appreciate how generous he always is, but I don't need to be showered in expensive gifts to be happy.

On the way into town, he breaks open a bottle of champagne.

I break open a bottle of ibuprofen. We each take a couple of preventive painkillers since champagne gives us frightful headaches the next morning, and we'd like to indulge tonight.

When we each have a glass in hand, he puts his arm around me and draws me close to him. "Oh damn, what's that?" He withdraws a velvet box from his pocket. "Where did that come from?"

"What is it?"

"I don't know. You should open it and find out."

"I will not open it, because I told you not to buy me anything."

"Did you? I don't recall you saying that."

I stare at him, incredulous. "You do *too* remember me saying it, because I said it *two days* ago."

He shakes his head. "Not ringing any bells."

"No wonder you're up for all these awards. You're a truly gifted actor."

"Why thank you, sweetheart. Now how about you make me happy on my big night and open that."

"If I open it, I'll like it. If I like it, that'll encourage you to do this again when I told you I don't want you to."

"Hmm," he says, scratching at the stubble on his jaw, "I can see your dilemma. On the one hand, you're burning up with curiosity because you really, *really* want to see what's in there. But if you go along with me on this, chances are you're setting a precedent for our entire marriage. I mean, can you *imagine* if I get a big idea to buy you something new for every formal event we attend together? With the way we pat ourselves on the back in Hollywood, you'll need a storage unit for your jewelry. It is indeed a dilemma."

"You're totally making fun of me."

"I am not! I'm simply summarizing the situation and the impasse at which we find ourselves." Every beautiful inch of him is sexy in yet another tuxedo, this one by Armani.

His eyes dance with mirth as he pushes my buttons and tries to win me over to his way of thinking. He's absolutely right about one thing—if I accept this gift, I will be setting a precedent, and that concerns me.

"Open it."

"No."

"Yes."

"No."

"How about I open it for you, and if you don't like it, you don't have to keep it."

"What kind of BS is that? Of course I'm going to like it."

"Do you ever actually swear? BS doesn't count unless you actually say it."

I get very close to his face and say, "Bull. Shit."

He takes full advantage of my closeness to kiss me. "I love you, Mrs. G, and I love to pick out shiny things I think you'll like. You'll hurt my feelings if you make me take it back, so I suppose you ought to just open it so my feelings won't be hurt."

"Oh my God. You're really going to play the hurt-feelings card?"

"I believe I just did."

I snatch the velvet box out of his hand and open it. I think I actually go blind for a second or two from the shine of diamonds sitting in blue velvet. "Flynn… What? I mean…" I sigh, deeply. He's too much for me. I lost this battle before it ever began.

He takes my glass and puts both of them in cup holders so he can remove the dazzling diamond bracelet from the box and affix it to my wrist. "There. Now I'm happy."

"It's beautiful, but—"

Laying a finger over my lips, he stops me before I can finish the thought. "No buts. You're my wife, and that gives me the legal right to buy you anything I want whenever I want."

I raise a brow. "The legal right?"

"Uh-huh. And the law says you gotta take whatever I buy for you, no matter what it is."

"Where does the law say that?"

"Like you want an actual paragraph or something?"

"That'd be good."

"I'll ask Emmett to get it for you."

"You do that." I look down again at the bracelet. "It's too much, Flynn. I'm not comfortable with being spoiled like this."

"Give it time. You'll get used to it."

"No, I don't think I will."

"Why do I suddenly fear there's a deeper issue afoot here?"

I take a moment to collect myself, swallowing the knot of emotion that has gathered in my throat. "You're so incredibly generous. I've never known anyone who thinks of others as selflessly as you do. I don't want you to ever think I don't appreciate your thoughtfulness or your generosity, because I do. I appreciate it very much."

"But?"

"But it makes me uncomfortable to be showered with things like diamonds when I can barely buy you dinner right now." A glance at my online bank balance earlier in the day left me feeling rather ill. He mentioned me getting paid for my work on the foundation, but that hasn't kicked in yet.

"Wow. Well, I don't even know where to begin to reply to that. You're my *wife*, Natalie, which means everything I have is now yours, too. You can buy me anything you want to. You can buy yourself anything you want or need. Tomorrow, we're getting you access to money. I should've done that sooner, and I'm sorry that I didn't think of it before now."

"I'm not asking you to do that."

"I know you're not. I'm *telling* you that that's what's going to happen."

I'm not sure I like being *told*. I decide to let it drop for now so we can enjoy this special evening, but the subject is far from closed.

CHAPTER 15

Flynn

My beautiful, sweet wife is worried about *money*? It makes me fucking crazy to hear her say she can't buy me dinner. She has no idea what she's married into or the resources that are now hers—and that's entirely my fault. Why didn't I think of it sooner? Of course she's worried about money. She lost her job because of me, for fuck's sake.

I feel like I'm learning every lesson with her the hard way, and once again I'm berating myself for not anticipating her concerns. She's gone quiet, which means she's pissed. My Natalie is a fighter, and she doesn't back down. Silence, where she's concerned, is not golden.

"Nat."

She looks at me.

"I didn't mean to say it that way. You have to understand where I'm coming from. To have what I have and then to hear that my wife is worried about money… That sort of hits me right here." I lay my hand on my heart.

"I'm not worried about it. I'm just out of it because I'm not getting paid anymore."

"You'll be getting paid soon from the foundation work, and you're far from out of money, sweetheart. We're married now. Your worries are my worries. If you have bills to pay or things you need to take care of, you only have to tell me and it'll be done."

"I don't want to take advantage of you."

"I'm your *husband*. It's my job to take care of you."

"This is not the Stone Age, Flynn. I've always been independent, and I've always taken care of myself. I don't know how to be any other way."

"I understand and respect that tremendously. It's extremely refreshing to be with a woman who wants to earn her own way. I'll never stand in the way of you following your dreams. What you want, I want. But you will never, ever, *ever* worry about money again. Are we clear on that?"

"I suppose I'll eventually get used to my change in circumstances, but it's not going to happen overnight. I appreciate that you want to take care of me, but you have to understand that taking care of me doesn't mean buying me diamonds for every occasion. Put that money toward the foundation. That would make me much happier."

"I hear what you're saying. I really do, but you have to let me spoil you a little bit."

"I have a feeling your idea of a *little bit* and mine are vastly different."

I nuzzle her neck, focusing on all the spots that make her sigh. "We'll find common ground. Eventually."

"Until then, no more diamonds."

"No more diamonds. Now, about your student loans…"

"Flynn!"

Laughing, I squeeze her tight and kiss the indignation off her lips.

"You messed up my lipstick."

"I'll buy you more."

"You're incorrigible."

"I love my wife."

"She loves you, too, even when you're incorrigible."

"I have more fun with you than I've ever had with anyone, Nat. Even when we're bickering. Especially then."

"I keep waiting to discover something about you that I don't like."

Her words are like an arrow to my heart. God… she can't ever know about the one part of me that she'd definitely not like or understand.

"But so far, there's nothing not to like."

"Same here, sweetheart, although I'm not waiting to find something bad. I know there's nothing to find."

When we arrive a short time later at the Shrine Auditorium, my anxiety kicks up a few notches. Our security detail has been in close touch with the event security to ensure there won't be any issues with getting us into the building. But after I was stabbed in a rope line at an event last year in London, public appearances aren't what they used to be. People are fucking crazy, and I expect the crazy to be a thousand times worse than usual since this is our first public appearance since we tied the knot. The thought of exposing Natalie to that level of crazy makes me extremely uneasy.

We've been told to wait in the car until the security detail comes for us.

Natalie holds my hand between both of hers. "You're vibrating."

"This shit makes me nuts after what happened in London. Especially now that we've given them the story of the year by getting married."

"Tonight will be nuts, and after that, they'll get used to us, and we'll be just another old married couple."

"Right," I say with a laugh. "Somehow I don't think that'll happen for a while. This is going to be insane, so just hold on to me, smile and wave if you want to, but don't let go of me. Okay?"

"I won't let go. Ever."

"Promise?"

She lays her head on my shoulder. "I believe I already made that promise in Vegas."

She soothes and calms me with her sweetness. Knowing that I get to go home with her—tonight and every night—eases my anxiety.

The door opens, and it's show time. I get out first, generating a roar from the crowd that has gathered to watch the red carpet festivities. As I extend my hand to Natalie to help her out, the decibel level increases exponentially. The crowd literally goes wild over my gorgeous wife.

She glances at me nervously, but then seems to recover, smiling widely as she takes hold of my arm and holds on—tight.

People scream our names, and flashes nearly blind us. The red carpet unfolds before us, and we move forward with the security guys keeping a slight distance so as not to hide us from the crowd. I don't want that. It's a fine line between being safe and being standoffish. I've always been hands-on with my fans, and I never forget that they're the ones who made me a star.

But a knife slashing across your ribs in a rope line tends to change your outlook on crowds and fans and celebrity. I keep a bit of distance now that wasn't there before, and while it saddens me to have to do that, I won't risk my safety, and I certainly won't expose Natalie to any danger.

Taking her cues from me, she waves and smiles like an old pro. People are calling out her name and telling her they love her. I'm amazed and humbled by the show of support for my wife. We pause for a huge group of photographers who leave me half-blind from the blast of flashes.

Out of the corner of my eye, I notice a disturbance that draws my attention. One of the reporters for the show *Hollywood Starz*, a woman who has interviewed me many times in the past, is crying—on the air—as one celebrity after another walks by her without so much as a glance in her direction.

The boycott is on. I lean closer to Natalie. "Check it out—to the right. They're the ones that broke your story. Everyone's blowing them off."

She takes a subtle look. "Wow. Is she crying on the air?"

"Looks that way." I keep my arm around her. "Congratulations, sweetheart. You've got all of Hollywood on Team Natalie."

A *Hollywood Starz* producer tries to get our attention as we go past their setup on the red carpet. Like the rest of my peers, I keep walking when I'd normally stop for a quick chat with them. Instead, I head for their competitors across the way and introduce my wife to the reporters.

"What do you have to say about the boycott of the *Hollywood Starz* red carpet show?"

"I think the acting community is sending a strong message that we won't tolerate the exploitation of our loved ones in the name of ratings or clicks. What was done to Natalie shouldn't happen to anyone."

"What do you have to say, Natalie?"

She glances at me, and I nod, hoping to encourage her to speak her mind. "I've been extremely moved by all the love and support I've received from Flynn, his friends and family, as well as the larger Hollywood community. It's been overwhelming, to say the least."

"Flynn, you have to know the whole world is talking about you and your lovely wife today. You once said very publicly that you'd never marry again. What was it about Natalie that made you change your mind?"

I look at her gazing up at me with those expressive eyes that had me from the first second I met her. "Everything. Every. Single. Thing."

She smiles at me, and I'm simply dazzled. There's no other word for the way I feel when she looks at me as if I hung the moon just for her.

"It's safe to say that every woman in America just swooned."

We laugh, say our good-byes and move on to the next interviewer. The questions are similar, and the good wishes are genuine, as is the support for Natalie. I love the way my community has come together to back us both.

On the way into the auditorium, we're stopped every few feet by people who want to say hello and meet Natalie. I introduce her to some of the biggest names in the business. She is gracious and adorable as she tries to hold on to her composure and not turn into a giddy fangirl.

"Oh my God, oh my God, *oh my God*," she whispers after she meets Julia Roberts. "I had posters of her in my room when I was little."

"She's a doll. I'm glad you got to meet her."

"Could I hit the restroom before we go in? The champagne and excitement are catching up to me."

"Sure thing. I could go, too." I gesture to the security detail to let them know we're going to the restroom. "I'll meet you right here, sweetheart."

"I'll be quick."

Natalie

Everyone is so incredibly nice. I'm not sure what I was expecting, but the outpouring from the Hollywood community has been overwhelming. Running into Julia Roberts and having her *call me by name* was the craziest thing that's ever happened. Well, other than meeting Flynn, of course.

As I'm headed into a stall, a woman comes out of the next one. I do a double take when I recognize Valerie Ward, Flynn's ex-wife. Oh God...

"Well, what do we have here?" she asks with one of those small, nasty smiles catty women do so well. "The *new* Mrs. Godfrey. Congratulations. You've managed to do what so many others have failed to accomplish. You're the Valerie antidote."

I know she wants me to react, to say something I'll regret, but I refuse to let her goad me. Rather than take her bait, I start to duck into the stall, but she grabs the door, refusing to let me close it.

Leaning into the stall, she says, "What's a nice, sweet girl like you doing with a beast like him? Has he tied you up yet? Beat you? Clamped your nipples? Plugged your ass?" She takes a breath, her eyes glittering maniacally. "Yeah, I didn't think so. Good luck, *sweetheart*. You're going to need it." With the palm of her hand, she smacks the door shut in my face. It narrowly misses hitting the side of my head.

My hands tremble as I slide the lock into place. What was she talking about? Valerie's words race through my mind as I try to make sense of what she said. The man she described bears no resemblance to my Flynn. And the way she called me *sweetheart* in that condescending tone. Is that what he called her, too? Am I foolish to think that name belongs only to me?

The encounter with Valerie lasted a matter of seconds, but she's left me reeling and wondering if there's any truth at all to what she said. She's good. I have to give her that. Somehow I manage to take care of business, but I need more time than I have to regain my composure.

Did Flynn see Valerie come out? Is he talking to her now? Are they having a contentious reunion? Or is he unhappy to see her and worried about what she might've said to me? A line has formed inside the ladies' room, and I feel the eyes of everyone on me as I wash my hands and reapply my lipstick. I take a few deep breaths, hoping I'm not giving anything away to the curious women who are watching me. Some of them I recognize.

I murmur a hello to everyone who speaks to me on the way out.

When he sees me coming, Flynn pushes off the wall between the men's and women's rooms and smiles widely. He doesn't look upset or pissed, which leads me to believe his path and Valerie's didn't cross. Lucky him. I decide to keep my encounter with Valerie to myself so as not to upset him on his big night.

He puts his arm around my shoulders and brings me close enough to kiss my temple. "How bad do I have it when I miss you in the time it takes you to pee?"

His sweetness puts me immediately at ease, despite the ugliness Valerie spewed at me. "Pretty bad."

"If this is bad, baby, I don't want to see good."

Everyone is looking at us. Everyone is interested. Everyone is curious. I'm the woman who changed Flynn Godfrey's mind about marriage. I realize that for the rest of my life, I'll always be the woman who changed his mind about marriage. I can live with that.

Once again, we're seated with Flynn's Quantum colleagues, Hayden, Jasper, Marlowe and Kristian. Marlowe, Jasper and Kristian hug us, and they congratulate us again on our marriage. Hayden is the last to greet us, and he hugs us both, which I take as a hopeful sign.

We take our seats and pick at the dinner we're served until the show begins a short time later. While the conversation buzzes around me, I find my mind drifting, puzzling over the things Valerie said to me.

"Has he tied you up yet? Beat you? Clamped your nipples? Plugged your ass?" Flynn had *beaten* Valerie? There's no way that's true. He's never been anything but a perfect gentleman with me. Sure, things got particularly heated a few times, like on the plane and our wedding night before my meltdown. Everything between us has been hot and entirely consensual, though. The things Valerie described don't sound consensual.

Then there's the possibility that Valerie is screwing with me because she's jealous. I wish I knew what she hoped to achieve by saying that stuff to me.

"You okay?" Flynn asks during a break.

"Yeah. It's hot in here."

"Is it? Feels okay to me."

"How much longer until your category?"

He smiles and winks when he says, "It's toward the end."

Someone taps him on the shoulder, and he gets up to say hello.

Marlowe slides into the seat next to mine. "How's it going, Mrs. G?"

"Is it hot in here, or is it only me?"

"I'm fucking roasting. It's always hot at these things. Too many people and not enough air."

My stomach flutters at the thought of asking Marlowe about Valerie. But I need to know. "Hey, Marlowe."

"What's up?"

I glance over my shoulder to make sure Flynn is still actively engaged in his conversation. "Tell me about Valerie. What's she like?"

"She's a viperous bitch. I hate her guts, and not just because of the hell she put Flynn through, but because she's not a nice person. People in this town are seriously over her. I don't know too many directors who will still work with her."

"Hmm, interesting."

"Why do you ask?"

"I ran into her in the ladies' room. She was a little… less than friendly."

Marlowe snorts in a most unladylike fashion that makes me like her more than I already do. "I imagine she was. Not only did she lose Flynn, but for years he told the world she permanently turned him off marriage. That's gonna leave a mark. Did you tell Flynn you saw her?"

"No. I didn't want to upset him on his big night, and I knew he'd be pissed at what she said to me."

Marlowe leans in closer. "What'd she say?"

"It's not even worth repeating. I suppose if I was stupid enough to lose the love of a man like Flynn, I'd be a jealous bitch, too."

"You will never, in the history of the universe, be capable of the kind of shit that woman spews. And P.S., you did the right thing not saying anything to him about it. He sees red where she's concerned, and it is a big night for him. Or I expect it will be anyway."

"Don't jinx him."

She smiles at me. "You really love him, don't you?"

"I really do."

"Good. You're just what he needs in his life."

"You think Hayden will ever come around to seeing that?"

"Hayden has his own demons," Marlowe says, looking at the man in question as he laughs and jokes with friends. "I don't think his reaction has anything to do with you or Flynn, and you shouldn't take it seriously."

"It hurts Flynn's feelings."

"Those two have always had their ups and downs. It's the nature of their relationship. They always get past the bumps, so try not to worry."

An announcement is made that the commercial break is about to end and everyone is asked to return to their seats.

"Hey, Marlowe, thanks. You've been a good friend to me. I appreciate it."

She gives me a quick hug. "I hope we'll become very good friends."

Marlowe Sloane wants to be good friends with me. How crazy is that? She returns to her seat, and Flynn slips his arm around me.

"How you doing?"

"I'm good. How're you?"

"Ready to get out of here."

"And hit the parties?"

He shakes his head. "I'm a newlywed. I'm skipping the parties."

"What if you win?"

"I'm going to pretend you didn't say that…"

"You can't skip the parties."

"Watch me."

The way he says those two little words—and how he looks at me as he says them—does crazy things to my insides. I love how much he desires me and how badly he wants to be alone with me. I lean back against him while we wait for his category to be announced.

Marlowe is the presenter for Outstanding Performance by a Male Actor in a Leading Role. She announces the nominees, and when she gets to Flynn's clip, the audience goes crazy. He smiles for the cameras, but under the table he's gripping my hand.

I give him a squeeze in support.

"And the Actor goes to… my friend Flynn Godfrey for *Camouflage*!"

The place goes bonkers.

He kisses me, hugs Hayden, Jasper and Kristian and then heads for the stage. We're all on our feet clapping, cheering and, in my case, trying not to cry. Marlowe greets him with a hug and hands him the award.

It takes a long time for the applause to die down. Wearing that humble smile I love so much, Flynn stands before his peers, holding his award and drinking in his big moment.

Even if I'd been watching the show at home having never met Flynn, I'd be happy for him because *Camouflage* is one of the best movies I've ever seen. But as his wife and the woman who loves him... I'm over the moon with happiness and pride in his accomplishments.

"Thank you so much to the Screen Actors Guild for this incredible honor," he says after the crowd finally settles. "I've been blessed to work with so many of you and to call you my friends and colleagues. We're the luckiest people in the world to be able to do this job we love. To be recognized for the work is frosting on a pretty nice cake. You all know this film is very near and dear to me and to everyone at Quantum. Jeremy's story took me on an amazing journey and gave me an all-new appreciation for the sacrifices our military members and their families make for us every day. Please do your part to support our veterans and their families. We owe them everything." Another round of enthusiastic applause follows that statement.

"No one gets here," he says, holding up the statue, "without a lot of help, and I have the best people in the world working with me as well as the greatest family anyone could hope to have. And now..." He takes a moment and seems to be collecting himself as he looks directly at me.

My heart stops and I hold my breath, waiting to hear what he will say.

"Now I have Natalie, too. It's no secret that these last few weeks have been rough for my *wife*—I sure do love saying that—and for me. Neither of us will ever forget the love and support we've received from this community. I owe a huge debt of gratitude to Natalie's wildebeest dog, Fluff-o-Nutter," he says to a crackle of laughter from the crowd. "Without Fluff's bad behavior, Natalie might've walked right by the park where I was filming in New York, and I never would've known that the love of my life was getting away. So thank you, Fluff." Looking directly at me, he adds, "Natalie, I love you with all my heart, and I can't wait to spend forever with you."

He holds up the award. "Thank you very much for this incredible honor."

I wipe away a monsoon of tears as Flynn and Marlowe leave the stage arm in arm, laughing as they go. I can't believe he actually thanked Fluff! He's back a few minutes later with the *Camouflage* cast to accept the award for Outstanding Performance by a Cast in a Motion Picture.

What an amazing moment to witness, even if I had nothing at all to do with it. His joy is mine, and I'm filled to overflowing with pride for this man who has swept me off my feet and captured my heart. That day in the park feels like a lifetime ago, when it was only a couple of weeks. Flynn and I have packed a year's worth of living into that short time, and I'm so excited to see what's next for us.

As the show ends, Flynn comes down the stairs from the stage. Even with an award in each hand, he manages to lift me right off my feet and kiss the daylights out of me with most of Hollywood looking on.

I put my arms around him and kiss him back.

He seems to finally remember where we are and breaks the kiss, but I can feel his reluctance.

"I'm so proud of you and so happy for you," I whisper into his ear so he can hear me over the din around us. "Thank you for recognizing Fluff's contribution to our relationship."

"She played an essential role. Best supporting actress."

I smile up at him, and he hugs me again. Since I'm wearing sky-high heels, I can see over his shoulder. My gaze locks on Valerie, who's looking at us with barely restrained hatred. I'm not sure what comes over me, but I smile at her as I hug my handsome, successful husband. Let her eat her heart out, because she let him get away.

The look she gives me is positively vile, and I realize that with one smile, I've made an enemy for life. That's okay. I hold on tighter to Flynn. We'll get our revenge by being happy together.

"Let's get out of here," he says in a low growl.

"Don't you have to do interviews and stuff?"

He moans. "Yeah, I do, and then we're getting out of here."

"I'm with you, love."

"Yes, you certainly are."

CHAPTER 16

Natalie

I love watching him do the interviews. With his Actor statues in hand, he's all the things I love best about him—humble, charming, funny and sincere. The reporters ask the same question over and over: How does he feel about being the front-runner for the Oscar? It's exciting, he says, but a lot of things in his life are exciting these days. The last reporter wants to know how he's enjoying married life.

"It's spectacular," he says with a smile for me. "And about to be more so if you're done with me."

"Far be it from us to keep the newlyweds apart any longer," the giddy female reporter says. "Congratulations again, Flynn. *Camouflage* was amazing. You deserve all the acclaim and awards."

"Thanks very much." He comes to claim me. "Let's get the fuck outta here."

We follow the security detail to the limo, which they have standing by, ready to whisk us away.

"Are people going to be mad if you don't go to the parties?"

"I don't care if they are." The second we're settled in the car, he puts his arm around me and draws me to him, his eyes glittering with happiness and intent. "Kiss me, sweetheart, before I die from wanting you to."

What else can I do when he puts it that way? I reach for him and bring him to me, laying my lips over his and breathing in his endlessly appealing scent. It always makes me want to burrow into his neck. For the longest time, we don't do anything more than kiss, lips pressed against lips, sharing the same air. The sheer intimacy of the moment hits me like an arrow to my heart. This man who could have any woman in the world has chosen to spend the rest of his life with me.

He frames my face in his big hands and pulls back to study me. "How can you be so beautiful and all mine?"

"I was just wondering the same thing about you." I curl my hand around his wrist. "I really loved what you said up there. Fluff will be pleased when she hears about it, too. It was very sweet of you to include her."

"You know I meant what I said about how close we came to never meeting. If she hadn't broken free, if you hadn't chased her... It makes me ache to think about what we could've missed."

He kisses me again, his mouth sliding over mine, his tongue coaxing its way in. His hand slides up my leg, pushing up my skirt as he drags his fingertips over my inner thigh and beyond. Breaking the kiss, he says, "Take off your panties. I want to taste you. Right now."

"Flynn..." I glance at the closed partition that seals us off from the driver. "Not here. We'll be home soon."

"Right here. Right now." He tugs on my panties to make his point.

The thought of doing that now, here, makes my heart beat fast and my palms sweaty, not to mention the flood of heat between my legs. "Flynn..."

"Shhh." The panties come down my legs and get stuffed into the pocket of his suit coat. He kneels on the floor in front of me. Then I'm on my back, my skirt hiked up to my waist and my legs propped open on his shoulders. God, is this really my life now? As he parts me and licks me from front to back before dipping inside me, I realize I was only half-alive before I met him and found out how much more was possible.

Speaking of more, he slides his fingers into me. He moans against my most sensitive flesh. "Fuck, I love how you taste, Nat. I'll never get enough of you." The stubble on his jaw rubs against me, the sting only adding to the assault on my senses. Every one of them is engaged as he licks and sucks and strokes me to a screaming orgasm. As I come back down from the incredible high, I remember where we are.

"Ah, the driver…"

"Won't hear a thing. I told him to turn up the music."

He keeps going, as if he didn't just make me come harder than I ever have before. "I want another one."

"I *can't*."

"Yes, you can, baby." He sets out to prove me wrong, and makes me scream all over again as I grasp a handful of his hair and hold on for dear life.

I'm desperately trying to get air into my starved lungs when I feel him press against me. "Has it been seven days yet?" he asks, sounding as desperate as I feel.

Raising my hips to encourage him, I say, "Yes. Close enough." I open my eyes to look up at him as he enters me in one smooth stroke that fills me to capacity and nearly makes me come—again. I can't believe I'm having sex in the back of a limo.

"You've turned me into a regular sex fiend, Mr. Godfrey. Airplanes *and* limos."

"Mmmm, so many other places to explore and a lifetime to do it—and now with no more fucking condoms. God this amazing, Nat."

"For me, too." My hands find their way inside his suit coat to his sweat-dampened back and down to grasp his ass as he thrusts into me. I love the way that feels, his muscles working in harmony to make love to me.

He has the same idea as he reaches under me to take hold of my ass to keep me in place for his absolute possession. For the first time since my meltdown on our wedding night, I feel like he's letting go of the tight hold on his control.

I want to let him know I love what he's doing. "Yes, Flynn, *yes*… Don't stop."

My words are like gas on his fire. He picks up the pace, and his lips come down on mine. I open to his tongue, which takes fierce possession of my mouth. I've forgotten all about where we are or that there's a driver on the other side of a thin screen. I can't think about anything other than the magnificent pleasure of making love with my beautiful husband.

He raises his head, opens his eyes and looks down at me, and I lose my heart to him all over again when I realize he's checking on me. Even when swept away by passion and desire, he takes care of me in a way that no one else ever has or ever will.

I reach up and put my hands around his neck. "I'm okay. Come down here and kiss me again. I love to kiss you."

He gives me exactly what I want and need until we're both coming, his fingers digging into my bottom as he pins me down with the force of his body and lets himself go.

I gather him into my embrace, holding him close.

"Love you so much, Nat. So, so much. Every guy in that room tonight wanted to be me because you're so amazing and beautiful, inside and out."

"So are you. And we're even more beautiful together."

He lifts his head to look out the steamed-up window. "We'd better get ourselves together. We're almost to Malibu." Smiling down at me, he withdraws and produces tissues from a box that came with the limo.

"They're prepared for backseat hookups, huh?"

"Don't think about the leftover DNA on the seats."

"That's gross. You need to get your own limo so the only DNA on the seats will be ours."

His eyes get wide and animated. "Other than you, nothing turns me on more than being told I need to buy another car."

"Because the sixty you have aren't enough."

"Never enough." He pulls up his pants and lands on the seat next to me. "Seriously, baby, new cars make me hot. Not as hot as you make me, but pretty damned close. That smell… Mmm… I can only think of one thing on this earth that smells better than a new car."

"And you are *not* going to say what that is."

Offering a wolfish smile, he says, "Okay, I won't say it." He pulls my panties from his pocket, brings them to his face and takes a deep breath.

I've never seen anything so earthy or erotic in my life.

"Do I shock you terribly?"

"No."

He tips his head, eyeing me skeptically.

"You make me feel like I've been half-asleep my whole life until I met you and came alive."

"That's the most incredible thing you've ever said to me." The panties return to his pocket. He puts his arms around me and holds me and kisses me until we arrive at Hayden's beach house.

"I think it's probably safe to go home to my place tomorrow," he says when we're inside, where a very enthusiastic Fluff greets us like we've been gone for six months. She even seems rather happy to see Flynn.

"She must've been watching tonight when you made her famous."

"Maybe we'll be friends now." Flynn goes to answer a knock on the door. "Thanks a lot." He returns holding two bags.

"What's that?"

"Dinner from In-N-Out. Best burgers in LA."

"How did you pull that off?"

"I texted the security guys and asked some of them to stop on the way home. I can't think of a better way to celebrate tonight than with some In-N-Out," he says with a dirty wink.

"Are we still talking burgers?"

"Of course we are. What else would we be talking about?" ·

Flynn lights the gas fireplace, and, still decked out in formal attire, we enjoy a picnic on the living room floor.

"I gotta say, this burger is amazing."

"Told ya," he replies, his mouth full. He dips fries in ketchup and holds them up to feed me, slipping a couple to Fluff, too.

Burgers and fries have never tasted better than they do tonight. I reach over to wipe a dab of ketchup off his lip. "Is this what happy feels like?"

"Sweetheart," he says gruffly, clearly moved by my question, "this is what *ecstatic* feels like."

"I have to go into the office today," Flynn says in the morning, "even though I'd much rather be with you."

"It's okay. I'm going to sleep some more and then get organized with some foundation stuff, not to mention a ton of laundry that needs to be done and packed to go back to your place. I've got plenty to keep me busy. Don't worry about me."

"I will worry about you. I'll always worry about you." He sits next to me on the bed. He's freshly showered and shaven and is dressed in a formfitting black T-shirt and faded jeans that hug him in all the right places. As always, he makes my mouth water just looking at him. "This'll be the first time we've spent apart since we got married."

"We can't spend every waking minute together. What about when you're filming in some exotic location?"

"You'll be there with me."

"What if I get my job back?"

His brows knit with what appears to be consternation, but he quickly shakes it off and bends to kiss me. "We'll figure it out, sweetheart. I gotta go before Hayden has me killed." After one more kiss, this one longer and more involved, he groans and pulls himself away. "I'll be back as soon as I can. There're security people right outside. If you want to go anywhere, just check in with them. They also have the code to get back in here."

"I'll be fine. Go to work, dear."

"We're going on a fucking honeymoon," he says as he leaves the room. "A long-ass fucking honeymoon. As soon as we possibly can."

"I thought we've been on our honeymoon?"

"No way does hanging around here count. We're going somewhere awesome."

"This has been pretty awesome as far as I'm concerned."

"I can do better than this."

He leaves me with a big silly smile on my face as I snuggle under the covers, hoping to go back to sleep after having been up half the night making love to my insatiable husband. I'm on my way to dozing off when my phone rings.

I grab it off the bedside table and see Leah's name on the screen. "Hey," I say, curbing a yawn. "What's up?" It's eight here, so eleven there. "Why aren't you in class?"

"I am in class," she whispers. "I'm hiding in the supply closet, but I've got the door cracked so I can watch the monsters."

"Why are you in the supply closet?"

"I have news. Sue told me this morning that the board wants to reinstate you, but Mrs. Heffernan refused. She said it was either you or her. According to Sue, they chose you."

I sit straight up in bed. "Are you kidding me? They picked *me* over *her*?"

"Before you take that as a huge compliment, you should know that Flynn's lawyers were playing hardball with them. They were looking at a huge lawsuit if they didn't reinstate you. But Sue said they all felt that it was wrong for Mrs. Heffernan to let you go for the reasons she did, especially when the parents were so pleased with the job you were doing."

"Wow. I don't know what to say."

"Apparently, you're going to hear from the board chair later today. I wanted to give you a heads-up, but don't tell them I told you."

"I never would. Don't worry."

"What'll you do, Nat? Do you want to come back?"

If she asked me that on the day I was fired, I would have said of course I want to go back. But now… now everything is different. "I don't know. I need to talk to Flynn and figure out our plans."

"Well, no matter what you decide, they're doing the right thing offering you your job back. People here have been in an uproar over the whole incident. The way she treated you was wrong, Natalie. Everyone thinks so."

"Thanks for that, and please tell the others, too."

"I will. I gotta go before the little bastards get a big idea to lock me in here."

"They are *not* little bastards!"

"Yes, they are. Call me later and let me know what happens."

"I will. Thanks for the info."

"No problem."

I end the call with Leah and call Flynn.

"Miss me already, baby?"

"You know it, but I just got off the phone with Leah, and there's news on the job front." I relay to him what Leah told me. When I'm finished, he's totally silent. "Flynn?"

"I'm here, sweetheart, just processing it all. What're you thinking?"

"I don't know. On the one hand, I feel sort of glad that Mrs. Heffernan is leaving because she wasn't mean to just me. Everyone dislikes her."

"What's on the other hand?"

"You, me, our life together. You're here. Not so sure I want to be three thousand miles from you for even a day or two."

"While this is entirely and completely your decision to make any way you see fit, your thinking matches mine on the three-thousand-mile thing."

"I had a feeling it might."

"Do you have to give them an answer right away?"

"I'm not sure. Leah said they're going to call me today sometime to ask me to come back."

"See if you can think about it for a day or two, and we'll talk it over tonight when I get home."

"All right. I will."

"I'm happy for you that a terrible wrong is going to be righted, no matter what happens next."

"I'm happy, too. Leah said the board was intimidated by whatever Emmett said to them."

"Good, they should be intimidated. What Mrs. Heffernan did set them up for a huge liability. I'm glad they were able to see that." He pauses before he adds, "Are you okay?"

"Yeah, I'm fine. Just processing it all."

"We'll talk more later, okay?"

"Sure. I'll see you then."

"Love you, baby. So glad they're doing the right thing."

"Love you, too. Thanks for not letting them off the hook."

"Never. I'll be home as soon as I can."

"I'll be here. See you then."

I return the phone to the table and snuggle into bed, my mind racing with the implications of getting my job back. After lying there for half an hour, it's clear I won't be going back to sleep. I decide to get up and make myself useful by doing the ton of laundry that has accumulated over the last two weeks.

I gather our clothes into a basket I find in the master bedroom closet. Flynn told me the laundry room was "up there somewhere," gesturing to the second floor of Hayden's sprawling house.

I head up the stairs, enjoying the view of the beach through the two-story windows as I go. I try to imagine what it would be like to make enough money to afford a place like this. "Not going to happen in this lifetime," I mutter to Fluff, who follows me upstairs. Because there are six doors to choose from, I put down the basket at the top of the stairs and head for the end of the hallway to find the laundry room.

The first three doors open to spacious bedrooms that look out over the beach. There isn't a bad view to be had in this place. Behind the fourth door is a massive master bedroom. Intrigued, I venture inside to check out the biggest bed I've ever seen. It is easily twice the size of Flynn's California king. What does a single guy need with a bed that size?

Off the bedroom is an equally huge bathroom, where I find the full-size washer and dryer tucked behind a closed door. I'm going to get the basket when the closet catches my eye, and apparently Fluff's eye, too, as she wanders into the walk-in closet. I call out to her to come back, but she doesn't. No surprise there, so I go after her.

Holy shit, the guy has some clothes! Most of them in muted colors—grays, blacks, browns. Everything is color-coordinated and neatly arranged. I venture farther into the closet, past rows of shoes and drawers of all sizes to another door that Fluff has nudged open.

"Fluff, come here. We shouldn't be in here." She's in the far corner, sniffing up a storm. The second room appears to be a gym of some sort—until I look more closely at the equipment. I've never seen any of this stuff at the gyms I've frequented. What the hell is it? On one wall, a set of drawers beckons me.

At this point, I have to acknowledge that what I am doing counts as snooping. I found the laundry room and checked out the amazing closet. If I open these drawers to see what's inside them, I will cross a line that can't be uncrossed. But I can't seem to help myself. I want to know what all this stuff is for.

I look down at Fluff. "What would you do?"

She barks, which I take to mean, "Go for it."

"You're a bad influence. You have no moral compass whatsoever."

Her reply is two more sharp barks that sound like agreement.

I can't explain what makes me do it. This is way out of character for someone who has kept to herself and out of other people's business for most of her life. Because I kept a low profile, no one paid much attention to me, and I liked it that way. I have no experience at all in minding other people's business.

But I want to know what's in those drawers, so I walk over to them and begin opening them. They are filled with a variety of objects I don't recognize—most of them rubbery materials in odd shapes and sizes. In the second drawer, I find more of the same, only these are shaped like penises—very big penises. Why in the hell does Hayden keep large rubber penises in his house?

The question makes me giggle nervously. Does Flynn know about this? The thought of telling him only adds to my nervous laughter. In the third drawer, I find shiny metal objects that look like clips of some sort alongside feathers and strips of velvet.

I take another long look around the room, at the oddly shaped weight bench and the big cross that takes up most of the space. On the wall, wooden paddles that look like oversized Ping-Pong paddles hang next to what might be a collection of riding crops. Affixed to the ceiling are a series of ropes attached to pulleys. "What the hell, Fluff?"

Then I open the bottom drawer to find boxes of condoms and bottles of lubricant. "Oh my God." Suddenly, I want out of there. I've seen more than enough to ensure that I'll never again be able to look Hayden Roth in the eyes.

I shoo Fluff from the room and go grab the laundry. As I start the wash, I try not to think about what I saw in Hayden's secret room. What does it mean? How does it work? What does he do with all those items? With the washing machine running, I go downstairs, my mind racing as I try to process it all.

I go straight to the laptop in Hayden's office and begin poking around online, my curiosity only growing as I realize that what I've stumbled upon is Hayden's "playroom." I learn that these rooms are frequently found in the homes of sexual dominants.

Clicking from one website to another, I follow a trail of information and pictures that make my eyes pop out of my head. People actually *do* this stuff?

I see a woman stretched over what I now realize is a spanking bench while her "Dom" uses a paddle on her ass. Another woman is strapped to the St. Andrew's cross with clamps on her nipples. A chain connects them as well as the one that's apparently affixed to her clitoris.

I cross my legs against the tingle between them. What would that feel like? How badly would it hurt? Or would the pleasure override the pain? My curiosity leads me to click on videos that demonstrate how the equipment upstairs is used in sexual situations. I cannot look away.

By the time I come up for air, two hours have gone by. I make a point of clearing the browser history on the computer before I stand on trembling legs and leave the office with more questions than I had going in. I now know that the smaller rubber and glass objects are butt plugs. That had been what Valerie meant when she asked if Flynn had "plugged" my ass. My whole body tingles at the thought of that. Does the tingling mean I want it or that I don't?

I'm such a neophyte when it comes to sex. I stayed away from men and anything to do with sex for so long that I lack the context I need to satisfy my curiosity. Judging by the heat between my legs, however, I'm incredibly aroused by what I've seen. Does that mean I want to try it?

Not necessarily. The thought of being tied down or shackled makes me feel light-headed—and not in a good way.

The most pressing questions I have after seeing Hayden's room and two hours of "research" are whether my husband is into the same things as his best friend, and how will I ever work up the nerve to ask him that?

I need help dealing with this situation. Professional help. I scroll through my contacts for a number I haven't called in six years. When I moved into my new cell phone, Natalie's phone, I made sure to include the number just in case I ever needed it. I'm not even entirely sure it is still his number.

"One way to find out." Fluff lifts her head to check on me. I give her a pat to settle her and place the call.

He answers on the fourth ring. Hearing his voice takes me right back to the dark days after the attack, when he'd been a big part of the group who put me back together. Dr. Curtis Bancroft specializes in post-traumatic stress and counseling sexual assault survivors.

"This is Curt. Hello?"

"Dr. Bancroft… This is April. April Genovese." He's never known me by my new name, as I stopped seeing him before I changed it.

"April," he says on a long exhale, "it's so great to hear your voice. I've been worried sick about you. I really hoped you'd call. How are you?"

"I'm doing surprisingly well, all things considered. Am I catching you at a bad time?"

"I'm on vacation in the Caribbean with my family, but I'm very happy to talk to you."

"Are you sure?"

"I'm positive. So you got married! That's wonderful news. That's going well?"

"Yes, Flynn… He's amazing. He's been very sweet and understanding."

"Is this the first relationship you've had?"

I know he means sexual relationship. "Yes."

"April? Are you coping with everything?"

"I think so. I'm able to… to make love with him."

"That's wonderful. And are you able to enjoy it?"

God, it's embarrassing to talk about such personal things, even to someone from whom I have few secrets. "Yes, it's … It's incredible. I love it."

"I'm very happy to hear that. You've worked so hard to get free of your past, and I hope you're giving yourself permission to be happy."

"I am. It's just… Flynn, he… Well, I had a flashback on our wedding night. He… He held down my hands, and…"

"That was a trigger for you?"

"Yes! I didn't even think about that until he did it, and then I totally lost it. And now… He's so afraid of it happening again. He's holding back. I told him that having sex with me is like juggling dynamite. You never know when it will blow—and not in a good way."

His low chuckle rumbles through the phone. "While that's an interesting metaphor, if your husband loves you—"

"He does. I have no doubt at all about that."

"Then I'm sure he's just trying to be careful as you get used to your first sexual relationship."

"A few times, before he knew everything about what happened to me... He was different."

"How so?"

"He was more unrestrained, earthy... He said things and did things."

"Did you like that?"

"Yes. I liked it because it was Flynn, and I trust him. But since the thing with my hands, he's... different. I worry that there are things he wants, and I'll never know because he's afraid to tell me."

"Have you talked to him about this?"

"Sort of. It's hard, though. This is so new to me. And his friends... Well, one of them at least, is into some really hard-core stuff, which makes me wonder what Flynn is interested in. I sound ridiculous because I can't even find the right words to describe all this to you. How will I ever talk to him about it?"

"You're doing a great job explaining it to me."

"That's easy. You're not my husband. And I ran into his ex-wife at the SAG Awards." I go on to tell Curt what Valerie said to me.

"Wow, well... You have to remember the source is someone who has an ax to grind with him—and with you."

"I know. I've thought of that. But she's got me wondering."

"It sounds to me as if he truly cares for you, and when I saw you together on TV, he was very attentive."

"He does, and he is. He's more than I ever hoped to dream possible."

"Then trust him, April. Trust him to know how to be what you need. But he's not a mind reader. He can't know what you're thinking if you don't tell him."

"It's strange to be called April after all this time."

"Do you prefer Natalie?"

"I'm not sure what I prefer. It's weird to be talking about April when I've been Natalie for so long now."

"I'd just like to say that as much as I hate how it happened, I'm so glad to know you're doing well in your new life. I've wondered about you for years and hoped I'd hear from you."

"I should've checked in. I'm sorry."

"Don't be. You were off living your life, and all your hard work with me made that possible."

"Would it be okay if I checked in from time to time?"

"It would be absolutely fine. I'll always be happy to hear from you."

"Thank you again. I'm not being dramatic when I say you saved my life."

"No, April… You saved your own life. I only helped. Your inner strength got you through before, and it will again. Don't be afraid to rely on it."

"I won't. I'll call again soon."

"I'll look forward to it. Take care, and talk to your husband."

"I will. Thanks again."

I end the call feeling more confident that I can handle the conversation I need to have with Flynn.

CHAPTER 17

Flynn

Arriving at the Quantum offices, I pull into a parking space and sit for a moment, the engine in the Mercedes idling as I think about what Natalie told me. She's going to get her job back, which means she'll return to New York while I have to be here for the next couple of months.

If the thought of a single day without her in it is unbearable, how will I ever stand to have her in New York for weeks on end while I'm here? I could go to New York with her, and I probably will if it comes to that, but I'd rather be here.

I hate the way life is interfering with my desire to be completely alone with my new wife. And then I call bullshit on myself. I can do whatever the fuck I want to, so why am I not doing whatever the fuck I want to?

With my security detail following close behind, I head into the office, which is abuzz with activity. Everyone is still ecstatic about the SAG Awards as well as the Oscar nominations for *Camouflage*, especially after all the campaigning that was done to ensure the film got the recognition it deserves from the Academy. For the most part, I've stayed out of that fray, letting others do the heavy lifting. The idea of campaigning for awards has never sat well with me, but it's a necessary evil in our world.

After accepting congratulations for the SAGs from everyone I see along the way, I head for Hayden's office, where I'm told he's in the editing room. I take the elevator up one floor. I find him in the dark, staring at two huge monitors, headphones on. I tap his shoulder to get his attention.

He pauses the video and removes the headphones. "Look what the cat dragged in. It's my long-lost partner in crime who is now an Oscar nominee. Congrats again."

"Same to you, and I apologize for everything I've done to piss you off in the last few weeks."

"Well, that fixes it. Thanks."

The sarcasm isn't lost on me. "I am sorry, Hayden. I know I picked a hell of a time to punch out on you."

He shrugs. "Shit happens. I get that. Are you back now?"

"Sort of."

"What does that mean?"

"It means I need a break. I need some real time off. I've been working nonstop for years, and I'm burned-out."

After a long pause, he says, "Maybe you could, at the very least, be honest about why you want to take time off. You're not burned-out. You don't get burned-out. You want to spend time with your new wife. Why not call a spade a spade?"

"Fine. You're right. But call me crazy if I'm not willing to talk to you about her when you've made your feelings where she's concerned very clear."

"I have no bad feelings toward her. I barely know her. My feelings, as you call them, have been toward you, not her."

Sighing, I take a seat next to him. "I hate having this shit between us."

"As do I."

"Look, I know I've dropped the ball with work and left you to deal with things on your own, and I'm sorry about that. This whole thing with Natalie… It just… happened. And then it blew up in our faces. I had to be with her during all of that, Hayden."

"Of course you did, but did you have to marry her?"

"I did that because I wanted to. Not for any other reason."

"You gotta see this from my side, Flynn. I've known you all my life, and I've never seen you like this before. It's… It's unsettling."

"It's *love*."

"So you say."

"I understand that it's difficult for you to watch me do things that seem out of character to you."

"Out of character... That's a good way of putting it."

"But I can only hope that someday you'll allow yourself to feel for someone what I feel for her. It's the best thing that's ever happened to me, and I refuse to apologize to anyone, even you, for being happier than I've ever been in my life."

"Fair enough," he says begrudgingly. "So what do you want to do?"

"I want to get away from everything for a while with her. I know we've got shit to do, but I can do it from anywhere. I can review the edits and provide feedback. I can make decisions about future projects. I don't have to be here to do that."

Hayden scratches at the stubble on his cheek as he thinks it over.

"Where're you going to be?"

"I don't know yet. Could be New York or maybe Mexico. Depends on what she decides to do about her job."

"I thought she lost her job."

"Apparently, the board has removed the principal who fired her and is preparing to invite Natalie back."

"Wow, that's amazing. There was nothing else they could do."

"Especially after Emmett threatened them with a ten-million-dollar wrongful termination suit."

Hayden smiles. "That's awesome."

"But I don't think that's the only reason they buckled. They know it's the right thing to do."

"Yeah, it is. So she might be living back in New York?"

"We haven't decided anything yet."

"I want you to know... I'm happy for you. I really am. She seems like a very nice person, and the way she held up during all the shit says a lot about who she really is."

"She's incredibly courageous. You have no idea just how courageous she is. We could all learn from her."

"It's admirable. I mean that sincerely. What she endured at such a young age… To come through it whole and intact… It's amazing, and I get why you're so gone over her."

"Why do I hear a 'but' coming?"

"I just worry about you and the sacrifices you're making to be with her. I worry about my best friend Flynn, who is one of the smartest, savviest people I've ever known, getting married without a prenup. That's not the Flynn Godfrey I know and love. The Flynn I know and love understands the way things work in this world we live in and how the best of situations can go bad in the blink of an eye."

I don't want to talk about my relationship with Natalie going bad. That isn't going to happen. "I hear you, and I appreciate what you're saying. You should know that Natalie asked me about a prenup and wanted to have one."

"And you still said no?"

"I still said no."

"You're crazy, man. Seriously insane."

"If the day ever comes when I have to give her half of everything I have, I'm not going to care enough to quibble over that. And let's face it. I could live in high style for the rest of my life on half of what I have. I wanted to go into this marriage with nothing between us but love. Putting a prenup in front of her would have made it a business thing, and I didn't want that. I know it's hard for you to understand, but I really believe it's the right thing for us not to have one. She needs to be able to have faith in me, and I need to believe she's not in it for the money."

"How do you know she isn't?"

"Because she got totally pissed when I bought her a diamond bracelet after she told me not to buy her any more jewelry. She's not into all that. After the show last night, we sat in your living room and ate In-N-Out burgers and fries. You know what she said to me?"

"What?"

"'Is this what happy feels like?'"

Hayden looks down at the control board and fiddles with some knobs.

"Most of the women we know would've been pissed to miss out on the parties and the photo ops. Natalie was perfectly content to go home and eat fast food and dip her fries in ketchup. That's all she needs to be happy, Hayden. Do you know how refreshing that is?"

"I can definitely see the appeal."

"And yet you're still not convinced?"

"What about the other side of the equation?"

"Are you actually asking me how the sex is with my wife?"

"Yes, I'm asking you that! I know how you like it, and I can't for the life of me see you behaving that way with a woman who's been through what she has."

"I can't see it either, but the sex with her is still incredible. There's a connection with her that I've never had with anyone else. It's always been mechanical. With her it's… Divine."

He's quiet again, but I can see his wheels turning.

"What? Just say it so we can clear the air."

"Don't shoot me for playing devil's advocate, but you felt that way about Valerie at first, too."

"I *never* felt for Valerie what I feel for Natalie. *Ever.*"

"Okay, but you were really into her at first, and after a while you found it difficult to deny yourself the things you wanted from her. And we all know how she felt about what you wanted. All I'm saying is it was hard to watch that happen and to see you crushed in the aftermath. It affected everything for a long time, including the work. I don't want to see that happen again. None of us does."

"That's not going to happen." As I say the words, a tingle of anxiety works its way down my spine.

"You've convinced yourself that you'd rather live without the lifestyle than without her. Am I right?"

"Something like that."

"Believe it or not, I almost understand. You've tuned in to my… affection, I guess you'd call it, for Addie."

"Yeah, and I'm hoping you're going to do something about that one of these days. I'm sure she is, too."

"I'm never going to do anything about it, because I know myself and what I can live without—and what I can't. There's no way I'd put either of us through that kind of hell. And that's what it would be as soon as the blush wore off the rose and I accepted that I had to spend the rest of my life denying who and what I am. If you can do that, I give you credit. I can't."

Hayden's words hit me in the chest like an arrow, filling me with irrational fear. What if I can't either? What will become of us if my inner Dom tries to break loose with her? Remembering the panic in her eyes after I pinned down her hands makes me break out in a cold sweat.

Addie knocks and pokes her head in. "Flynn."

"Yeah?"

"Can you, um, can you come here, please?"

My first thought is of Natalie. Has something happened? "What's wrong?"

"There's an FBI agent here to see you."

Hayden and I look at each other and then at her. "To see me? Why?"

"He didn't say. He's waiting in your office."

"Did you call Emmett?"

"He and the rest of the legal team are off-site today at a training session," Addie says. "I can call him, if you think we need him."

"Let's see what he wants with me first."

No words are spoken as Hayden gets up to come with me. The three of us are silent in the elevator that delivers us to the floor where our offices are housed. We step into my office, where a man in a suit is standing at the window, admiring the view. He turns when he hears us come in.

"Mr. Godfrey, I'm FBI Special Agent Vickers."

I shake his hand. "My business partner, Hayden Roth."

"Good to meet you. I admire your work. Both of you."

"Thank you." I'm anxious to dispense with the small talk. "What can we do for you?"

"A lawyer named David Rogers in Lincoln, Nebraska, was found murdered in his office this morning. Does that name ring a bell with you?"

I know a moment of pure, unmitigated joy at hearing the man who screwed Natalie over so badly is now dead. "As you and everyone else in America is aware, I know exactly who he is. What does it have to do with me?"

"On the Carolyn Justice show, you made a statement that has sparked the interest of law enforcement." He consults a notebook he withdraws from his pocket. "You said, 'I've never thought I was capable of murder, but in this case…'"

"Are you inferring that I killed him?"

"I'm inferring that you said you'd like to."

"Yes, I did, but I didn't actually *do* it."

"Did you get someone else to do it?"

"No, I didn't. I haven't given that guy a thought in days other than to keep tabs on the efforts of my attorneys to ensure that he never had a chance to do to anyone else what he did to my wife."

"By having him killed?"

"No, by having him disbarred. I'm not a murderer, Mr. Vickers."

"That's Special Agent Vickers."

The guy is full of his own importance.

"We can put a halt to this immediately," Addie says. "Mr. Godfrey has been surrounded by security personnel for days. He hasn't left the state of California since he returned from New York two weeks ago this coming Wednesday."

"That would rule him out," Vickers said, "but it wouldn't rule out a contract job."

"Are you listening to yourself?" Hayden asks, incredulously. "Are you actually accusing *Flynn Godfrey* of hiring someone to kill a lawyer in Nebraska?"

"I'm not accusing him of anything. I'm simply pointing out that he had both motive and opportunity. He has the resources to procure any service he might need."

"Well, I didn't *procure* the service of murder. I was much more interested in legal ways to make Mr. Rogers suffer for what he did to my wife. We were going to ensure his life was a living hell for the next decade. I'm actually a little disappointed that we won't get to do that now."

"If you think he had this guy murdered, you're going to have to prove it," Hayden says.

"I'm well aware of that." He produces a piece of paper from a binder and hands it to me.

"What's this?"

"A warrant for your phone and computer, just so we can rule you out as a suspect."

I withdraw the phone from my pocket and hand it to him. "Have at it." I gesture to the computer on my desk. "I haven't touched a computer in three weeks, but knock yourselves out."

"Is this the only cell phone you own?"

"Yep."

"We may acquire additional warrants for the phones belonging to your employees."

Out of the corner of my eye, I see Addie stiffen and have to quell the urge to laugh. The idea of Addie without her phone for even an hour is hilarious. She'd go into convulsions.

"And your wife is where?"

All thoughts of laughter flee as I straighten my spine. "At home. Why?"

"I'd like to speak with her as well."

"She's been with me every minute of every day for two weeks. She has neither the desire nor the wherewithal to kill anyone."

"She certainly had motive."

"You know, Mr. Vickers," I say, enjoying the flush that appears on his face when I refuse to use his title, "I've found that when someone is a snake like Rogers was, there's usually more than one person who's been screwed over by him. I certainly hope you're looking beyond the obvious here. There's probably a long list of people who'd like to see him dead."

"We're conducting a thorough investigation."

"When will I get my phone back?"

"Hopefully we can return it to you tomorrow, providing there's nothing on it that could be used as evidence in this case."

"I'm leaving for my honeymoon in Mexico in the next few days. I'd like to have it back before I go." I wait for him to tell me I'm not to leave the country.

"What's the code?"

I try not to show my relief that he hasn't objected to me leaving the country, which confirms he's on a fishing expedition with this visit, and I'm not an actual suspect. "Nine six three two." And then I remember the photos of Natalie I took on our wedding night, and a feeling of profound dread overtakes me. "There're very personal photos on that phone that I'd like to remove before you take it."

"I'm afraid that won't be possible. Everything on here is evidence."

"Pictures of my wife from our wedding night are *not* evidence. Give me the phone."

Vickers stares at me, a mulish expression on his face.

"My father and I are great friends and supporters of the president. Give me the phone, or I'll have your job." I hold out my hand and engage in a stare-down with the agent.

He blinks first and puts the phone in my hand.

It pains me to delete the suggestive, sexy photos of Natalie from our wedding night, but there's no way I'm letting them out of my custody. The phone is backed up to the cloud, so we still have access to them.

"There you go. Was that so hard?"

"People like you are so entitled. You think you're above it all, even the law."

"I think our business is finished, Mr. Vickers. You can find your way out."

We are quiet until after he leaves, slamming the door behind him.

Addie breaks the silence. "Holy. *Shit*. Did that really just happen?"

"They're just ruling you out," Hayden says. "You haven't left California, so there's no way they can pin it on you."

"Sure there is. There're all sorts of ways they can pin this on me if they really want to."

"They'd be foolish to try," Addie says. "No jury in this world would convict you even if you had done it."

While I appreciate her support, I'm not so naïve as to believe there aren't plenty of regular Americans who'd love to see a big-time, self-important movie star knocked off his high horse.

"I need to go home and talk to Natalie. Will you text her and tell her I'm on my way?"

"Sure," Addie says. "And I'll get you another phone to hold you over."

"Don't bother. You've got Natalie's number if you need to reach me, and I'll tell my folks." To Hayden, I say, "Are we good on the plan for the film and the other stuff?"

"Yeah, we're good. I'll email you when there's new footage to view."

"And I'll work some part of every day until it's done."

"In the meantime, we need a fucking name for this movie."

"I've been thinking about that, too. I'll send you some suggestions."

We had what we considered the perfect title until the studio that's distributing the film rejected it. We're so married to the original title, we're having trouble coming up with something else.

"If anyone else hears from the FBI, let me know."

"We will."

"By the way," Hayden says, "there're your Critics' Choice awards."

I hadn't even noticed the two crystal statues on my desk until he points them out to me. "Thanks for accepting for me."

"No problem."

Before I leave the office, I ask for a moment with Addie, gesturing for her to close the door behind Hayden.

"What's up?"

"I need to get Natalie on all my personal accounts. She needs an ATM card, credit cards, etc. Can you take care of that for me?"

"Sure, I'll call the bank and have them call you on her phone if they have any questions."

"Thank you."

She gives me a questioning look.

"What? Do I have spinach in my teeth or something?"

"No," she says with a laugh. "I'm still trying to get my head around the fact that you're actually *married*. Flynn Godfrey is *married*."

I'm amused by her comments. "Yes, he is and very happily so. I'll be happier when my wife has access to money. Apparently, she's been concerned about her lack thereof."

Addie's eyes bug out of her head. "Has she *no idea*?"

"No, she doesn't, but she will."

"I'll take care of that right away."

"Thanks. We might need some travel help tomorrow or the next day."

"Where to?"

"Either Mexico or New York, I guess, depending on whether she decides to accept the offer to go back to school."

"I'm so glad to hear they're asking her to come back."

"So am I. No matter what happens now, it's up to her, which is the way it should be."

Addie writes a number on a piece of paper and hands it to me.

"What's this?"

"My phone number. It's been programmed into yours for so long, you probably don't know it. Call me when you decide where you're going."

"I will, thanks."

"And before I forget, Liza sent these over for you." She puts copies of all the major industry magazines on the desk in front of me.

We're on the covers of all of them. *People* magazine went with the huge headline, "Well, hello, Mrs. Godfrey!" *US* magazine proclaims "Off the market!" and *In Touch* has, "Flynn says 'I do.'"

"And check this out." Addie flips open the copy of *People* to the page where Natalie is named as one of the best-dressed women at the Golden Globes. Inside *US*, one of the top designers refers to her as an instant fashion icon. I know a moment of pure, unadulterated pride at how beautiful my wife looks in all the pictures. "Pretty cool, huh?"

"Very cool. I guess our wedding bumped the crap about her past off the front pages."

"Looks that way."

"Can I take these?"

"They're all yours. One other thing... Danielle wants to talk to you."

Everyone goes through Addie to get to me, even my manager. "What does she need?"

"She wants to talk about all the offers that are rolling in for Natalie and how you want her to handle them. It's been everything from cosmetic companies to designers to modeling agencies to casting agents."

"Casting? Seriously?"

"Yep. She said they've been bombed with calls since you guys were on Carolyn's show."

"I told her that would happen. I'll get in touch with Danielle when I get a chance."

Before I leave the office, I call Emmett. After I tell him the latest from Natalie's school, I say, "And you're not going to believe what just happened at the office."

"What now?"

"Our friend David Rogers got himself murdered, and the FBI came to talk to me about it."

"Are you fucking kidding me?"

"Wish I was. They took my phone into evidence and everything."

"Flynn… Jesus."

"Don't sweat it. I didn't do it, so I have nothing to worry about."

"The fucking FBI actually talked to you about it."

"Yeah, because of what I said on Carolyn's show the other night, about being capable of murder."

"Anyone would say that after what he did to your girlfriend—now wife."

"I guess I made it easy for whoever actually killed him to try to pin it on me by spouting off on national TV."

"I wouldn't worry about it. You haven't been anywhere near Nebraska, and we both know you didn't actually hire someone to bump the guy off." After a short pause, Emmett says, "You didn't do that, did you?"

"No," I say, laughing, "but I'm not even kinda sad that he's dead."

"People get what's coming to them. I'm sure you're not the only enemy he's made. He owes a lot of people money. They've got motive all over the place."

"Do you think you ought to call this FBI guy?"

"No," he says. "Nothing says 'I've got something to hide' quite like a call from a lawyer. Let's wait and see what happens. But I don't want you talking to him again without me with you. Okay?"

"Right. Gotcha. Thanks, Emmett."

"This whole thing is so fucking unreal, isn't it?"

"Yeah, especially what Natalie had to endure—alone—at fifteen."

"No kidding. Keep me posted."

"Will do."

A few minutes later, I pull out of the parking lot at the office and head for Malibu, eager to get home to my wife.

CHAPTER 18

Natalie

My phone chimes with a message from Addie to tell me Flynn is on his way home, which sends a thrill of anticipation rippling through me. I thought I had hours to kill until I'd see him again.

I run for the shower, and I'm drying my hair when he comes in. I turn off the hair dryer and start to say hello, but he has other ideas. His arms are around me and he's kissing me before I can get a word out.

He lifts me onto the countertop and steps between my legs, tugging my robe open.

Fluff goes crazy barking and circling Flynn's feet. Fearing she might take another piece out of him, I break the kiss. "Go lie down, Fluff. Mommy's fine. Go on."

Pacified, she slinks out of the bathroom into the bedroom.

"Missed you," Flynn whispers. His lips are soft and persuasive against my neck.

"You were only gone a couple of hours."

"Too long." Recapturing my lips for another heated kiss, he fumbles with the button of his jeans until I push his hands out of the way and take over.

He's commando under there and falls into my hand, hot and hard and ready to go.

Grasping my bottom, he pulls me to the edge of the counter and plunges into me.

My head falls back in surrender to the overwhelming sensation of being possessed by him.

"God, Nat… This is gonna be fast." True to his word, he takes us on a quick, wild ride. He reaches down to where we're joined and caresses me to an explosive finish.

I arch into him as he goes with me, crying out as he comes.

I'm still recovering when he lifts me right off the counter and carries me to the bed I haven't made yet.

"I want to do something new," he says, looking down at me. "Is that okay?"

"Yes." I'm onboard for anything he wants right about now.

He helps me remove the robe and pulls off the rest of his clothes. "Turn over on your belly."

I experience a twinge of apprehension but do as he asks because I'm dying of curiosity.

"I won't be able to see your face in this position, so I'm counting on you to remember your safe word, okay?"

I read about safe words this morning, and how they're an essential element of the BDSM lifestyle. Does his use of that term indicate that he's familiar with the lifestyle?

"Nat?"

"I remember."

He puts a couple of pillows under my hips, which leaves my bottom on full display. Before I can be embarrassed, his hands are coasting over my cheeks, squeezing and spreading them. "You have the sexiest ass I've ever seen. I can't get enough of it." Then his tongue is between my legs, and he leaves *nothing* untouched. I'm shocked and aroused by how much I like everything he's doing. Until him, until us, I didn't even know people did these things to each other. He has me on the verge of another orgasm within minutes, but then he pulls away, leaving me bereft.

"*Flynn!*"

"Hang on, sweetheart." He takes hold of my hips and gently pulls me back toward him, pushing into me and triggering the release he had started with his talented tongue. "Is this okay?"

I can't believe he expects me to talk right now. "Mmm."

"I need words, Nat."

"Yes! Don't stop!"

"Those are good words."

I feel like I'm being split in two—in a good way—as he pounds into me, deeper than he's been before. It's already the best thing I've ever felt, and then he makes it better by tweaking my nipples.

"Ahh, fuck, *yes*…" His hoarse whisper raises goose bumps on my back. "Do that again."

I tighten my internal muscles, drawing another long groan from him.

"Tell me you're okay."

"So okay. Don't stop."

He picks up the pace, his fingers digging into my hips and then one of them is sliding through the dampness between my legs and teasing my back entrance.

Dear God… He's done this before, and I loved it, and this time is no different. I never would've imagined I'd like that.

"Still okay?"

"Mmm. Do it, Flynn."

Growling, he drives his finger into my ass, and I come immediately.

"Holy Christ," he whispers before he surges into me one more time, filling me with the heat of his release. "Nat… God, I love you."

"Love you, too."

He withdraws from me slowly, carefully, and then removes the pillows that are propping me up. Kissing my shoulder, he says, "I'll be right back."

I hear water running in the bathroom before he returns with a towel that he uses to clean me up. Then he crawls back into bed with me, molding his body to my back. His hand comes around to land between my breasts. "So good, baby. So, so good."

"Mmm, sure is." I want to tell him about Hayden's room upstairs and ask him the million questions I have, but he's sexed me into a stupor. "If that's what happens after a few hours apart, what's going to happen when we're apart for weeks at a time?"

"We are *not* going to be apart for weeks at a time."

"We will be at some point."

"No, we won't."

"Flynn, you're not being realistic."

"Yes, I am. I want to be wherever you are, and I want you wherever I am."

"So what does that mean for my job in New York?"

"If you want to go back, I'll go with you."

"Your life is here."

"My *life* is wherever you are."

"What about when you have to go on location to film?"

"I'll set up my schedule so I only film in the summer so you can go with me."

I turn over to face him, my hand flat against his chest. "You're talking crazy now."

"No, I'm not. At this point in my career, I can do whatever I want to. I don't need to shoot three films a year anymore. One is plenty, and I can do it in the summer so you can teach."

"What'll you do the rest of the time?"

"Produce other projects. Maybe check out the theater. There's lots I can do from New York."

"You'd be bored out of your mind."

He nuzzles my neck and sets off another attack of goose bumps. "Not if I have you in my bed every night. I could never be bored."

My cell phone rings, and I reach for it on the table. The display shows a 212 number I don't recognize. "This could be it."

"Take the call, sweetheart. Do whatever you want to. We'll make it work."

I draw in a deep breath and accept the call. "This is Natalie."

"Natalie, this is James Poole, chairman of the board at the Emerson School in New York."

"Hi, Mr. Poole. How are you?"

"I'm doing fine, and hope you're well?"

I squeeze Flynn's hand. "Yes, I am."

"Very good. I'm calling with what I hope you will think is good news. The board of directors has voted to reinstate your position, effective immediately, with back pay, of course. And to address your next question, Mrs. Heffernan has decided to retire."

I find it interesting, in light of what Leah told me earlier, that they are spinning Mrs. Heffernan's departure as retirement rather than dismissal.

"I understand that you may feel less than inclined to accept our offer in light of what's happened, but we all hope that you'll consider returning to your class and serving out the remainder of your contract as planned. We've heard nothing but wonderful things about you from the parents of your students. You've made a big impression on them."

"That's nice to hear."

"I'd just like to say… I'm very sorry for the way this was handled. Mrs. Heffernan's actions do not, in any way, reflect the feelings of the board of directors. We believe she acted far too hastily and before she had all the information. I hope that no matter what you decide to do, you'll accept our heartfelt apology that this happened in the first place."

"I do. I accept your apology. Thank you."

"And how do you feel about returning to your class?"

"I'd love to return to my class, but before I decide anything, I need a few days to talk it over with my husband and figure out our plans. I hope you understand."

"Of course. Please, take your time and let us know your decision when you're ready. Again, my sincere apologies and best wishes to you no matter what you decide. On a personal note, you have my admiration for what you've endured and how you've persevered."

"Thank you," I say softly, moved by his kind words even if part of me suspects he's far more concerned about dodging lawsuits than he is about me. "One question…" I figure I'll never be in a better position to bargain, so why not go for it?

"Of course."

"I have an elderly twenty-pound dog named Fluff who sleeps all day. I wondered if I come back, if the board would permit her to sleep under my desk. No one will know she's there, and she's great with children. She loves them."

After a hesitant pause, he says, "I'm sure some accommodation could be made."

"Wonderful. Thank you so much. I'll be in touch."

"I look forward to hearing from you."

We say our good-byes, and I return the phone to the table. "Could you hear all that?" I ask Flynn.

"Yep, and I'm very happy for you that they have realized the error of their ways."

"I think you and your lawyers helped them to see the error of their ways."

"However it happened, as long as it happened. I'm sure it has much more to do with the outrage of the parents and the staff than it did with lawyers."

I'm not as convinced, but I let him believe what he wants to.

"Great move with Fluff, too. Way to work your advantage."

Smiling at his praise, I say, "You didn't give me a chance to ask what you were doing home so early. I thought you'd be gone all day."

"Are you complaining?" he asks with a sexy smile.

"Not at all. Just wondering what's up."

His smile fades, and he looks away from me.

"Did you have another fight with Hayden?" I hate that I've come between lifelong friends.

"No, we actually had a really good talk. I think we've reached an understanding of sorts."

"That's a relief. So what's wrong, then?"

He twirls a strand of my hair around his finger. "While I was at the office, I had a visit from an FBI agent who told me that David Rogers was found murdered in his office this morning."

The news hits me like a fist to the gut, and I sit up. "What? Why did they want to talk to you? Oh God, what you said on Carolyn's show! Are you a *suspect*?"

"Take it easy, sweetheart. It was a formality. They needed to rule me out, and they did. He took my phone, though."

"The pictures…"

"Were removed from the phone, but they are still safely stored in the cloud where no one but me can see them."

"Oh, good. Okay." I relax into the pillow once again. "Did you talk to Emmett?"

"Yes, before I left the office. He says it's bullshit and we have nothing to worry about because I only said I *wanted* to kill him. I didn't actually do it."

"I can't believe he's dead. Did the FBI agent say what happened?"

"No, and I didn't ask."

"I guess it doesn't matter."

"Emmett said Rogers owed a lot of people money. There's plenty of motive to go around, and they probably needed to rule me out. He said we shouldn't worry about it."

"Okay."

"Why do you still look worried?"

"I just hate that something from my past has caused you trouble."

"Now you know how I felt when my fame caused you trouble."

"It sucks."

"Yes, it does, but we're fine, sweetheart. There's nothing to worry about. We're together and we have each other and everything else is just…noise. Speaking of noise… What do you say we get away from it all for a little while and go on an actual honeymoon?"

"Where do you want to go?"

"How about Mexico? Unless you want to go back to New York right away, and I'll totally understand if you do."

"Jeez, what a decision. Sunny Mexico or freezing New York."

"You love New York in the winter."

"Yes, I do." I love New York in the winter, but I'm not sure I can go back to who and what I was before I met Flynn. Don't I belong wherever my husband is?

"It's completely up to you. Just say the word on what you want to do, and I'll make it happen."

"You'd be okay with going back to New York?"

"If that's where you want to be, that's where I want to be."

"What about Hayden and the movie and work and everything?"

"He and I have come to an understanding. He knows I want and need to be with you right now. I'll work some part of every day from wherever we are, and he was cool with that."

"Can I think about it a little?"

"Take all the time you need." He lets out a huge yawn that tells me he's as tired as I am from staying up half the night before. "What do you want to do today?"

He's given me the perfect opening to ask the questions I have about the room I discovered upstairs. He runs a finger over the furrow between my brows. "What's wrong?"

"Nothing."

"Come on, Nat. Whatever it is, just tell me."

"I'd rather show you, if that's okay."

"Sure."

I get up out of bed, retrieve my robe from the floor and tie it around my waist.

Flynn groans. "You didn't say I had to get dressed for this."

"You don't have to if you don't want to."

"I don't want to."

I take him by the hand, and he follows me up the stairs, caressing my bottom as we go. "Flynn, stop!"

"I'll never stop. This is my favorite ass in the whole world."

I lead him into Hayden's bedroom. "What do you want to show me in here besides the biggest bed in the universe?"

"I know! What does he need with a bed that big?"

He doesn't reply.

"What I want to show you is in here."

"How did you happen to end up in Hayden's closet?"

"I was looking for the laundry room and Fluff came in here. I chased after her, and one thing led to another, which led to this."

CHAPTER 19

Flynn

Natalie steps aside, and I nearly gasp at what I see. Hayden's fucking playroom. Natalie is in Hayden's fucking playroom, and I have no idea what to say right now. I'm feeling panicked. I knew Hayden had a room in his house in town but I didn't know he had one here, too. If I'd known that, I never would've left Natalie alone in the house. And why in the name of fucking hell isn't it locked?

"Flynn?"

I glance over at her to find her looking at me curiously. That's when I realize my dick is hard and giving away my true feelings about the room.

"I guess Hayden has his secrets." I don't know what else to say.

"So you didn't know about this?"

I'm on a very slippery slope, and it's getting slipperier by the second. "No," I say, because it's the truth. I didn't know he has a room here.

"Oh."

Does she sound disappointed or is that my hopeful imagination at work?

"Do you know what goes on here?"

"Yeah, I guess." I venture a glance at her. "Do you?"

"I looked it up."

"Oh." The thought of her looking up information about sex playrooms and other such things only makes me harder, which she notices but thankfully doesn't comment on. I'm dying to ask her what she thinks of it and whether she wants to try it, but then I remember what happened when I pinned her hands above her head. So I don't ask. Rather, I dodge the subject. "Since we're moving home tonight, we should hit the beach while we can."

After a long pause, she says, "Sure, whatever you want to do. Let me put the clothes in the dryer, and I'll be right down."

She goes out ahead of me, and I close the door to the playroom. My heart is hammering on the way downstairs. Fuck, fuck, *FUCK!* If she ever finds out what I've kept from her, she'll never forgive me, especially after all the painful things she's shared with me and no one else.

Maybe I should see this as an opportunity and just tell her the fucking truth once and for all. But the thought of that makes my skin feel hot and tight the way it did when I had hives once as a kid. I can't tell her. I just can't, even though I know I should.

We pass a relaxing afternoon at the beach. At least she's relaxed. I'm wound so tightly, my chest aches from the stress. After dinner, we pack up our belongings and head back to my place in the Hollywood Hills. The paparazzi gave up when they saw no sign of us there for more than a week.

Natalie has been unusually quiet, which I chalk up to the decision about her job that's hanging over her. I want to ask her what she's thinking, but I'm afraid of what she might say. I don't want to go back to New York. I want to take her to Mexico on the honeymoon she deserves. I want to spend some more time completely alone with my wife.

Then it occurs to me that she probably doesn't have a passport. "Hey, Nat," I say from my perch in bed. Thrilled to be back in my own bed, I'm waiting for her to join me.

"Yeah?"

"Do you have a passport?"

"Uh-huh. I got one when I changed my name." She comes into the bedroom rubbing lotion into her hands and wearing a gorgeous nightgown I haven't seen before. "Ironically, David Rogers suggested I get one while we were taking care of everything else."

"Is it here or in New York?"

"It's here. I keep it zipped into my purse so I have ID on me since I don't have a driver's license. Why?"

"Just wondering, if we end up going to Mexico. Have you ever used it?"

"Nope. Never been out of the country. My parents weren't comfortable with me being out of the country when I traveled with the Stones, so I never went on those trips."

"Now I really want to go to Mexico so I can be with you for another first."

She slides into bed and turns to face me. "I want to go to Mexico, too, Flynn. I want a honeymoon."

I take hold of her hand and link our fingers. "What about your job?"

"I'm going to call tomorrow and ask if I can have next week to figure things out. I'm sure they'll be willing to give me some time since I thought I'd been permanently fired."

"Do you have Addie's number in your phone?"

"Yes, she texted me earlier."

"Will you text her and tell her Mexico is a go for tomorrow?"

"Tomorrow? She'll be up all night making plans if we go tomorrow."

"Nah, I have a house down there, so all we need is the plane and to let the staff there know I'm coming."

"You have a house in Mexico."

"Uh-huh."

"Where else do you have houses?"

"I have a place in Aspen and one in the south of France. And the place in New York. That's it, though."

"Oh, thank goodness. For a minute there, I wondered if your house collection is as big as your car collection."

"Smart-ass." I smile as I kiss her. "Now will you send that text, please? I feel like I've had an arm amputated without my phone."

"Awww, poor baby. Yes, I'll send the text."

Addie replies right away. *Got it. I'm on it.*

Natalie

"Does that poor girl ever sleep?" I put my phone on the bedside table and snuggle up to Flynn.

"Yes, she gets plenty of sleep."

"When? You're bugging her morning, noon and night."

"She loves her job."

"Sure she does."

"She does! I'm great to work for. I pay her a ton of money. I bought her an awesome car. I set her up rent-free in a condo we own in Santa Monica. She's doing just fine."

"It does sound like a pretty sweet deal, especially since she gets to work for you."

"I know, right?" he says with a cocky grin.

I poke his belly, and he laughs. "If we go to Mexico, when will I be able to see my sisters?" I've texted with both of them every day, and all we talk about is getting together as soon as we're all free at the same time.

"Addie has been in touch with them about the logistics, and it seems like the weekend after next is better for them because of school and work and everything they've got going on. Will that be okay?"

"Sure. That'll be great." We've waited this long. Another week or so won't make a difference. Everything in my life feels so uncertain and up in the air. Except for the man currently wrapped around me, who begins to snore softly.

I stroke his hair and caress the stubble on his cheeks. He's so beautiful all the time, but he's even more so when he's asleep. Even with the gorgeous rings on my fingers, I still can't believe that this incredible man is my husband, that I get to keep him forever.

My phone rings, and I pounce on it, hoping it won't wake Flynn.

"Hello?" I get out of bed and leave the bedroom, closing the door behind me.

"You were looking awfully smug last night, which leads me to wonder how much you know about the man you married."

"Who is this?"

"The *first* Mrs. Godfrey."

I feel like I've been punched in the gut. How did she get my number? "I have nothing to say to you."

"I have a few things to say to you. I'm sure you've heard about all the ways I ruined his life, but you should know how he ruined mine. Have you seen his sick little playroom in the basement yet? If you don't believe me, you should check it out for yourself. He keeps it locked, but there's a key in the kitchen. It's hanging on a hook by the door."

I need to end this call right now, because I know how awful she's been to Flynn. But remembering his obvious physical reaction to Hayden's playroom keeps me from ending the call. "Why're you telling me this?"

"Because. You look like a nice enough girl. And I'd hate to see him do to you what he did to me, both in private and in public."

"It's not because you want him back, is it?"

She snorts loudly. "I'd rather be single and celibate for the rest of my life than to spend one more minute with that man."

"Good thing you don't have to, then."

"Check out the basement, Natalie. Don't be naïve."

"Don't call me again." I hit the End button and hold the phone in my trembling hands. For long minutes, I stand in the dark living room that looks down over the glittering lights of Los Angeles. I can't move. I can't think or process what just happened.

Why is she doing this to me? It's no secret that she and Flynn hate each other, so of course she doesn't want him to be happy with his new wife. I'd be wise to forget what she said and go on with my life. But how am I supposed to do that without knowing if what she said is true?

And what if it is? What then?

"One thing at a time." I return to the bedroom, where Flynn is still asleep. Fluff has moved into my spot, and Flynn's hand is on her back. Tears fill my eyes at the sight of the two "people" I love best snuggled up to each other. How far we've all come since that day in the park.

And in all that time, has he been keeping something huge from me? Something I should've known before I married him and tied my life to his forever? Have I been a total fool? In hindsight, there have been signs that there's more to my husband than what he has shown me. Things he's said and done. "I want to fuck you here," he said while fingering my ass.

Later, he showed regret for his blunt language and for introducing things I wasn't ready for. But I liked it, and he's done it again since then. Standing there, watching him sleep, I'm so confused. I should wake him up and just ask him if what Valerie said is true. Is he into the same things Hayden is, and if so, what does that mean for us?

But how will I know if he's being truthful? When it comes right down to it, I don't know everything there is to know about this man I married after a whirlwind romance.

Leaving him and Fluff to sleep, I step out of the bedroom and close the door. I return to the living room where I sit in the dark for more than an hour, trying to reject what Valerie said as the words of a vindictive bitch who lost the love of an amazing man and earned his eternal scorn. I want to put all my faith in him because he's given me no reason not to, but she was so specific, right down to where the key is located.

It becomes clear to me that I have to see for myself if it's true before I ask him. There'll be no peace in my mind or in my life until I know for certain. In the kitchen, I find the key right where Valerie said it would be, which is a reminder that she once lived in this house. Did she choose all the furniture? Were the dishes once hers?

"Ugh." *Focus, Natalie. One thing at a time.*

The door to the basement is in the hallway. In the short amount of time I've spent in this house, I haven't paid it much attention. That's how I managed to miss the fact that there's a dead-bolt lock on the door. I insert the key and turn the lock, which disengages with a loud click that sends my anxiety into the red zone. I'm fully aware that if I open that door and go down those stairs, I'm violating his privacy. That once I do this, it can't be undone.

Other than my accidental foray into Hayden's closet, I've never done anything even close to this before. I mind my own business. That's who I am. But there's a first—and second—time for everything. I flip on the light and start down the stairs, my heart beating so hard I can hear the flutter of it echoing in my ears.

My throat is tight and my mouth is dry. What will I find here, and will it change everything? I don't have to go far to confirm that Valerie was telling the truth. "Oh my God," I whisper. Flynn's playroom is bigger and even more elaborate than Hayden's. There are numerous pieces of equipment, one of them an S-shaped chaise that I didn't see on any of the sites I visited online.

Like in Hayden's room, ropes fall from the ceiling and a row of paddles in various sizes as well as floggers and whips hang from a pegboard on the wall. I don't bother to cross the room to the armoire because I already know what I'll find inside.

I've seen more than enough to know the truth about my husband and his true preferences. Half-expecting to find him waiting for me, I trudge up the stairs, my mind whirling as I relive every moment we've spent together and every sexual encounter. I've been blown away by our physical connection. I thought he was, too. But is he only pretending to be satisfied while wishing for so much more than his broken wife can give him?

I turn off the light, lock the door and return the key to the hook in the kitchen. There's no way I'll sleep, so I fix myself a cup of hot chocolate and take it to the sofa. I'm so far out of my league with this situation that I don't know how to begin to wrap my mind around it.

Over the course of the next few hours, I sit in the darkness and dissect every minute, every second, every conversation, every caress, every word that has passed between us. There were clues, here and there, little things that didn't make sense at the time, but in this new context, I realize they were red flags that I missed. Such as his insistence on a safe word, which is a mainstay of the BDSM lifestyle. I recall something he once said: *"I've been with a lot of women. Probably too many. I've kissed them and fucked them and done things with them you'd no doubt find distasteful at best, objectionable at worst."*

Is this what he meant by objectionable? I never suspected my husband was a dominant or that he participated in things so far outside my realm of understanding I wouldn't have recognized them if they slapped me in the face.

Among all those moments we spent together were the ones in which I'd bared my soul to him, sharing my painful past and bringing him into my life. I have been closer to him in the few weeks we've spent together than I've been to anyone in my life. He knows me in ways that no one else ever has.

While I was giving him everything, he was lying to me about who and what he really is. If not for his ex-wife clueing me in, I might never have known. Now I'm angry—that he kept his truth from me, that his ex-wife, a woman he despises, was the one to tell me and not him. Was he ever going to tell me? What was his plan? Initiate me to regular sex and then change the rules?

Or is it possible that he never planned to tell me? Probably... I recall our wedding night and the panic attack I had when he pinned down my hands. After hearing my story, I can see why he might've decided to keep the dominant side of himself hidden from me. Though I don't approve of him entering into a marriage with such a big secret between us, I understand that he thought he was protecting me. And I love him for that, even though I can't condone the keeping of secrets of this magnitude.

I think about all the good things that have happened between us. I remember his generosity toward Aileen and her family, the way he paid the rent on our New York apartment for a year, paid for meals for all the kids in my school, hosted the gathering of my students, put up with my hostile dog in his bed and went to war over my wrongful termination. I relive his heartfelt proposal, the acceptance and love his family has shown me, and the tenderness he has given me when I needed it most.

I've seen his heart, over and over again. He loves me. I have no doubt about that. But does he love me enough to tell me the truth? Does he love me enough to figure this out together? Does he love me enough to let me see the rest of him? The part he has kept hidden from me?

What I won't tolerate are lies and secrets. I've had enough of both those things in my life already. I want the truth. I want him to *want* to tell me. What will I do if he looks me in the eye and lies?

My heart is breaking as it becomes clear to me that if he lies, I'll have no choice but to leave him. I can't—and I won't—be in a relationship built on lies. Even if he had my best interests at heart by keeping this from me, it's time now to come clean. I'll give him the chance to tell the truth, and if he does, we'll figure out our next steps together. If he lies... Well, then I know what I have to do.

CHAPTER 20

Flynn

I wake up to the most god-awful smell. I'm almost afraid to open my eyes to see what it is. When I do, I realize I'm sharing my pillow with the wildebeest, and she's got some nasty morning breath.

"Christ on a stick," I mutter as I realize that not only is she sharing my pillow, but apparently I'm snuggling with her, too. I long for the days when she was snapping at me. How in the hell did I end up snuggled up to Fluff rather than my gorgeous wife? And speaking of my gorgeous wife, where is she?

I roll out of bed, leaving the beast snoring, go into the bathroom to take a leak and brush my teeth. I find a pair of gym shorts that I pull on before I go looking for Natalie. In the living room, I spot her rolled up in a ball on the sofa, her dark hair spread out on a pillow.

Why is she sleeping on the sofa and not with me?

I sit next to her and lean over to kiss her awake. Her eyes flutter open, and for a second she looks happy to see me before the light in her eyes goes dull. What's that about?

"What're you doing out here, sweetheart?"

"Couldn't sleep and didn't want to bother you."

"You wouldn't have bothered me. I much prefer you and your sweetness to Fluff and her gorilla breath."

"She doesn't have gorilla breath."

"Yes, she does. And that's me being kind." I tug on her hand. "Come back to bed for a while. It's still early, and we have nowhere to be until later." Addie will know to book us on a late-day flight so we can have some time to regroup before we head to Mexico.

Natalie resists my efforts to lure her back to bed.

"What?" I ask.

"Could I talk to you about something?"

"Of course."

Her brows furrow and her lips purse, like she's screwing up the courage to tell me what's on her mind.

"Sweetheart, tell me what's wrong."

She looks at me, and it occurs to me that I still haven't seen the true color of her eyes without the brown contact lenses she wears. I want to see the real color. Maybe she'll show me while we're in Mexico.

"If I ask you something personal, will you tell me the truth?" she asks.

"I'll always tell you the truth."

"Do you promise?"

"What's this about, Natalie?"

"The room at Hayden's…"

Oh fuck… "What about it?"

"Are you into that stuff, too?"

For a second, my brain totally freezes. I just promised to tell her the truth, but if I do, then she'll know that I've kept it from her until now. She'll think I've been unsatisfied every time we made love when I'm the opposite of unsatisfied.

"Flynn?"

"No, I'm not into it. That's his thing, not mine. I'm into *you*. You're all I need, Natalie." I lean in to kiss her forehead. "Can we go back to bed now?"

"You go ahead. I'm going to take a shower."

"Let me get you dirty first." I turn my attention to her neck, but she slides out from under me, her face set in an unreadable expression, which is all new. I can always read her. "Nat? What's going on?"

"Nothing. I just want a shower."

"Okay, then…" She leaves the room, and I sit there for a minute, confused by her behavior. What the hell just happened here? I return to the bedroom and get back into bed to wait for her. She comes out of the bathroom thirty minutes later, fully dressed for much colder weather than what we're experiencing in Southern California.

Then I see the suitcase she's pulling behind her. I get out of bed. "What're you doing?"

"I'm going home to New York. I'm returning to school and my apartment with Leah."

I feel like I've been knifed in the heart. "What the fuck, Natalie? You're *leaving* me?"

Her eyes fill and her jaw sets before she nods.

"*Why?*"

"Because you're a liar, and I won't be married to a man who lies to me about who and what he really is."

That's when I realize two things—one, she's seriously leaving me, and two, she knows the truth about me. How in the fuck did she find out?

"Natalie, wait. Let's talk about this."

"We did talk, and I gave you the opportunity to tell me the truth. Instead, you looked me in the eye and lied."

"How do you know that?"

"We both know you lied."

"And that's a deal breaker? After everything we've been through, you're actually going to walk away from me? I thought you loved me."

"I do love you. I love you with my whole heart and soul. I've shared every part of myself with you, even the most painful parts. I've been closer to you in the last month than I've been to anyone else in my life. I've kept *nothing* secret. Can you say the same?"

"Natalie… You don't understand."

"I understand perfectly. You didn't think I could handle it, so you kept it from me."

"Yes! That! *Exactly.*"

"Except, when I gave you the chance to fix it, you continued to lie. That's the part I can't live with. How will I ever know what else you're keeping from me? How will I ever know if you're satisfied with me when you obviously want more than you think I can give?"

The ground is shifting under me, and I can't find my footing in this situation. A sense of desperation unlike anything I've ever experienced overtakes me. I want the last hour to do over again more than I've ever wanted anything, ever.

"If you leave, there's no chance we'll ever find our way through this."

"If I stay, there's no way I'll ever know that I truly have all of you. I've lived half a life for long enough, Flynn." Her voice catches, but she recovers her composure. "I've loved every minute we've spent together. You've been so extraordinarily generous and tender toward me from the beginning, and you'll never know how much I appreciate that."

"I don't want your goddamn appreciation."

"And I don't want your goddamn lies. Come on, Fluff. Let's go home."

Fluff launches off the bed and follows Natalie and her suitcase out of the bedroom.

"Natalie, wait. This is insane. You can't go back to who you were before. The press will be all over you. You won't be safe."

"I'll be fine. After a while, they'll lose interest in the boring schoolteacher from New York who was briefly married to the movie star."

Hearing her describe our marriage in the past tense fills me with panic. "You're just going to give up on us that quickly? Without even giving me a chance?"

"I've given you every chance. You've had more than enough time to tell me the truth, and you didn't. And this morning, you lied to my face."

"How do you know? Who told you?"

"Valerie."

Hearing that, I want to roar from the rage that surges through me like a tidal wave, sucking me under and making me see red. I'll fucking kill her for this. I somehow manage to find the words to ask the one question that has to be asked. "When did you see Valerie?"

"The other night in the ladies' room at the SAGs. She gave me quite the earful, but I didn't believe her. The Flynn I know and love bears no resemblance whatsoever to the man she described to me, so I blew it off as meaningless jealousy. Then when she called me last night, after you were asleep, to tell me about your room downstairs and where I could find the key, I had a feeling she wasn't making it up after all."

I feel like I've been shot straight through the heart. I never got around to getting rid of the stuff in the basement, and now she's seen it. This can't be happening.

"After I saw what you have down there, you know what occurred to me?"

"What?" I ask through gritted teeth.

"Yesterday, when we were in Hayden's room, you were naked and hard as a rock. It turned you on to be in that room with me, didn't it?"

"*Yes,*" I hiss. "So what?"

"It's too bad you couldn't have just told me that. Now we'll never know what might've been, will we?"

"You can't leave me over this. I won't let you!"

"You won't *let* me? What're you going to do?"

I make an effort to soften my tone so I don't make this worse, if that's even possible. "You're overreacting, baby. I kept it from you because I didn't want to scare you after everything you've been through."

"And I understand that. I even appreciate it. But when I asked you straight out and you lied to me, that's something else altogether."

"I realize that now. I shouldn't have done that. I swear to God, I've never lied to you about anything else—and I never will again. Can't we please talk this through and figure it out together?"

She wants to. I can see that, yet I also know there's a backbone made of steel in her that's gotten her through worse than this.

"So many times," I say, "I told myself I should walk away because you deserve better than me. Remember after our first date when I didn't call you? It was because Hayden convinced me that a nice girl like you had no business getting tangled up with the likes of me. Then you texted me and asked me to see Aileen. I took one look at you that day and knew I could never walk away from you. I love you so much, Nat. I put your needs ahead of my own. That's what this comes down to."

Her eyes are full of unshed tears that break my heart. "I had a right to know about your needs. You should've told me, especially before you married me."

"Yes, I should have. You're absolutely right—and I was wrong. So very, very wrong. I screwed up. I'll never deny that. But we can fix this. I *know* we can. We've already endured more than some people do in a lifetime. Please don't give up on us, Nat. You told me the night we got married that you wouldn't." I take a step closer to her and put my hands on her shoulders. "You made promises to me."

She pushes my hands away. "You *lied* to me! Don't talk to me about promises, Flynn. This is why Hayden can't bear to look at me, because he knew the truth about you—and I didn't."

I gather her in close to me, breathing in the scent of her hair. "You can't leave me, Nat. You'll ruin me."

She begins to cry in earnest. "I don't want to leave you, but I can't live with someone who lies to me as easily as you did this morning, especially over something so important."

"It's not important! That's what I'm trying to tell you!"

She wiggles out of my embrace, pushing me back. "If it's not important to you, then *why* do you have a room full of BDSM equipment *in your house*? And don't make it worse by telling me it's not yours or some other line of bullshit."

Before I can form a response to that, Fluff begins to bark and snarl at me the way she did when Natalie and I were first together.

"I have to go."

"You can't leave without security."

"I'll let them drive me to the airport, and then I'll put my hair up and wear glasses. No one will recognize me."

"Yes, they *will*, Natalie. You're being naïve."

"I've been naïve from the beginning where you're concerned. Why stop now?" She goes into the kitchen to retrieve her purse and then returns to the foyer, where she bends to clip Fluff's leash to her collar.

"So that's it? Just like that it's over?"

After a long, endless pause during which I die a thousand times, she finally looks at me. "I need some time."

"How much time?"

"I don't know. I'll call you when I'm ready to talk to you."

"I'll give you a week, and then I'm coming after you." As I say the words, I wonder how I'll survive a week without her, the same week we were supposed to spend on our honeymoon.

"Don't do that. I won't see you until I'm ready to."

"I'm sorry, Natalie. I fucked this up. I freely admit that. Please don't go. I love you so much. Please." I have never once, in all my life, begged a woman for anything.

Until now.

"I don't want to go, but it's what I need right now. I will call you. When I'm ready." With Fluff's leash attached to one hand and her suitcase in the other, she opens the door but turns back once more. "I love you, too. You are the best thing to ever happen to me."

The door closes with a click that echoes throughout the house like a gunshot.

Through the beveled glass on the side of the door, I watch her approach the security detail. I see one of them open the back door of an SUV for her. I see her and Fluff get in. Right before the door closes, Natalie wipes tears from her face. And then they're gone. Almost as fast as they entered my life, they've exited it.

Motherfucker.

I pick up a heavy crystal vase that sits on a table next to the door and throw it across the room, shattering one of the plate-glass windows in the back of the house.

I stand there breathing hard and filled with rage, most of it directed at the venomous bitch who is my ex-wife. I want to find her and kill her, except even that wouldn't be what she deserves.

I'm also fucking furious at myself for not getting rid of the equipment in the basement before I brought Natalie here, but that's not exactly something I could ask Addie to take care of for me since she knows nothing about it. And there hasn't been time, without Natalie here with me, to do it myself.

The rage slowly drains from my system, leaving only pain behind. I'll give Natalie the time she says she needs, and then I'll go after her. I'll get her back or die trying. I will tell her everything I should've told her from the beginning, and this time, I'll hold nothing back.

244 | MARIE FORCE

She's *mine*. She will *always* be mine.

The doorbell rings, and I run for the door, hoping Natalie has come back, that she's changed her mind about leaving me.

But it's not Natalie. It's the FBI agent. Vickers.

"Mr. Godfrey, I'm afraid we have a problem."

Other Titles by
Marie Force

Book 5: Hoping for Love

Book 6: Season for Love

Book 7: Longing for Love

Book 8: Waiting for Love

Book 9: Time for Love

Book 10: Meant for Love

Book 10.5: Chance for Love,
A Gansett Island Novella

Book 11: Gansett After Dark

Book 12: Kisses After Dark

The Green Mountain Series
Book 1: All You Need Is Love

Book 2: I Want to Hold Your Hand

Book 3: I Saw Her Standing There

Book 4: And I Love Her

Novella: *You'll Be Mine* in the *Ask Me Why* Anthology, July 7, 2015

Book 5: It's Only Love, November 3, 2015

Single Titles
The Singles Titles Boxed Set

Georgia on My Mind

True North

The Fall

Everyone Loves a Hero

Love at First Flight

Line of Scrimmage

About the Author

M.S. Force is the erotic alter-ego of *New York Times* bestselling author Marie Force. The Quantum Trilogy is M.S. Force's first foray into erotic romance, but it won't be the last!

With more than 3.5 million books sold, Marie Force is the *New York Times*, *USA Today* and *Wall Street Journal* bestselling, award-winning author of 40 contemporary romances. Her New York Times bestselling self-published McCarthys of Gansett Island Series has sold more than 1.8 million e-books since *Maid for Love* was released in 2011. She is also the author of the *New York Times* bestselling Fatal Series from Harlequin's Carina Press, as well as the *New York Times* bestselling Green Mountain Series from Berkley Sensation, among other books and series, including the new Quantum Trilogy, written as M.S. Force.

While her husband was in the Navy, Marie lived in Spain, Maryland and Florida, and she is now settled in her home state of Rhode Island. She is the mother of two teenagers and two feisty dogs, Brandy and Louie.

Join Marie's mailing list for news about new books and possible appearances in your area. Join one of Marie's many reader groups at marieforce.com/connect. Contact Marie at *marie@marieforce.com*.

Follow her on Facebook at Facebook.com/MarieForceAuthor, on Twitter @ marieforce and Instagram at marieforceauthor.

CPSIA information can be obtained at www.ICGtesting.com
Printed in the USA
LVOW10s0840050415

432873LV00028B/209/P